James Hadley Chase (born René
born in London in 1906. He work
which time he was inspired by American crime-writers and went on to write his own thrillers and gangster stories, also set in the United States. He first found success with *No Orchids for Miss Blandish* which was published in 1939 and was one of the most successful books of the thirties, selling several million copies. George Orwell described it as 'a brilliant piece of writing with hardly a wasted word or a jarring note anywhere'. It was subsequently dramatised and performed on London's West End and also made into a film. Chase went on to gain popularity for his numerous other gangster stories, and by the end of the war he was one of Britain's most successful thriller writers. During his career he produced some ninety books, also writing under the names of James L Dochery, Ambrose Grant and Raymond Marshall. He travelled widely, though only visited the USA late in life. He died in 1985 whilst in Switzerland.

BY THE SAME AUTHOR
ALL PUBLISHED BY HOUSE OF STRATUS

An Ace Up My Sleeve
An Ear to the Ground
The Fast Buck
Goldfish Have No Hiding Place
The Guilty are Afraid
Hand Me a Fig-Leaf
Have a Change of Scene
Have This One On Me
Hit Them Where it Hurts
Just a Matter of Time
Knock, Knock! Who's There?
Like a Hole in the Head
Make the Corpse Walk
More Deadly Than the Male
My Laugh Comes Last
Not My Thing
So What Happens to Me?
Tell it to the Birds
The Whiff of Money
You Have Yourself a Deal
You're Dead Without Money

JAMES HADLEY
CHASE

Hit and Run

This edition published in 2000 by The House of Stratus, an imprint of Stratus Books Ltd., 21 Beeching Park, Kelly Bray, Cornwall, PL17 8QS, UK.

www.houseofstratus.com

Typeset, printed and bound by The House of Stratus.

A catalogue record for this book is available from the British Library and the Library of Congress.

ISBN 1-84232-108-0

Cover design: Marc Burville-Riley
Cover image: Photonica

1

I

Roger Aitken was the kind of boss who never mixed his home life with his business life. It wasn't until he fell down the Plaza Grill steps and broke his leg that I went to his home and I met his wife.

It had never bothered me that he hadn't ever invited me back to his house. To my thinking there is nothing worse than the Big Wheel who looks on his employees as part of his family. I have always regarded the man who invites his employees to his home for a monthly nightmare dinner where no one dares take a drink or raise his voice as a boss to be avoided like a plague.

There was nothing like that about Roger Aitken. He was strictly the feudal type of boss. He picked the men and women who worked for him with searching care, paid them a quarter more than any other advertising agency, and if they didn't make good in their first week, he'd put his foot under their tails and out they'd go. You weren't given a second chance with Aitken: it was strictly deliver or out!

Before coming to work for the International and Pacific Agency, the biggest and best agency on the coast and which was managed by Aitken, I had been working for a crummy little outfit that had one foot in the financial grave, and a boss who was later hauled off to a home for incurable alcoholics. This was some two years ago. At the time I remember I was sitting at my desk wrestling with a scheme to promote a new kind of dishwasher that couldn't even shift the gravy stains off a plate when I had a call from Roger Aitken's secretary. She said Aitken wanted to talk to me on a personal matter and would I come over around six o'clock?

I knew Aitken, of course, by reputation. I knew he ran the agency for a board of rich businessmen and had made a wonderful thing out of it. Naturally enough I wondered if he were going to offer me a job. Naturally enough I was pretty excited: a job with the International was the ambition of every ad man on the coast.

At six, dead on the second, I was in his outer office, and at five past six, I was standing before his desk, getting the treatment from a pair of steely blue eyes that went through to the back of my head like the proverbial hot knife through the proverbial pat of butter.

Aitken was a big man, just over six foot two, massively built, with a whisky complexion, a mouth like a gin trap and a high executive's aggressive jaw. He was around fifty-seven and thick around the middle, but if it was fat, it was hard, solid fat. He looked the kind of man who kept himself in pretty good condition.

He stared at me for maybe ten seconds before he got up and thrust out his hand with a knuckle-cracking grip.

'You Chester Scott?' he demanded in a voice you could hear in the outer office without having your ear to the keyhole.

I don't know who else he thought I could be since I had had to give my name to at least four minor officials before breaking into his office.

I said I was Chester Scott.

He opened a file on his desk and tapped the contents with a thick finger.

'This your work?'

The folder contained about two dozen layouts clipped from various newspapers and journals I had been working on over a period of four or five months.

I said they were my work.

He closed the folder and began to prowl around the room.

'They're not bad,' he said. 'I can use a man like you. What are they paying you?'

I told him.

He paused in his prowling to stare at me as if he wasn't sure if he had heard aright.

'Do you know you're worth more?'

I said I did.

'Then why haven't you done something about it?'

I said I had been pretty busy recently and hadn't had time to get around to it.

'Work more important to you than money, huh?'

'I wouldn't say that,' I said. 'It's just that I've been pretty busy.'

He stared at me some more, then went behind his desk and sat down.

'I'll give you a hundred a week more than you're getting now: you can start Monday.'

That's how I came to work for the International.

And now, two years after this meeting, I was second in charge and only responsible to Aitken himself. I was pulling down a salary that two years ago would have seemed just a pipe dream. I had a Cadillac convertible, a three-bedroom bungalow that faced the sea, a Filipino boy to take care of me, and a respectable balance in the bank.

Don't imagine I moved into this class by sitting on my seat and smoking cigarettes. When you go to work for Aitken, you go to work. I was at my desk at nine o'clock every morning, including Saturdays, and there were times when I didn't get away until around midnight. If the International paid well, Aitken took good care he got his pound of flesh. I don't think I have ever worked so hard, but I enjoyed it, and I had a good team working with me: every one of them was a hand-picked Aitken man or woman, and that meant something. I was sitting right on top of the world. I looked set to go on sitting right on top of the world, but it didn't work out that way.

One hot July evening, the whole set-up suddenly exploded in my face. I was working late at the office. The time was just after nine o'clock. Only Pat Henessey, my secretary, and Joe Fellowes, my layout artist, were with me. The rest of the staff had gone home. We were working on a promotion scheme to put over a new toilet soap. It was a big job, with a TV hook-up and a two-million-dollar allocation.

Fellowes was showing me some pulls of the ad he intended to run in the weeklies: good stuff, and Pat and I were chewing the rag about it when the telephone bell on Pat's desk came alive.

She went over and lifted the receiver.

Pat was a lovely looking girl: tall and long-legged with honey-colour hair, big blue eyes and a complexion that looked too good to be real, but was. She was around twenty-six and as sharp as a razor. She and I worked as a team. Without her to nudge my memory I would have been hard pressed to keep pace with the stuff Aitken kept piling into my lap.

I didn't pay any attention to what she was saying on the telephone. Joe and I were altering one of his layouts. I wasn't too satisfied with the girl he was using as a model.

'Look, Joe, if a girl had a bosom like this in real life,' I said, 'she'd get it caught in the first revolving door she tried to go through.'

'That's the idea,' Joe said with his direct simplicity. 'That's exactly what I want to convey. I want the fellas, as soon as they see this ad, to ask themselves what a dame like this one does when she gets to a revolving door. It's a psychological drawing.'

I threw the layout at him, but that didn't stop me from laughing, then Pat hung up and said in her quiet calm voice, 'Mr Aitken has broken his leg.'

'Now if you had said he had broken his neck ...' Joe began, then broke off to gape. 'You kidding?'

Pat looked at me.

'That was Mr Aitken's housekeeper,' she said. 'Mr Aitken slipped on the steps of the Plaza Grill. He has broken his leg.'

'That's just like RA,' Joe said unfeelingly. 'Trust him to break his leg somewhere high toned. Did she say which leg?'

'Will you shut up, Joe?' I said. To Pat: 'Where is he? In hospital?'

'They took him home. He wants you. The housekeeper said for you to go right on over.'

It was then I realized I didn't even know where Aitken lived.

'Where do I find him?' I asked, getting to my feet.

'He has a little shack out on Palm Boulevard,' Joe said with a cynical smile. 'A twenty-four-bedroom job with a lounge big enough to serve as a bus garage; just a throw away: a weekend cabin.'

I ignored him, looking at Pat.

'The Gables, Palm Boulevard,' she said briskly. 'Third house up on the right.'

She began to open drawers and files, taking out papers and dumping them in a folder.

'What are you up to?' I asked, staring at her.

'You may need these. I can't imagine RA wants to see you so you can hold his hand. There's a board meeting tomorrow. You'll have to handle it. He'll want to see all the papers, and here they are,' and she thrust the folder at me.

'But he's broken his leg! He won't want to talk business. He'll be in pain. Maybe they'll have given him a shot by now.'

'I'd take them, Ches,' Pat said seriously. 'You could need them.'

And as it turned out, she was right. I did need them.

The Gables was a vast house standing in a two-acre garden with a view over the sea and the distant hills. I wouldn't have said it had twenty-four bedrooms, but it had at least ten. It was a nice house: the kind of house I would have liked to have owned. The kind of house your friends would have to admire even if they secretly hated you.

There was a fair-sized swimming-pool to the left of the house and a four-car garage which housed RA's Bentley, a Cadillac tourer, a Buick estate wagon and TR2 runabout.

The garden, a mass of rose trees, begonias, petunias and such like, was floodlit. The swimming-pool was floodlit too, and looked lonely as I drove up the sanded drive: it was the kind of pool that would only look its best when dressed with bikini-clad beauties.

I was slightly stunned by this affluence. I knew RA was a Big Wheel, but I had no idea his earnings could run to a show this big and this lavish.

I left my car, toiled up twenty marble steps that led to the front door and rang the bell.

There was the usual short delay before the door opened and a tall, fat man wearing an English butler's outfit raised white eyebrows at me. I learned later his name was Watkins, and he had been imported from England at a considerable cost.

'I'm Chester Scott,' I said. 'Mr Aitken is expecting me.'

'Yes, sir. Will you step this way?'

I followed him through a large hall, down some stairs and into a room RA obviously used as his workroom. There was a desk, a dictaphone, four lounging chairs, a radio and about two thousand books lining the walls.

'How is he?' I asked as Watkins turned on the lights and made ready to fold his tent and steal away into the distant spaces of the house.

'As comfortable as can be expected, sir,' he told me in a voice a mortician would have envied. 'If you will wait a few minutes, I will tell him you have arrived.'

He went away, and I took a turn around the room, staring at the book titles.

After a while Watkins came back.

'Mr Aitken will see you now.'

Clutching the bulky folder Pat had forced on to me, I followed him along a passage and into an elevator that hauled us up two storeys. We walked across a fair-sized landing to a door. Watkins rapped, turned the handle and stood aside.

'Mr Scott, sir.'

Aitken was lying in a single divan type of bed. The room was large and one hundred per cent masculine. The drapes were drawn back from the big window that looked on to the moonlit sea.

Aitken looked as he always looked, except it seemed odd to find him lying down instead of standing up. He had a cigar between his teeth, and there were papers strewn over the bedspread. A bedside lamp made a pool of light around him, the rest of the room was in shadows.

'Come in, Scott,' he said, and I could tell by the rasp in his voice that he was pretty testy. 'This is something, isn't it? Pull up a chair. I'm going to make some fool pay for this! I've sent my attorney down to take a look at those steps: they're a damn death trap. I'm going to sue the ears off them for this, but that doesn't mend my leg.'

I pulled up a chair near him and sat down. I started to express my sympathy, but he brushed that aside.

'Save it,' he said irritably. 'Talking about it won't do any good. I'm going to be out of action for at least four weeks if I can believe that fool of a doctor. When you get to my age and weight a broken leg can be tricky. If I don't watch out, I'll be lame, and that's one thing I'm not going to be. So I'll have to stick here. There's that board meeting tomorrow. You'll have to handle it.' He stared at me. 'Think you can do it?'

This was no time to be modest.

'You tell me how you want it handled,' I said, 'and I'll handle it.'

'Got the papers with you?'

That's when I blessed Pat. I would have looked four kinds of a dumb cluck if I hadn't listened to her. I took the papers from the folder and offered them to him.

He looked at me for a long ten seconds, then his hard face creased into the resemblance of a smile.

'You know, Scott,' he said as he took the papers, 'you're a pretty smart fella. What made you bring these? What made you imagine I wouldn't be laid low and unable to work?'

'I couldn't imagine you being laid low, Mr Aitken,' I said. 'You're a man who isn't laid low easily.'

'That's a fact.' I could see I had said absolutely the right thing. He put the papers down and reached forward to knock ash off his cigar into the ashtray on the bedside table.

'Tell me something, Scott: have you got any money?'

This unexpected question startled me, and for a moment I stared at him.

'I have just over twenty thousand dollars,' I said.

It was his turn to look surprised.

'Twenty thousand, eh? As much as that?' Then he chuckled. This was the first time since I had known him I had ever seen him look jovial. 'I guess I haven't given you much time to spend your money, huh?'

'It's not that bad,' I said. 'Most of it came to me in a legacy.'

'I'll tell you why I asked,' he said. 'I'm getting tired of working for a bunch of egg-heads. I'm planning to set up on my own in New York. For the next four weeks you're going to run the International. I'll tell you what to do, but you'll have to do it, and there will be times when you will have to make a snap decision without consulting me. I don't expect you to keep calling me up and asking me this and that. I'll give you the broad policy to work on, but you will have to implement it. If you make a success of it, and when I get back, I'll give you a chance every man in this racket would give his ears to have. I'll make you my partner in New York if you are willing to put your money into the business. It'll mean you'll run the place up there while I keep the International going. That way both of us will make a lot of money, Scott. What do you think?'

'Why, sure.' I sat forward, my heart thumping. 'You can count on me, Mr Aitken.'

'Okay, we'll see. You run the International without a mistake and you're in. Slip up and you're out. Understand?'

I hadn't any time to think what this chance would mean, for we got right down then to the board meeting, but later, when I had the time to think about it, I realized how big this chance could be. It could easily give me the opportunity to break into Aitken's class, and sooner or later set up on my own. With a twenty-thousand-dollar stake, with the opportunities New York can offer to a go-ahead advertising man and with Aitken's backing, I really had a chance, as he had said, that any man in the racket would give his ears to have.

I was with Aitken for two and a half hours: going through the board meeting minutes, and then on to policy matters that he would have had to tackle himself during the coming week. Pat had given me every paper we needed. She hadn't missed out on one, and that made a big impression on Aitken. Finally, around eleven-thirty, a tall, thin woman in a black silk dress, who I afterwards learned was Mrs Hepple, his housekeeper, came in and broke it up.

'It's time you had a little sleep now, Mr Roger,' she said with a I'm standing no nonsense-from-you expression in her eyes. 'Dr Schulberg said you had to be asleep by eleven, and it's gone half past.'

I expected RA to tell her to go to hell, but he didn't.

'That damned quack,' he grumbled, not looking at her as he pushed the collection of papers towards me. 'Well, all right. Take this junk, will you, Scott?'

As I put the papers in the folder, he went on: 'This is what I'll have to put up with for the next four weeks. Give me a call as soon as the board meeting is over. Watch out for Templeman. He's the troublemaker. Come and see me tomorrow night. I want to know how you're handling the Wasserman account. That and Beauty Soap have got to be watched every second or we'll lose them.'

I said I would take care of everything, hoped he would get a good sleep and eased myself out of the room.

I crossed to the elevator, pushed the call button, but nothing happened. Someone who had used the elevator must have left the grille gate open, I decided, and I moved along the corridor to the stairs.

Halfway down, I saw below me a landing with several doors opening on to it. One of the doors stood wide open, and a light came out and made a bright rectangular pattern on the green and white carpet.

The carpet on the stairs was thick and muffled my footfalls. I guess that was why she hadn't heard me coming down.

She was standing before a full-length mirror, looking at herself, her hands lifting her long, chestnut-coloured hair off her shoulders, her head a little on one side. She had on one of those fancy things called shorties that reached only to within four inches of her knees. Her legs and feet were bare.

She was the loveliest thing I have ever seen in my life. Maybe she was twenty-two, but I doubted it, twenty would be nearer it. She was young and beautiful and fresh, and everything about her was exciting from her thick, long glossy hair to her small bare feet.

The sight of her touched off a spark inside me that had been waiting to be touched off ever since I had become what is technically known as a man, and which no woman had up to now succeeded in touching off.

The spark ignited with a flash that knocked me mentally backwards and sent a flame through me that dried my mouth, made my heart pound and left me breathless.

I stood motionless in the semi-darkness looking at her, aware that my blood was racing, my heart was thumping and aware that I had never seen a woman I wanted so badly as this one.

Maybe she had an instinctive feeling that she was being watched or maybe she had finished admiring herself in the mirror; anyway, she suddenly stepped back out of my sight, and the door was pushed to.

For perhaps ten seconds I stood motionless, staring at the half-closed door, then I went on down the stairs, down the next flight to the hall. It was only when I reached the hall that I paused to take out my handkerchief and wipe my sweating face.

Watkins came out of the lounge.

'A warm night, sir,' he said and his old shrewd eyes peered at me. 'You had no hat?'

I put my handkerchief back into my pocket.

'No.'

'You have a car, sir?'

'Yes.'

I made a move to the front door. He opened it for me.

'Good night, sir.'

I said good night and walked out into the warm, silent darkness. I was glad to get into the car and sit behind the driving wheel.

Although she must have been thirty-five years younger than Aitken, I was sure she wasn't his daughter nor his mistress. I felt in my bones she was his wife, and that knowledge turned me sick to my stomach.

II

I didn't sleep much that night.

I had a lot on my mind. There was this business of the New York partnership which I knew was a chance in a lifetime. There was tomorrow's board meeting that could be tricky.

There were five directors of the International and Pacific Agency. Four of them were bankers and they were co-operative and admirers of Aitken. The fifth member was an attorney, Selwyn Templeman, a know-all and a nuisance and the thought I had to handle him bothered me.

Then there was the Wasserman account. Joe Wasserman was the biggest manufacturer of TV sets on the Pacific coast. He was one of our most important clients and our biggest spender, and he knew it. Every so often he'd threatened to take the account away and give it to some other agency, but so far we had managed to hold on to him. Aitken always dealt direct with him: one of the very few accounts Aitken handled himself. Now I had it in my lap and that bothered me too.

Then there was the thought that from tomorrow for a possible four weeks I would be boss of the International with a hundred and fifteen men and women working under me, and two hundred and three clients who were liable to write or telephone about their problems any hour of the working day and expect me to have the answers at my fingertips. Up to now this thought hadn't bothered me because I knew if the going got tough I could always go to RA and drop the sticky end into his lap. I could still do that, of course, but if I did, I knew he wouldn't think much of me. A man with a broken leg doesn't want to deal with anything except an emergency, so that bothered me too.

As I lay in bed with the moonlight coming through the window and hearing the sound of the sea breaking on the shore, all these problems seemed pretty overpowering until I took a look at them. It was then that I realized the real reason why I was sweating it out in the semi-darkness was because my mind was obsessed with the picture of Roger Aitken's wife as I had seen her standing before the mirror.

That was the thing that kept me from sleeping: the picture of her lifting her thick, chestnut-coloured hair off her white shoulders, the shape of her breasts under the frilly shortie, the young, fresh beauty of her, and the realization that she was Aitken's wife and the burning need I felt for her. It was that picture that kept my mind feverish and stopped me from sleeping.

Why had Aitken married her: a girl young enough to be his daughter? I kept asking myself. More important still: why had she married him? Surely no young girl could fall in love with a man like RA?

Don't imagine I didn't try to snap out of this mood. I did my best to stop thinking about her. I told myself she was RA's wife and therefore sacrosanct. She wasn't for me. She couldn't possibly be for me. I was crazy to think of her the way I was thinking of her, but it didn't help. I didn't sleep much that night. I just couldn't get her out of my mind.

I got to the office after nine o'clock the following morning. I arrived as Pat was entering the express elevator and I joined her. We were huddled against the wall, surrounded by other workers, and we smiled at each other, but we didn't speak because there were ears all around us.

It wasn't until we were in my office that I told her about the New York project.

'Oh, Ches, how wonderful!' she exclaimed. 'I've always wondered why he didn't set up on his own and in New York. To think you'll be in charge!'

'It's not certain. I could make a hash here, and then I'm out.'

'You won't make a hash here. You'll handle it. You mustn't even think you could make a hash of it.'

'I'll want you in New York, Pat. I couldn't handle the job without you.'

Her eyes sparkled as she said, 'You couldn't keep me away from New York. I've always wanted to work there.'

It was while I was going through the mail that Joe Fellowes wandered in.

'Hey, boss,' he said, grinning at me. 'How was the old man?'

'The only difference was he was lying in bed and not pacing up and down,' I said. 'Look Joe, I'm busy. I've got this board meeting in a few minutes. What do you want?'

Joe sat on the corner of my desk.

'Relax, boy. That board meeting isn't anything. I just want to be told the old man is writhing in pain. I like to think of him suffering. I bet he was screaming the roof off.'

'He wasn't. He's the original stoic. Sorry to disappoint you, Joe, and now if you'll beat it, I'll get on with the mail.'

Joe didn't move. He stared at me, a puzzled expression on his face.

'You look bothered. What's biting you?'

I had worked with him now for two years, and I liked him. He was the best layout artist in the racket. He had often said he wished I were his boss, rather than Aitken, and if ever I thought of opening up on my own, he would like to join me.

So I told him about the New York project.

'That's wonderful!' he said when I was through. 'You, Pat and me could make a world-beating team. If you don't land this job, Ches, I'll strangle you.'

'I'll do my best if it's like that,' I said and grinned at him.

He slid off the desk.

'Did you see RA's wife when you were at the house?'

I felt myself turn hot. I was collecting some papers together so I didn't have to look at him otherwise I think I might have given myself away.

'His wife?' I tried to make my voice sound casual. 'No, I didn't see her.'

'Then you've missed something. Phew! What a dish! I've only set eyes on her once, but she's been haunting my dreams ever since.'

By now I had enough control over myself to look up and meet his eyes.

'What's so special about her, then?'

'Wait until you see her, then you will realize you've asked the silliest question of the year. What's special about her? For one thing she has more sex appeal in her little finger than any other girl I've seen. She can't be more than twenty, and what a beaut! It kills me to think she's married to that whisky-pickled, flint-hearted old sourpuss.'

'How do you know she isn't happy with him?'

'If you were young and beautiful, would you be happy married to RA?' Joe asked and grinned. 'It's the old, old story, of course. The only reason why she could possibly have married him is she was after his cheque book. So now she lives in a twelve-bedroom house. So now she can hang a diamond necklace around her pretty neck. So now she can have RA all to herself. But I bet she's not happy.'

'You know it's funny, but I don't remember hearing he had a wife. Where did she come from?'

'I wouldn't know. The front row of some snappy chorus, I'd imagine. He married her about a year before you joined us,' Joe said. 'That would make her scarcely seventeen when he hooked her – talk about cradle-snatching. Anyway, you look out for her. She's really worth seeing.'

'Suppose you stop gossiping and get out of here?' I said. 'I've only ten more minutes before the board.'

I hadn't time then to think about what Joe had said, but later I did think about it. It made me feel pretty bad to think she had thrown herself away for the sake of RA's money. I felt sure Joe was right. There couldn't be any other reason why she had married him.

Around three o'clock in the afternoon, I called Aitken. I was feeling as if I had been fed through a wringer. The board meeting had been tougher than I had thought possible, and Templeman, finding Aitken wasn't there to keep him under control, had come out with his ten-inch guns blazing. But I had handled him, and I had handled the rest of the board. I had finally got them to agree to the items RA was anxious about, and that in itself was a major triumph.

So I called RA's house without even waiting to get back to my own office, and the ringing tone had scarcely started up, when I heard a click and a girl's voice said, 'Hello? Who is that?'

I knew it was her, and the sound of her voice made me short of breath. For a moment I couldn't speak, and I sat there motionless, with the receiver against my ear, listening to her gentle breathing.

'Hello? Who is that?' she asked again.

'This is Chester Scott,' I managed to get out. 'Can I speak to Mr Aitken?'

'Mr Scott?' she said. 'Why, yes, of course. Will you hold on, please? He is expecting you.'

'How is he?' I said because I wanted to go on listening to this soft, exciting voice.

'He's getting along very well.' Was I imagining that her tone lacked enthusiasm? 'The doctor is very pleased with him,' then she pulled the plug out, and after a moment or so, RA came on the line.

2

I

I got to the Gables just after eight o'clock.

While I drove to the house I wondered if I would see her again. The thought of her gave me a sick, dry feeling in my mouth and made my heart thump hard and unevenly.

When I reached the house I saw someone had turned off the flood-lighting in the garden and the swimming-pool, but the place still looked pretty impressive in the hard, white light of the moon.

I left the car before the front entrance, climbed the steps and rang the bell. After the usual delay, Watkins opened the door.

'Good evening, sir,' he said. 'A fine night.'

'Yes,' I said, and moved past him into the hall. 'How is Mr Aitken?'

'Fairly well, I would say. Perhaps he is a little nervous tonight. If I may suggest, I wouldn't stay longer than necessary.'

'I'll cut it as short as I can.'

'That would be good of you, sir.'

We rode up in the elevator. The old boy breathed heavily and I could hear the starched front of his shirt creaking every time he dragged down a breath.

Aitken was propped up in bed, a cigar gripped between his teeth. Across his knees lay a couple of financial papers, and a pencil and scratch pad lay by his side. He looked a little flushed, and the light from the bedside lamp showed up the sweat beads on his forehead. His mouth turned down at the corners and his eyes looked heavy. He didn't look as good as he had done the previous night.

'Come in, Scott,' he said, and the growl in his voice warned me he could be irritable.

I came over to the bed and sat down in the easy chair.

'How's the leg?' I asked, not looking at him, but concentrating on opening the briefcase I had brought with me.

'It's all right.' He swept the financial papers off the bed onto the floor. 'Hamilton called me. He said you did a good job at the meeting.'

'I'm glad he thinks so. I didn't handle Templeman too well,' I said. 'He gave me a rough ride.'

Aitken's mouth twisted into a smile.

'You handled him all right. Hamilton told me. The old fool went away with a flea in his ear. Got the minutes?'

I handed them to him.

'While I'm reading them, have a drink, and give me one too.' He waved to where a collection of bottles and glasses stood on a table against the wall. 'Give me a whisky, and I mean, put some whisky in the glass.'

The note in his voice warned me not to argue with him, so I went over to the table and made two drinks. I came back and offered him one of the glasses. He stared at it and his brows came down. He looked a real bad-tempered hellion at that moment.

'I said put some whisky in it! Didn't you hear me?'

I returned to the table and sloshed more whisky into the glass and brought it back to him. He took the glass, stared at it, then drank the lot. For a long moment he held the glass while he stared over the top of my head, then he thrust the glass at me.

'Fix me another and come and sit down.'

I repeated the dose, put the glass on the table at his side and sat down.

We looked at each other, and he suddenly grinned.

'Don't mind me, Scott,' he said. 'When you break a leg you're helpless. There's a plot going on in this house to treat me like a sick man. I've been waiting all day for you to come and give me a drink.'

'I should have thought it was the worst thing you could have had,' I said.

'Think so?' He laughed. 'You leave me to judge that.' He took up the minutes. 'Smoke if you want to.'

I lit a cigarette and drank some of the Scotch. It took him about ten minutes to finish reading the minutes, then he dropped the papers on his knees, reached for his glass and took another drink.

'A pretty good beginning,' he said. 'More than that: I couldn't have handled them better myself. You go on like this, and the New York job is yours.'

This was praise indeed.

'Now let's see how you're going to make use of concessions we've got from them,' he went on. 'Let's have your ideas.'

I had thought he might ask this question, and I had discussed it with the heads of the departments before I had left the office so I was ready for him.

For the next half hour I explained my ideas. He lay still, listening, sipping his whisky, and every now and then nodding his head. I was pretty sure I was saying the right things. When I was through, he said: 'Not bad; not bad at all. Now I'll tell you a better way of handling it.'

It was my turn to listen to him and it was an object lesson. He used all my ideas, but in a slightly different way, and I saw at once where I had gone wrong. My way was just that much more expensive. His way gave us a saving of ten per cent, and made him a better businessman than I was.

By now it was a little after nine o'clock, and I remembered what Watkins had said about cutting the meeting short.

'Okay, sir,' I said and began to put the papers back into my briefcase. 'I'll take care of it. And now if it's all right with you, I'll run along. I have a date at ten.'

He grinned at me.

'You're a liar, Scott. You've been listening to that old fool, Watkins. But that's all right. You get off. Come and see me tomorrow at eight.' He finished his whisky, and as he set his glass down, he asked, 'Have you got a girl, Scott?'

The question startled me. I let some papers slip out of my fingers on to the floor. As I bent to pick them up, I said: 'No one in particular, if that's what you mean.'

'I don't mean that. A man needs a woman every now and then. Don't get yourself involved with them, but make use of them. That's what they are here for.' The cynical note in his voice riled me. 'I don't want you to be working all the time. I want you to get in some relaxation. Maybe you have lived long enough to know a woman can be a very satisfactory form of relaxation, providing you don't let her get her hooks into you. Let her do that, and you're a goner.'

'Yes, sir,' I said and stuffed the papers back into the briefcase. I was surprised. I didn't expect this kind of thing from him, and his cynicism made me angry. 'I'll be along tomorrow at eight.'

He lay back against his pillows, staring at me.

'You'll take the weekend off. I don't want to see you on Friday night. Give me a call on Monday morning. What's today – Tuesday? You make plans for the weekend, Scott. I want you to get some relaxation. Do you play golf?'

I said I played golf.

'Finest game in the world if you don't take it seriously. Golf is like a woman. Take either of them seriously, let either of them get a hook into you, and you're sunk. What do you go around in?'

I said on my best days I shot 72.

He stared at me as if he were seeing me for the first time.

'Why, you're quite a golfer!'

'I should be. I've played since I was five. My old man was wild about golf. He even got my mother to play.'

I started to drift towards the door. 'I'll be in tomorrow night at eight.'

'Do that, Scott.' He was still staring at me, his eyes quizzing. 'And arrange to play golf over the weekend.' His hard mouth twisted into an ugly little smile. 'Then find yourself a pretty girl for the night: golf and a woman are the two best relaxations in life.'

I was glad to get out of the room. His cynicism left a nasty taste in my mouth, and I was in two minds whether to take the elevator or walk down the stairs. Then the picture she had made, standing before that mirror, came surging into my mind, and I walked away from the elevator to the head of the stairs.

There I paused and looked down on the landing below. It was in darkness, and the pang of disappointment that stabbed me hurt. Then I realized that it was only ten minutes after nine o'clock. It wasn't likely she would be in her bedroom at this hour.

I turned back and took the elevator down to the ground floor.

Watkins was waiting for me in the hall.

'I don't think Mr Aitken looks so well tonight,' I said as I walked with him to the front door.

'He is a little feverish, sir. I imagine it is to be expected.'

'Yes. I'll be in again tomorrow night.'

'I'm sure Mr Aitken looks forward to your visits,' he said as he opened the front door.

I said good night to him and stepped out into the hot moonlit night. The big door closed behind me.

I walked slowly down the steps to where I had left the Cadillac. When I reached the bottom step, I turned and looked up at the house. Except for Aitken's room, which showed a light, the rest of the many windows were shiny, black eyes that stared down at me. I wondered where she was. Was she out or was she somewhere at the back of the house?

All day I had been waiting for this chance to see her again. I had to make a considerable effort not to remain there, staring up at the house in the hope a light would come up in one of the windows and I would see her.

For all I knew Mrs Hepple or even Watkins was watching me from behind the darkness of one of the windows. This was no time to stand staring, so I went over to the car, opened the door, pitched my briefcase on to the back seat and slid under the driving wheel.

She was there, sitting beside me, her hands folded in her lap. Although it was dark in the car, I could just make out the shape of her head which she held a little on one side as she looked at me. I knew it was her. It had to be her. It couldn't have been anyone else or I wouldn't have felt the way I was feeling. My heart wouldn't be pounding like this.

For perhaps five seconds I stared at her, aware of the faint smell of the perfume she was wearing and hearing her quick, gentle breathing, and in those five seconds everything around me went out of focus.

It was a moment in my life I will never forget.

II

'Hello,' she said. 'Did I startle you? I didn't think you would be out so soon.'

'Well, perhaps you did.' My voice sounded husky. 'I didn't expect ...'

She laughed.

'Is this your car?'

'Yes.'

'It's a lovely car. I'm crazy about cars. When I saw it, I just had to get in. I like it better than Roger's Bentley. I bet it's fast.'

'Yes: it's pretty fast.'

She leaned back against the cushion of the seat and stared up at the roof. The moonlight coming in through the open window lit up her profile. She looked breathtakingly beautiful.

'Roger was telling me about you,' she said. 'He says you're going to be his new partner.'

'It's not absolutely fixed.'

I was sitting bolt upright, my clenched fists resting on my knees, my mind still stupid with the surprise of finding her here, talking to me as if she had known me all her life.

'He told me it was. Will you like living in New York?'

'Very much.'

'I wish I could live there.' She lifted her arms and clasped her hands behind her head. I could see her breasts lift and strain against the thin wool of the sweater she was wearing. 'Palm City is dreadfully dull, don't you think?'

'I suppose it must be for someone your age.'

She turned her head and stared at me.

'You sound as if you're old, but you're not. You're not thirty yet, are you?'

'I'm thirty-one.'

'You must be awfully clever. Roger says you are putting twenty thousand dollars into the business. How did you get all that money when you're only thirty-one?'

'My father left me most of it. The rest I've saved.'

'Do you want to put all that money into Roger's business?'

I was bewildered by her calm, direct questions.

'You sound very interested,' I said.

'I am.' She turned her head and smiled at me. 'I've always been interested in the way men make money. The only certain way a girl can become rich is to get married. Men can go out and make money. I think it's a much more satisfactory way. Of course you were lucky to have a father to leave you something, weren't you?'

'I guess I was.'

She sat up and, reaching out, she rested her hand on the dashboard.

'I love this car. Will you teach me to drive?'

'There's nothing to teach.' My voice was unsteady. 'It's an automatic drive. You press the starter and it drives itself.' She looked at me.

'Believe it or not, I've never driven a car. Roger won't let me touch any of his, and he has four.'

'Why is that?'

'He's terribly possessive. If I want to go anywhere, I go on a bicycle. It's fantastic, isn't it? His excuse is I can't drive. If I learned, then he would have to lend me a car. Will you teach me?'

I didn't hesitate.

'Why, yes. If that's what you want.'

She clasped her hands around her knees and pulled her knees up to her chin. I could see now she was wearing light-coloured slacks. 'I want that more than anything else in the world. Will you teach me now or have you something else to do?'

'You mean right now?'

'Yes, if you can spare the time.'

'Well, all right. We'd better change places,' and I began to get out of the car, but she put her hand on my coat sleeve, stopping me. The feel of her fingers sent a hot wave of blood crawling up my spine.

'Not here. They'll see us and they'll tell Roger. Let's go somewhere where no one can see us.'

'They? Who do you mean?'

'Mrs Hepple and Watkins. Have you met Mrs Hepple?'

'Yes.'

'I don't like her. She's sneaky. Don't you think she's sneaky?'

'I wouldn't know. I just saw her last night. I haven't spoken to her.'

'She doesn't approve of me. She likes to get me into trouble. Roger listens to her.'

I suddenly saw the danger of this.

'If Mr Aitken doesn't want you to learn to drive ...'

She put her hand on my arm, and that stopped me short.

'Don't tell me you're another one of them who is afraid of him. If you are, I'll find someone else to teach me to drive.'

'It's not that I'm afraid of him, but I can't very well do something that is against his wishes.'

She put her head a little on one side and looked searchingly at me.

'Don't my wishes mean anything, then?'

We looked at each other, then I turned on the ignition.

'If you want to learn how to drive, I'll teach you,' I said, my heart slamming against my ribs.

I moved the gear lever to 'drive' and trod down on the gas pedal. The car went down the long driveway like a bullet out of a gun. At the gates, I stood on the brake pedal and, when the tyres bit, I swung the car on to the main highway and again gave it the gun.

For about five minutes I drove fast with the speedometer needle flickering around the nineties, then I slowed and turned off on to a secondary road and pulled up.

'My!' she exclaimed, and she sounded a little breathless. 'You can drive! I've never been driven as fast as that before.'

I got out and walked around the car.

'Move over,' I said, opening the offside door. 'You can't drive where you're sitting.'

She slid across the bench seat and I got in and sat in her place. I could feel the slight warmth of her body still on the seat and that made the blood quicken in my veins.

'Look, it's simple. Here's the gear lever. All you have to do is shift it down a notch, like this, then you press down on the pedal by your right foot. When you want to stop, you take your foot off that pedal and put it on the big one here on your left. That's the brake. Got it?'

'Why, it's easy,' she said, and in one movement she flicked down the gear lever and trod down hard on the gas.

The car took off like a crazy thing. She had absolutely no idea how to steer a car. I doubt if she looked where she was going.

For two or three seconds I was so startled I couldn't do anything. In those seconds we shot off the road, mounted the grass verge, skated along it with the offside wheels skidding, and then we slammed back on to the road again. As we tore towards a hedge on the other side of the road I grabbed the wheel and got the car straight.

'Take your foot off the gas!' I yelled at her and I managed to kick her shoe off the pedal. Still holding the wheel, I stamped down on the brake and brought the car to a violent stop.

Those had been hectic seconds. In another moment we could have been wrecked.

I turned off the ignition and turned to look at her.

The moonlight was coming through the open car window and I could see her clearly. She was completely unruffled and she was smiling. She looked so lovely she took my breath away.

'It's got power,' she said. 'I was a little heavy-footed, wasn't I? I shouldn't have pressed down so hard. Let's try again.'

'Now, wait a minute,' I said. 'That's a terrific way to attempt suicide. You don't stamp down ...'

'I know,' she said impatiently. 'You don't have to tell me. I pressed down much too hard. Let's try again.'

'Will you watch the road when the car is moving? The idea is to keep straight.'

She looked quickly at me and laughed.

'I was taken by surprise,' she said. 'I didn't think it had so much power.'

'That makes two of us,' I said and turned on the ignition. 'Take it dead easy: gently with the gas.'

'Yes, I know.'

She moved the gear lever into position and we took off around twenty miles an hour. Again she showed she hadn't an idea how to steer a car. We bounced up on the grass verge and then back on to the road, only this time we were going at a reasonable speed and I could control the car. I kept my hand on the steering wheel and, for fifty yards, we kept a straight course.

'I don't see how I can possibly learn if you do everything,' she said and pushed my hand away.

We promptly darted towards the hedge. I got my foot on the brake pedal and stopped the car just in time.

'You don't seem to have the knack of this,' I said. 'Did Mr Aitken ever try to teach you to drive?'

'Roger?' She laughed. 'Oh, no, he wouldn't have the patience.'

'You're trying to drive too fast and you're not watching the road. Let's start again, and let's go a lot more slowly.'

This time she succeeded in driving a hundred yards at fifteen miles an hour, dead in the centre of the road.

'That's the idea,' I said. 'That's fine. Keep going like that and you'll get the feel of the thing.'

Then I saw, coming towards us, the headlights of a fast-moving car.

'Pull over to your right,' I said, 'and go slow. Watch the road.'

She pulled in too sharply and too far, and the offside wheels mounted the grass verge. The approaching car dipped its headlights and kept coming. I was sure she was going to pull the car off the verge and that would take her right into the path of the other car, so I stamped on the brake pedal and brought the Cadillac to a jerking stop. The other car swept past and went roaring on into the darkness.

'I wish you would let me do it,' she said a little impatiently. 'I could have managed.'

'Yeah, but it's the only car I've got.'

She turned to me and laughed.

'This is fun. I'm loving it. I know in a little while I'll be able to drive. Will you lend me your car sometimes if Roger won't let me use any of his?'

'You'll have to have a few more lessons before you go solo.'

'But when I can – will you lend me this car?'

'All right, but it will be difficult to fit in a time. I take it to work every day.'

'Perhaps when I want it, you could take the bus.'

'That's a thought, but I'm not wild about taking a bus. Besides, I use the car quite a lot when I'm at work.'

'On very special occasions, you could take a taxi, couldn't you?'

'I suppose I could.'

She peered at me.

'What you are trying to say is you don't want to lend me the car,' she said quietly. 'That's the truth, isn't it?'

If she had but known it, I would have given her the car if she had asked me for it: that's how far gone I was.

'It's not that,' I said. 'I'm just scared you'll hit something or someone will hit you. You will want a lot more practice before you can go out alone. Anyway, where do you want to go to on your own?'

'No particular place. I just want to drive. I want to feel the wind rushing by and to move fast. It's something I've always wanted to do.'

'Well, okay, when you can handle this car safely, you can borrow it.'

She put her hands on mine. The touch of her cool flesh really got me going.

'Do you mean that?'

'Yes, I mean it.'

'I can have the car when I want? All I have to do is to telephone and tell you when I want it and you'll let me have it?'

'That's all you have to do.'

'Honest?'

'Yes – honest.'

She sat staring at me for a long moment, then she gently patted my hand.

'I think you're the nicest man I have ever met.'

'I wouldn't say that,' I said, and my voice was husky. 'If you want the car you can have it. Now let's have another try at driving. Let's see if you can handle her better than last time.'

'Yes,' she said and turned on the ignition.

We drove along the road, and this time she was really pretty good, and even when two fast-moving cars snarled past her, she managed to keep the Cadillac on a straight course.

'I've got the hang of it now,' she said. 'I feel it,' and she increased speed.

I shifted a little closer to her so I could grab the wheel if I had to. My foot moved near the brake pedal, but she was keeping a straight course, and after a few moments, she really gunned the engine. The speedometer needle moved into the eighties.

'Better ease off,' I said. 'You're going too fast.'

'It's wonderful,' she exclaimed. 'I've always wanted to drive like this. What a car! What a beauty!'

'Ease off now!' I said sharply and put my foot gently on the brake pedal.

A car came out of the night with blazing headlights and stormed towards us. We were bang in the centre of the road. I trod on the brake.

'Get to your right!'

She swung the car to the right too sharply. If I hadn't trod down hard on the brake we would have hit the grass verge and we could have turned over. I grabbed the wheel and straightened the car as the other car stormed past us with a loud blast of its horn.

I stopped the Cadillac.

'Did you have to do that?' she asked, looking at me. 'I was going fine.'

'You certainly were.' I had had enough for one night. My nerves were sticking out of my skin. 'All you want is practice. That'll do for tonight. I'll take over now.'

'Well, all right.' She peered at the clock on the dashboard. 'Goodness! I must get back. He'll be wondering where I am.'

Those words made a conspiracy out of our association. They gave me a queer, bitter-sweet sensation.

'Will you drive really fast?' she went on as we changed places. 'Really fast?'

I pressed down on the gas pedal. In a few seconds, the Cadillac was tearing along at ninety miles an hour.

She hugged her knees and stared through the windshield at the two big blobs of light from the headlamps as they raced ahead of us. I had an idea she was surrendering herself to the sensation of speed and was revelling in it.

We reached the gates of the Gables at twenty minutes to eleven.

As I pulled up, she let out a long, deep sigh.

'You can drive,' she said. 'You really can. I loved that. I could have gone on at that speed forever. When am I going to have my second lesson?'

I hesitated for a brief moment. At the back of my mind, I knew this could be dangerous.

'Now look,' I said. 'I don't want to get you into trouble. If your husband really doesn't want you to drive ...'

She put her cool fingers on my wrist.

'He won't ever know – how could he know?'

Feeling her flesh on my flesh made me light-headed and utterly reckless.

'I'll be here at eight tomorrow night,' I said. 'I should be through just after nine.'

'I'll wait in the car.' She opened the door and got out. 'You don't know how much I've enjoyed this. I get so bored, but this has been the nicest and most exciting evening I've ever spent. I've really loved it.'

The hard white light of the moon showed me she was wearing lemon-coloured slacks and a bottle-green sweater. She had a shape on her under that sweater that made me catch my breath.

'My name is Lucille,' she said. 'Will you remember that?'

I said I would remember it.

She smiled at me.

'Then we meet tomorrow. Good night.'

She waved to me and then started to walk up the long drive towards the house.

I watched her go, my hands gripping the steering-wheel, my knuckles white. I sat there, breathing unevenly and quickly, watching her until I lost sight of her.

She was now in my blood like a virus: as deadly and as dangerous as that.

I didn't remember the drive back to the bungalow. I didn't remember getting into bed.

All I know of that night was I didn't sleep.

How could I sleep when my mind was on fire and the hours that separated our next meeting seemed like a hundred years?

3

I

The next three days followed a systematic pattern. I reached the office at nine o'clock every morning, left at seven, had a snack supper at an Italian restaurant on the highway that led past the Gables, and arrived at the big house at eight o'clock. I remained with Aitken for an hour and a half, discussing the business of the day and going through any letters that usually he would have dealt with, then I went down to the Cadillac, where Lucille waited for me.

It was this moment I lived for. The rest of the hours were just a chore to get through somehow and as quickly as possible. After I had said good night to Watkins and had heard him shut the front door, then, and only then, did I come really alive.

From nine-thirty until eleven o'clock, Lucille and I cruised the secondary roads. We didn't talk a great deal. For one thing she had to concentrate on her driving. I found her concentration failed and she was inclined to let the car wander about the road if I talked to her. Also she so obviously enjoyed handling the Cadillac that I could see she didn't really welcome any interruption to the sensation in which she revelled. It was only when we pulled up outside the big wrought iron gates of the Gables that we spent five or so minutes talking.

During those three evenings with her, my love for her grew to a degree that I had to exert a great deal of control not to show my feelings.

She did nothing to encourage me. She treated me as a friend whom she liked, and I knew she did like me. I could tell that by the way she spoke and the way she looked at me, but that was as far as it went.

It was my attitude towards her that bothered me. I knew if she gave me the slightest encouragement I could not have resisted making love to her.

I knew I was playing with fire. If ever Aitken found out what was going on, I was sure he would throw me out of the firm. She had said he was possessive, and by now I knew him well enough to realize he wouldn't for one moment tolerate me fooling around with his wife, no matter how platonic her feelings towards me were.

I kept telling myself that I should stop this before it got out of hand, then I tried to convince myself that, so long as Lucille wasn't falling in love with me, there surely could be no harm to continue the driving lessons.

As we were saying good night on the third evening, I reminded her I wouldn't be at the house the following night.

'Mr Aitken has given me the weekend off,' I explained. 'So I won't be up.'

'Does that mean I'm not going to have a lesson?' she asked twisting around in the car seat to look at me.

'Not until Monday night.'

'Are you going away, then?'

'No, I'm not going away.'

'Then why can't you come up as usual? You can meet me down here and not up at the house or perhaps you don't want to?'

'It's not that I don't want to, but I must admit this worries me sometimes,' I said, looking at her. 'I'm sure if your husband found out he would be furious.'

She laughed. She had the most infectious laugh I had ever heard. She put both her hands on my arm and rocked me a little.

'He would be absolutely livid, but we don't mind, do we? Besides, he will never find out.'

'Watkins or Mrs Hepple might see us ...'

'They never go out at night, but I tell you what we will do. I'll meet you at your place. I'll come down on my bicycle. May I do that? I'd like to see your bungalow.'

My heart began to beat fast.

'You'd better not. No, you mustn't come down there. If you really want a lesson tomorrow, then I'll be out here at nine o'clock but only if you really want it.'

She opened the car door and slid out, then she turned and looked in through the open window at me.

'I'll be here,' she said. 'Ches, I still think you're the nicest man I know. I am improving, aren't I? I'll soon be able to apply for a permit, won't I?'

'You're doing fine,' I said huskily. I would have given a lot to have taken her in my arms and felt her lips responding against mine. 'Okay, I'll see you tomorrow.'

Back in my big lounge, I lay in an easy chair, a double whisky and soda in my hand, while I considered my position.

I had known her now for five nights, and I knew I would never be more in love with any woman than I was with her. Was she aware of this or was she so naïve that she really believed I would risk Aitken's displeasure just to teach her to drive? That was something I just had to find out.

That suggestion of hers about coming to the bungalow bothered me. I had told her my house-boy left soon after seven, and I lived alone. Was this a hint that she was ready to return the love I felt for her?

I told myself reluctantly that this was unlikely. She had never encouraged me to think that she looked on me as anything more than a helpful friend who was teaching her to drive, and who was giving her a lot of pleasure with no expectation of favours in return.

I had to take this farther, I told myself. I had to find out if she realized the risk I was running. I was putting my whole future in the balance. If Aitken found out about us the New York job would go up in smoke.

I spent a restless night brooding over the situation. I was pretty short-tempered in the office the following morning, and it was a relief when I finally cleared my desk and collected a few papers I wanted to examine over the weekend.

Pat, who had borne my irritability without protest, came in with a few more letters for me to sign.

'For the love of Mike! I thought I had signed them all!' I barked at her.

'There are only six,' she said and laid them on the desk.

I took out my fountain pen and hurriedly scrawled my signature on the letters, then straightening and putting my pen away, I said: 'I'll be in first thing on Monday. I'll get off now. It's after six, isn't it?'

'It's nearly half past. Are you going away, Ches?'

I looked sharply at her, frowning.

'I don't know. I might. I'll probably play some golf.'

'I hope you get a little rest. You don't have to worry so much, Ches, you're doing fine.'

At any other time this would have encouraged me, but in my present mood it only irritated me.

'I'm not worrying,' I said curtly. 'See you on Monday,' and nodding, I left her, her eyes wide with surprise, her expression hurt.

Joe came out of his office as I walked down the corridor.

'Give me a lift to the station, Ches?'

'Okay.'

I didn't want him with me, but I couldn't very well refuse, as he knew I had to pass the station on my way to the bungalow.

We went together to the elevator.

As we were going down, Joe said: 'Seeing RA tonight?'

'No. He told me to take the weekend off. I've got the Wasserman TV script to look at. From what I've seen of it, it's not too bad.'

'Why don't you lay off work and take a rest?' Joe asked as we crossed the lobby. 'You're getting pretty nervy. What's biting you?'

'Nothing's biting me,' I said shortly as I made my way across the crowded sidewalk to where I had parked the Cadillac.

Joe slid in beside me.

'Well, for the past two days you've been snapping everyone's head off. You made Paula cry this afternoon.'

'Paula's a moron. I asked her three times to get Wasserman and she couldn't raise him.'

'He happened to be out. She can't perform miracles.'

I started the engine.

'What is this, Joe? Since when do I want your criticism?'

'Here we go,' Joe said, sinking down into the cushions of the bench seat. 'Now it's my turn. Well, okay, boy, if you think this is the way to act the Big Wheel, I won't stop you, but take my advice and try to relax. You're leaning too hard on the job.'

I knew he was right and I suddenly felt ashamed of myself.

'Yes. Sorry, Joe. I'll be okay after the weekend.'

'I guess I'd act the same,' Joe said generously. 'You have quite a job to hold down now.' Then changing the subject, he went on: 'You know I envy you this car – what a beaut!'

'I always wanted a Caddy. It cost me plenty, but it's worth every nickel. Although I've had it now for eighteen months, I still get a bang out of it.'

'I would too. When this New York job jells, and if RA ups my salary, I plan to buy one just for the hell of it.'

'If we land the job, Joe, I'll see you get a rise.'

'What are the prospects? Has he said anything about it again?'

'He was talking about it last night. I think it's in the bag. He asked me how soon I could raise the money.'

'Do you think it's a good idea to invest your money with him, Ches?'

'I'm sure of it. An office in New York can't go wrong. With a stake in the business, I get five per cent of the gross as well as my salary. I'd be crazy not to take the chance. Besides, I'll be running the business more or less myself so I can protect my stake.'

'Wish I had some dough,' Joe said. 'Five per cent of the gross! You're going to be rich, Ches.'

My hands tightened on the driving wheel. I could be rich if I wasn't found out, I thought. I might even be rich enough to take Lucille away from Aitken.

'Well, a lot depends on how we run the place, Joe.'

'How soon can you raise the dough?'

'I've told my brokers to go ahead and sell out. I should have it in a few days. The market's just right. A bit of luck that: I could have been stuck.'

I slowed down as we came to the station.

'Thanks, Ches,' Joe said as he got out of the car. 'Maybe I'll buy this off you one of these days,' he went on, patting the Cadillac's wing. 'You'll be able to get an Eldorado when you get to New York. Would you think of selling it to me?'

'You wait until you get some money,' I said and grinned at him, 'but I might. So long. Have a good weekend.'

I drove fast towards my bungalow.

II

At one minute to nine, I pulled up outside the tall wrought-iron gates that guarded the entrance to the Gables.

Lucille was standing in the shadows, waiting for me.

I let the driver's door swing open as she came quickly towards me. As she came out of the shadows and into the hard light of the moon I saw she was wearing a pale-blue dress with a flared skirt. Her hair was taken back by a narrow ribbon. She looked pretty enough to take any man's breath away.

She slid under the driving wheel as I moved along the bench seat out of her way.

'Hello,' she said, smiling at me. 'You're beautifully punctual. Do you like my dress? I put it on specially for you.'

'It's terrific,' I said, 'and you look terrific also.'

She laughed happily.

'Do you think so? Do you really think so?'

'Yes.'

Maybe there was something in my voice that startled her. Anyway, she looked quickly at me, but I had my back to the moonlight and she couldn't see much of my face.

'Well, where shall we go?' she said. 'Let's go down to the sea.'

'All right.'

This night she didn't seem in the mood for speed. She drove at a steady twenty-five miles an hour, and at that speed, she drove pretty well.

We turned off the highway and cruised along one of the secondary roads until we reached a narrow dirt road that led down to the sea.

She hummed to herself softly as she drove and she was relaxed, her hands no longer clenched the wheel in a knuckle-white grip. I felt a little pang as I realized that she would soon be competent enough to apply for a permit, and the lessons would come to an end.

We drove slowly down the dirt road and turning a sharp bend we saw ahead of us a great stretch of sand with palm trees and the sea glittering like a polished mirror in the moonlight.

'Isn't this wonderful?' she said. They were her first words since she had driven away from the Gables. 'You don't know how much pleasure I get from driving this car, Ches. There's no sensation like it. I can drive now, can't I? I'm really good now, aren't I?'

'You're not so bad. You want more practice before you apply for a permit. You haven't tried reversing yet. Do you want to have a shot at it now?'

She shook her head.

'Not now.'

We drove down the lonely beach road, and she slowed, drove the car off the road and on to the hard sand, then she pulled up and turned off the ignition.

I sat motionless, my hands damp and clenched, my heart beating fast while I stared at the vast expanse of sand, sea and palm trees. In the hard light of the moon, the beach was lit up for miles. There was no sign of anyone out there, no cars, nothing. We might have been the only two people left in the world.

'I'm going for a swim,' she said as she turned off the car's lights. 'Will you come?'

This was unexpected, and it took me by surprise.

'You're supposed to be learning to drive. You haven't a lot of time. It's twenty to ten.'

'I told Roger I was going to the movies. He doesn't expect me back until midnight.' She opened the car door and slid out on to the sand. 'There's no one here: no one at all. We have the beach to ourselves. If you don't want to swim, stay in the car and wait for me.'

She started to run across the sand towards a clump of palm trees.

For a long moment I sat in the car and watched her. Surely this sudden move of hers must be the answer to the question that had nagged me most of the night? If she didn't mean to let me make love to her, surely she wouldn't have brought me to this lonely spot?

Only briefly did I pay heed to the warning bell that rang sharply in my mind. You're fooling with Aitken's wife, I told myself. You go ahead with this now, and you could regret it for the rest of your life.

But that didn't stop me. Breathing hard, with my heart thumping, I got out of the car.

I could see her clearly. She had reached the clump of palm trees. She paused to kick off her shoes, then she zipped down her dress and stepped out of it. She had on a one-piece swimsuit under her dress.

I went around to the back of the car, opened the boot and took out a couple of towels and my swimming trunks I always kept there. I stripped off behind the car, left my clothes on the sand, and picking up the towels, I ran down to where she was now moving slowly towards the sea.

As I joined her, she turned and smiled at me.

'I knew you would come. I'll tell you something. I've always wanted to swim in the moonlight, but Roger would never let me. He makes out it's dangerous.'

'You seem to be doing all the things you're not supposed to do – and with me,' I said, walking across the hot sand with her.

'That's why I like you so much,' she said.

Then, breaking into a run, she raced across the remaining strip of sand and splashed into the water.

She may have been only a learner driver, but she certainly could swim. I went in after her, but I saw it was hopeless to attempt to catch up with her. After a while, she turned around and came back, almost as fast as she had gone out.

She circled around me.

'Aren't you glad you came in?'

'I guess so.'

I turned on my back and stared up at the big moon. The water was warm, but I wasn't in the mood to appreciate it. I was impatient for her to finish her swim and come out.

She swam away from me, came back, and then floated beside me.

We remained floating in silence for some minutes, and they were the longest minutes I have ever lived through. Finally, I could stand it no longer.

'We'd better get back.'

I began to swim towards the shore and she kept pace with me.

As we came out of the water and began walking across the sand to where she had left her dress, she said suddenly: 'What are you doing tomorrow, Ches?'

'I don't know ... nothing in particular. I might play golf.'

'I was wondering if we could meet. I've been invited out by a girl friend. I can easily put her off and we could go for a long drive in the country.'

We were in the shadow of the palm trees now. I picked up one of the towels and tossed it to her. Then taking the other I began to dry my hair.

'We might be seen,' I said, and sat down on the sand.

She stood over me, drying her arms, her back to the moon.

'We could be careful. I could come to your place on my bicycle and we could keep off the main roads.'

I found myself screwing the towel between my clenched fists.

'I don't think it would be wise for us to meet during the day, Lucille. Anyone could see us.'

She dropped the towel and came to sit beside me. She wrapped her arms around her knees and pulled her knees up to her chin.

'It's a bore, isn't it?'

'It's certainly that.'

'It would have been fun to have gone out all day in the car. We could have taken a picnic. Don't you think we could risk it?'

'Do you want to risk it?' I asked, my voice suddenly harsh.

'I don't see who would see us. I could wear a big shady hat and sunglasses. I could put my hair up. I bet no one would recognize me.'

'Would you mind, Lucille, if your husband found out?'

She dropped her chin on her knees.

'Well, yes.'

'What would he do, do you think?'

'He'd be angry, of course, but don't let's talk about that. Look, suppose I come to your place? We could spend the day together. It's lonely there, isn't it? We could swim and have a picnic, and no one would see us.'

'You're not serious, are you?'

She thought for a long moment, then she jumped to her feet. 'No, I don't think I am,' she said. 'I'm feeling chilly. I'm going to get dressed.'

She picked up her dress and shoes and ran off towards the car.

I sat like a stone man, my hands still gripping the towel. I remained like that for perhaps ten minutes, then I heard her calling me.

'Ches ...'

I didn't move and I didn't look around.

'Aren't you coming, Ches?'

Still I didn't look around.

Then I heard her running across the sand and in a few moments she paused at my side.

'Didn't you hear me call you?' she asked, standing over me, her long, slim legs level with my eyes.

I looked up.

She had on her dress now, but it didn't help me to know she had nothing on under the dress.

'Sit down. I want to talk to you.'

She dropped on the sand within a few feet of me and curled her legs under her.

'Yes, Ches?'

'Would you really like to go for a drive tomorrow and have a picnic – the two of us?'

The moonlight was directly on her face. She showed her surprise.

'I thought you said ...'

'Never mind what I said. Would you like to do it?'

'Why, yes, of course I would.'

'Okay. Tell your husband you want to spend the day with me and if he agrees, then we'll go.'

She stiffened.

'But I can't do that. You know I can't. He – he doesn't know I know you.'

'Then tell him we've got acquainted.'

'I don't understand.' She leaned forward and stared at me. 'You sound so angry. What is the matter, Ches?'

'Tell him we've got acquainted,' I repeated, not looking at her.

'But I can't do that. He wouldn't like it.'

'Why not?'

'Ches, I wish you would stop this. You know as well as I do why he wouldn't.'

'I don't know. You tell me.'

'He's jealous and silly about me. He wouldn't understand.'

'What wouldn't he understand?'

'Ches, you're being horrid. What's the matter?'

'I asked you what wouldn't he understand?' I said, turning to meet her eyes. 'You tell me. Just what wouldn't he understand?'

'He doesn't like me going around with other men.'

'Why? Doesn't he trust you?'

She remained silent and stiff, her eyes searching my face.

'Does he think you'll be unfaithful if you go out with some other man?' I demanded.

'Ches! What is the matter? Why are you so angry? Why are you speaking to me like this?'

'Would he think you'd be unfaithful to him if you went out with me?'

'I don't know. Ches, please, I don't like this. If you are going on like this I'm going to leave you.'

'Why don't you like it?' I said, suddenly furious. 'What's the matter with facing facts? You're a married woman, aren't you? You're not a virgin. You must know what a man thinks when a girl as lovely as you brings him to a lonely spot like this where there's no one about and at night. Or are you so dumb you don't know?'

She flinched back, her expression changing to shocked anger.

I leaned forward to stare at her.

'Are you in love with me, Lucille?'

She stiffened.

'In love with you? Why, no. What are you saying, Ches?'

The black bile of disappointment made me a little crazy.

'Then why bring me here? Why did you force yourself on me?' I demanded, my voice rising. 'What do you imagine I am? Do you think I'm made of stone?'

'I'm going ...'

She started to her feet. I reached out, grabbed her wrist and jerked her to me. She fell across my knees, her back arched, her face close to mine as I bent over her.

'Ches! Let me go!'

'I'm not made of stone,' I said, the blood hammering in my temples. I tried to get my mouth down on hers, but she began to struggle and I found her surprisingly strong. For a long, horrible moment I tried to subdue her. Then she got one hand free and struck me violently across my face.

The blow brought me to my senses.

I let go of her. She rolled clear of me and scrambled to her feet.

I sat there on the hot sand staring at her, my breathing fast.

She turned and ran towards the car.

I remained still, staring towards the sea, then I heard the engine of the Cadillac start up.

I got quickly to my feet.

The Cadillac was moving.

'Lucille! Don't ... Lucille!'

The car engine roared, then the car lurched into a wild, skidding circle and went away fast along the beach road.

'Lucille!'

I started to run, then stopped.

I stood motionless, my fists clenched, and listened to the steady roar of the car engine until it had died away.

4

I

It took me about forty minutes to walk back to my bungalow.

As I walked, I brooded over the scene I had had with Lucille. I told myself I must have been out of my mind to have done what I had done. It would serve me right if she went straight to Aitken and told him. Probably at this very moment she was telling him. I was too sick with myself to care. Again and again I saw her look of startled surprise when I had asked her if she loved me, and again and again I heard her reply: the words kept hammering in my mind.

My bungalow stood in a little garden, fifty yards from the sea. The nearest house was a quarter of a mile farther along the road: a house owned by a wealthy broker, Jack Seaborne, who only came for a month in the summer.

As I walked up the path from the beach, I saw there was a car parked before my front gate. I had only to take a few more steps up the path to see it was my Cadillac.

Then Lucille appeared from out of the shadows.

'Ches ...'

I came to an abrupt stop, staring at her.

'I've brought your car back,' she said in a small voice.

She too had stopped. A couple of yards separated us.

'Lucille, I'm sorry. I really am. I lost my head ...'

'Don't talk about it.'

'I'll take you home.'

'Could we go inside first? There's something I must tell you.'

'Better not. Come on, I'll take you home. You can tell me in the car.'

She lifted her thick hair off her shoulders with a movement that hinted oddly of despair.

'Please, can't we go inside for a moment?'

She was standing in the full light of the moon. She looked tense and there was a terror in her eyes that frightened me.

'We'll talk as I drive. You've got to get back ...' I stopped short as she began to sway. Her eyes suddenly rolled back and her knees buckled. I jumped forward as she began to fall and I caught her in my arms.

'Lucille! For God's sake! What is it?'

She collapsed against me, and I let her down gently to the ground. Kneeling beside her, her head against my chest, I held her to me. Her head dropped back. In the moonlight, she looked as white as a ghost. She looked so bad she frightened me.

Then her eyelids fluttered and opened. She stared up at me, then she tried to sit up.

'Take it easy,' I said. 'Don't move ...'

She rested her head against my shoulder and closed her eyes. I put my hand under her knees and lifted her. She was lighter than I expected her to be. I had no trouble carrying her up the path to the front entrance to the bungalow.

'I'll be all right now,' she said. 'Let me down. I'm sorry. I've never done this before.'

I set her down, holding her against me as I groped for my key. I found it, opened the door, then I picked her up again and carried her into the lounge. I laid her on the divan by the window.

'Stay quiet,' I said, and leaving her I went back into the hall and shut the front door. Then I came back and turned on the lights in the lounge.

She lay still, staring up at the ceiling, her eyes like holes cut in a sheet.

'I'll get you a drink,' I said. 'I can't say how sorry I am I behaved like this. A drink will pull you together.'

'I don't want one,' she said and covered her face with her hands. She began to cry.

I went over to the liquor cabinet, poured a little brandy into a glass and took it over to her.

'Drink this. It'll pull you together.'

'No, please.' She turned her head away. 'Ches, I'm terribly sorry. I've damaged your car.'

'There's no need to faint about that, and stop crying. You don't have to cry because you've damaged my car.'

She turned on her side and looked up at me. I was startled to see how white she was. There was a scraped bony look about her face that made her eyes look enormous.

'I didn't mean to do it,' she said, the words coming so fast it was difficult for me to follow what she was saying. 'He came up beside me and shouted at me. I didn't know he was behind me. I lost control of the car. There was an awful bang. There's a big scratch right along the door and the fender's dented.'

Suddenly I felt an icy chill start up my spine.

'What are you trying to tell me? Have you hit someone?'

She looked away from me and stared up at the ceiling. Her hands turned into fists.

'It wasn't my fault. I swear it wasn't. He came up from behind and shouted at me. I didn't even know he was there until he started shouting.'

'Who? Who shouted at you?'

'This policeman. He was on a motorcycle. He came up beside me and shouted ...'

I put down the glass of brandy and went over to the divan and sat beside her.

'You don't have to be frightened. Just tell me what happened.'

She began to beat her clenched fists together.

'I swerved when he started shouting. The side of the car hit him ...' She broke off and began to cry again.

I put my hands on my knees and squeezed until my knuckles turned white.

'Crying won't help,' I said sharply. 'What happened when you hit him?'

She drew in a long, shuddering breath.

'I don't know. I just kept on. I didn't look.'

I sat for a long moment, motionless, aware that my heart was beating heavily and sluggishly. Then I said: 'You mean you didn't stop?'

'No. I was frightened. I drove straight here.'

'Was he hurt?'

'I don't know.'

'Just where did this happen?'

'On the road leading from the beach.'

'You didn't hear him shout after you?'

'No. There was this awful bang against the side of the car, and that was all. I drove straight here. I've been waiting for you for more than half an hour.'

'Were you driving fast?'

'Yes.'

For a long moment I sat staring at her, then I got up.

'I'll be back in a moment. I want to look at the car.'

I got up and crossed the room to my desk. I took from one of the drawers a powerful flashlight. As I went out of the room, I heard her give a little sighing moan, and that chilled my blood as nothing else had done so far.

I walked down the path to the car. In the light of the moon I could see at once that the onside front fender had been damaged. When I turned on the flashlight I was able to see just how extensive the damage was.

The front headlamp was smashed and the fender buckled. There was a deep dent in the door panel and a long scar had been ripped into the paintwork. It ran in a jagged line the length of the door.

These details I took in with one brief glance. Then I moved around the car. There was a bright red stain that glistened in the light of my torch on the offside fender of the rear wheel. The white ring around the offside tyre was also sticky with the stuff. It didn't take me more than a second or so to accept the fact that this was blood, and I stared at it, feeling cold and sick.

It looked as if she had side-swiped the motorcycle, knocked the driver off, and had run over him with the rear wheel. And she hadn't stopped!

I turned off the flashlight and stepped back. The sweat on my face felt clammy and cold in the hot night air. He was probably in the road bleeding to death at this moment.

I went quickly back to the lounge.

She was still lying on her back, staring up at the ceiling, her fists clenched and her breath coming in quick, uneven gasps. She looked pretty bad.

I picked up the glass of brandy and went over to her.

'Here, drink some of this,' I said. 'Come on: it's no use crying.'

I lifted her head and made her drink a little. Then she pushed the glass away with a shudder.

'I'm going to see what has happened,' I said. 'Wait here. I'll be as quick as I can.'

She nodded, not looking at me.

I looked at the clock on the overmantel. The time was twenty minutes to eleven.

'Just wait here. I shouldn't be long.'

Again she nodded.

I left her and went down to the Cadillac. I paused and looked at the broken headlamp and the bent fender. I realized I would be crazy to take the car out on the road in this condition. If someone spotted the damage they might put two and two together when the news broke in the morning's papers as I knew it must break.

And yet I had to have a car and have it fast. Then I remembered that Seaborne who owned the house farther down the road kept a car in his garage for his vacation. I had been to his place off and on, and I knew he kept the key of the garage on a ledge above the garage doors. I decided to use his car.

I got in the Cadillac and drove fast down the road to the house. Leaving the Cadillac outside, I went to the garage, found the key and opened the double doors.

Seaborne's car was a battered 1950 Pontiac: a car he carted his six children around in when he came down here. I drove the Pontiac out on to the road, left it with its engine ticking over, then I got into the Cadillac and backed it into the garage, shut and locked the doors. I dropped the key into my pocket.

I got into the Pontiac and drove fast to the highway. It took me ten minutes to reach the beach road.

I approached the intersection cautiously. There were about six cars parked along the grass verge, their dipped headlamps making puddles of light along the road. A bunch of men and women were standing together looking towards the head of the beach road. Blocking the entrance to the road were two speed cops, standing beside their parked motorcycles.

With my heart slamming against my ribs, I pulled up behind the last of the parked cars and got out.

There was a fat man with a Panama hat resting on the back of his head standing alone by his car, his hands in his trouser pockets, staring at the speed cops.

I walked over to him.

'What goes on?' I said, trying to make my voice sound casual. 'What's the trouble?'

He turned to look at me. It was dark, and the lights from the headlights of the cars reflected downwards. He could see my legs and feet, but there wasn't much else of me he could see to recognize later.

'An accident,' he said. 'A cop got himself killed. I've always said these cops ask for trouble the way they get in front of you. Well, this one pulled that stunt once too often.'

I felt cold sweat break out on my face.

'Killed?'

'Yeah: a hit-and-run job. Can't say I blame the guy who did it. If I was unlucky enough to kill a cop, and there were no witnesses, damned if I would stick around and apologize. If they catch him, they'll crucify him. I've always said the cops in this town are no better than the Nazis were.'

'Killed him, did you say?' I scarcely recognized my voice.

'That's right: ran over his head. He must have hit the side of the car, and then the poor devil must have fallen under the rear wheel.' He pointed to a tall, thin man who was talking busily to the crowd. 'That's the fella who found him: the one in the grey suit. He told me. He said the poor guy's face was like a sponge of blood.'

Suddenly one of the speed cops came stalking across the road.

'Hey, you bunch of vultures!' he bawled, his voice violent and tough. 'I've had about enough of you. Get out of here! You hear me? It's swine like you in your hunks of metal who cause the accidents! Get out of here! Get out, the lot of you!'

The fat man said out of the corner of his mouth: 'See what I mean – a Nazi,' and he walked over to his car.

I went back to the Pontiac, started the engine, made a U-turn and drove back fast to the bungalow.

When I walked into the lounge, I found Lucille huddled up in one of the big easy chairs. She looked very small and defenceless and frightened, and her face was the colour of old parchment.

As I came into the lounge, she stiffened and stared up at me.

'Is it all right, Ches?'

I went over to the cocktail cabinet, poured myself a double whisky, added a little water and drank thirstily.

'No, I wouldn't say it is all right,' I said, moving to a chair near hers. I sat down, not looking at her.

'Oh.'

There was a long pause, then she said: 'Were you able ... did you see ...?'

'The police were there.' I couldn't bring myself to tell her she had killed him. 'I didn't see him.'

Again there was a pause, then: 'What do you think we should do, Ches?'

I looked at the clock on the overmantel. It was now twenty minutes past eleven.

'I don't think we can do anything,' I said.

I saw her stiffen.

'You mean we don't do anything at all?'

'That's what I mean. It's getting late. I'm going to take you home.'

She sat forward, her hands on her knees, and she stared at me.

'But, Ches, surely we must do something? I should have stopped. It was an accident, of course, but I should have stopped.' She began to beat her fists on her knees. 'He might recognize me if he sees me again. He might have taken the number of the car. Surely we must do something?'

I finished the whisky and put the glass down, then I got to my feet.

'Come on. I'll take you home.'

She remained motionless, her eyes wide and staring.

'You're keeping something from me, aren't you? What is it?'

'It's bad, Lucille,' I said. 'As bad as it can be, but you don't have to be frightened.'

'What do you mean?' Her voice was suddenly shrill.

'You ran over him.'

She clenched her fists.

'Oh, no! Is he badly hurt?'

'Yes.'

'Take me home, Ches. I must tell Roger.'

'You can't tell him,' I said. 'He can't do anything.'

'Oh, but he can. He's a friend of the Captain of Police. He'll be able to explain.'

'Explain what?'

'That I have only just learned to drive, of course. That it was an accident.'

'I'm afraid that won't make any impression.'

She became rigid, her eyes opening wide with terror.

'Is he so badly hurt? You don't mean – he's dead?'

'Yes. You'll have to know sooner or later. Yes, he's dead.'

She closed her eyes and her hands went to her breasts.

'Oh, Ches ...'

'Now, don't panic.' I tried to keep my voice steady. 'There's nothing we can do about it – anyway, for the moment. We're in a jam, but if we don't lose our heads ...'

She stared at me, her lips trembling.

'But you weren't in the car. It's nothing to do with you. It was my fault.'

'We're in this thing together, Lucille. If I hadn't behaved as I did, you wouldn't have rushed away like that. It's as much my fault as yours.'

'Oh, Ches ...'

She dropped her face down on the settee and began to sob. I watched her for a moment or so, then, getting up, I put my arms around her and pulled her against me.

'What will they do to us?' she gasped, her hands gripping my arms.

'You mustn't worry about that,' I said. 'There's nothing we can do until we see what the newspapers say tomorrow. Then we must decide.'

'Suppose someone saw me hit him?'

'No one did. There was no one on the beach.' My hands tightened around her. 'Did you pass any car after you hit him?'

She pushed away from me, got unsteadily to her feet and wandered over to the window.

'I don't think so. I can't remember.'

'It's important, Lucille. Try to remember.'

She came back to the divan and sat down.

'I don't think so.'

'All right. Now listen, we must discuss this tomorrow after we've seen the papers. Will you come down here? There's nowhere else I can think of where we can have an uninterrupted talk. Can you get here about ten?'

She was staring at me, her eyes empty holes in her face.

'Will they send me to prison?' she asked.

That gave me a horrible jolt. I realized if they caught her they would send her to prison. You can't kill a policeman and get away with it. You might kill anyone accidentally, and if you had a top-flight attorney you might beat the rap, but not if you killed a policeman.

'Stop talking like that! It won't get you anywhere. What time will you be here tomorrow? Can you get here by ten?'

'Are you sure we shouldn't do anything?' She began to beat her clenched fists together. 'If they find out ...'

'They won't find out. Will you listen to me, Lucille? We mustn't panic. We must first find out what the papers say. We mustn't do anything until we know all the facts. We'll know the facts tomorrow morning, then if you'll meet me, we can make up our minds what to do.'

She pressed her fingers to her temples.

'Don't you think I should tell Roger? He might be able to do something.'

If I had thought Aitken could have done something, I wouldn't have hesitated to go with her and tell him the whole sordid story, but I was certain he couldn't do a thing for her. If she went to him the truth would come out that she and I had been on the beach together. He would want to know why she had run off like that. Knowing Aitken, I felt sure he would have got the truth out of her, and then I would be sunk.

I drew in a long, slow breath.

'You can't tell him, Lucille. If you tell him, how will you explain what you were doing in my car? How will you explain what you were doing on the beach? How will you explain that you and I were on the beach together, that we undressed and swam together? If I thought your husband could do something, then I would go with you and tell him, but he can't. If you lose your head and tell him, you will give him grounds for a divorce, and I'll lose my job.'

She stared fixedly at me, then she said in a voice tight with panic: 'I'd rather be divorced than go to prison. Roger wouldn't let me go to prison. He has a lot of influence. I'm sure he wouldn't let me go to prison.'

I put my hands on her arms and shook her gently.

'Lucille! You're reasoning like a child. Once he knew you and I had been on the beach together, he would wash his hands of you. He wouldn't give a damn what happened to you. You must realize that.'

'That's not true,' she said desperately. 'He might divorce me, but he wouldn't let me go to prison. He's like that. He wouldn't allow it to be said his wife was in prison.'

'You still don't seem to realize how serious this is,' I said, trying to speak quietly and calmly. 'You have killed a policeman. All right, it was an accident, but you didn't stop and you haven't a driving permit. If you had killed anyone except a policeman, your husband might have been able to swing it, but even if he had more influence than Eisenhower, and he hasn't, he can't do a thing for you now.'

'So you mean I'll have to go to prison?'

Her face seemed to shrink and her eyes became rounder and larger. Terror spoilt her young, fresh beauty.

'No. They don't know you did it, and I don't think they will ever know. We would be fools to tell them until we know exactly what has happened. When we do know, then we'll be able to make up our minds just what we should do.'

She gnawed her underlip, looking at me.

'You mean we just don't do anything?'

'We don't do anything tonight. Have you understood about tomorrow? Will you come down here about ten? We can decide what to do then.'

She nodded.

'Well, come on, then. I'll take you home.'

She got up and walked ahead of me out of the lounge, across the hall and to the front door, then she stopped abruptly.

'We're not going back in the car, Ches? I don't think I could drive in it again.'

'I've another car. I borrowed it from a friend down the road.' I put my hand on her arm and eased her out on to the porch. 'We're not going back in the Cadillac.'

I turned off the light in the hall, closed the front door while she stood on the top of the porch. As I was turning the key in the lock, I heard a man's voice call out: 'Hey, is this your car?'

I felt as if I had put my hand out in the dark and had touched a naked electric cable. I don't suppose I started as much as I imagined, but I know I started pretty badly. I heard Lucille catch her breath sharply, but at least she had the sense to move quickly to one side into the shadows of the porch where she couldn't be seen.

I looked down the path. A man stood at the gate. It was too dark to see much of him, except that he was tall and bulky. Parked behind Seaborne's Pontiac was a Buick convertible, its bonnet lit by the Pontiac's tail lights.

'Stay where you are,' I whispered to Lucille, then I walked down the steps and down the path to where the tall man was standing.

'Sorry to give you such a start,' he said, and now I was close to him I could see he was around forty-five with a heavy moustache and a whisky-red, cheerful face. 'I thought you had seen me. Isn't that Jack Seaborne's car?'

'Yes,' I said, aware my breathing was too quick and too uneven. 'I've borrowed it while mine's in dock.'

'You Chester Scott?'

'That's right.'

'Glad to know you.' He thrust out his hand. 'I'm Tom Hackett. I don't know if Jack ever mentioned me. He's mentioned you to me often enough. I was passing and I wondered if the old sonofagun happened to be down here.'

I wondered if he had seen Lucille. We had come out of the lighted hall. It depended how long he had been standing at the gate.

I shook hands with him. My hand felt cold in his.

'No, Jack won't be down until August. He never comes down before then,' I said.

'I took a chance. I was on my way to Palm Bay. I'm staying at the Paradiso Hotel for a couple of weeks. The wife comes down by train tomorrow. She can't travel for long in a car: gets car sick.' He laughed easily. 'Not that

that's any skin off my nose. It gives me a little time to myself. I thought if Jack was here we might have a drink and a yarn together.'

'He won't be down until August.'

'Yeah, so you said.' He looked at me. 'If you've got nothing better to do, why don't we go some place and have a drink? The night's still young.'

'I'd like to, but I have a date.'

He looked past me towards the dark bungalow and he grinned.

'Well, if it's like that. I just had an idea we could make up a little party. Two's company, eh?' He moved back to look at the Pontiac. 'Good old bus. Going well?'

'Fine.'

'When you've nothing better to do, come over and see us,' he went on. 'The Paradiso. Pretty good joint: plenty of fun. Bring the girlfriend if she isn't too shy. Well, I mustn't keep you. So long for now.'

Waving his hand, he went back to the Buick, slid under the steering wheel, gunned the engine and drove away.

I stood motionless, watching his red tail lights disappearing down the road, my hands gripping the top rail of the gate, my heart slamming against my ribs.

'He saw me,' Lucille said, and her voice was unsteady. She came down the path and joined me at the gate.

'He saw I had a girl with me,' I said as calmly as I could, 'but he couldn't have seen enough of you to know you again. There's nothing to worry about.'

I took her arm and led her to the Pontiac. We got in.

'Are you quite sure I shouldn't tell Roger?' she asked in a small tight voice.

This was more than my jumping nerves could stand. I swung around, reached out, put my hands on her shoulders and gave her a hard little shake.

'Once and for all! I said no and I mean no! He can't do anything for you!' I was shouting at her now. 'If you tell him, you'll make him an accessory! Don't you realize that? If he doesn't hand you over to the police, he could get a sentence. You've got to leave this to me! I'll tell you what we will do tomorrow.'

She shrank away from me, and taking out her handkerchief she began to cry.

I drove fast towards Palm Boulevard.

II

On the highway I came suddenly on a long line of cars, crawling towards the city. I had never seen such a traffic jam, and I knew at once that it had to do with the death of this speed cop.

I had trouble in forcing my way out of the secondary road from my bungalow into the stream of traffic. Finally, someone gave way to me and I got into the line of the creeping cars.

Lucille stopped crying when she saw what was going on.

'What is it?'

'I don't know. There's nothing to worry about,' and I wished I really believed that.

We crawled on. Every now and then I looked at the clock on the dashboard. The hands showed ten minutes to twelve, and we still had about two miles to go before I got her home.

Suddenly the cars ahead of me crawled to a stop. I sat, gripping the wheel, staring into the darkness ahead of me, seeing only the red tail lights and maybe a hundred cars stretching in a long motionless line up the road.

Then I saw the cops. There must have been a dozen of them. They were moving down the line of cars, powerful flashlights in their hands, and as they passed, they threw the beams over each car.

That brought me out into a cold sweat.

'They're looking for me,' Lucille said in a voice tight with fear and she made as if to get out of the car.

I gripped her arm.

'Sit still!' My heart was thumping and I was thankful I had been smart enough to use Seaborne's car. 'They're not looking for you! They're looking for the car. Sit still and keep quiet!'

I could feel her shaking, but she had enough sense not to move as one of the cops neared us.

A big, broad-shouldered man got out of the car just ahead of us. As the cop came up to his car, the big man said in an explosion of rage: 'What the hell is this? I'm trying to get to Palm Bay. Can't you guys keep this goddamn road clear?'

The cop sent his beam over him.

'You can come down to the station and make a complaint if that's the way you feel about it,' he said in a voice that could have peeled rust off the keel of a ship. 'You'll go when we're good and ready for you to go, and not before.'

The big man seemed to lose some of his size.

'What's going on anyway, officer?' he asked in a much milder tone. 'Are we likely to be long?'

'A hit-and-run job. We're checking all cars going out of the city,' the cop said, 'and you won't be long.'

He checked the big man's car, then moved on to mine. I found myself gripping the wheel until my fingers hurt as he sent the beam of his flashlight over my wings, and then over the bumpers.

The cop, a thickset man with a face that could have been carved out of flint, looked at me, his light swinging first on me and then on Lucille, who cringed back, catching her breath sharply. He didn't seem to notice anything for he moved on to the car behind us.

I put my hand on her arm.

'Take it easy. There's nothing to be frightened about.'

Frightened? Cold sweat was rolling off me.

She didn't say anything. She sat, her hands gripped between her knees, and she breathed like an old woman of seventy after a climb up a flight of stairs.

The car ahead of me began to move, and I went after it. We crawled on in silence for four or five hundred yards, then the pace quickened.

'They were looking for me, weren't they, Ches?' she said, her voice shaking.

'They were looking for the car, and they didn't find it.'

'Where is it?'

'Where they won't find it. Now look, will you stop working yourself into a panic? Just sit still and keep quiet!'

Ahead of us was the intersection that led to Palm Boulevard. I pulled out of the line of traffic and increased speed. I reached the entrance to the Gables as the hands of the dashboard clock showed ten minutes after twelve.

I got out, went around to the offside door and opened it.

'I'll see you at my place tomorrow at ten,' I said.

Slowly, as if her legs were cast in lead, she got out of the car.

'Ches! I'm frightened! They were looking for me.'

'They were looking for the car. Now look, go to bed and try to get this thing out of your mind. There's nothing either of us can do until tomorrow.'

'But they're checking all the cars! The policeman said so.' She stood there, staring up at me, her eyes terrified. 'It's serious, Ches. It really is! Don't you think I should tell Roger? He's good at this sort of thing.'

I drew in a long, slow breath.

'No,' I said, trying to keep my voice from rising. 'He can't help you. I'm the only one who can handle this. You've got to trust me.'

'I just couldn't bear to go to prison.'

'You won't go to prison. You've got to stop working yourself into a panic. We'll discuss it tomorrow.'

She seemed to make an effort to pull herself together. 'Well, all right. I'll wait until tomorrow if you say so,' she said. 'But, Ches, if you don't think you can handle it, I must go to Roger.'

'I'll handle it. Now go to bed and leave it with me.'

For a long moment she stared at me, then turned and began to walk unsteadily up the drive towards the house.

I watched her go until I lost sight of her.

Then I got into the Pontiac and drove back to the bungalow.

While I drove, fear like a misshapen gnome, sat silently on my shoulder.

5

I

By ten minutes to ten the following morning, I was in such a state of jitter, I did something I have never done before. I drank two double whiskies, one after the other, in an attempt to steady my nerves and quell the sick apprehension that had been gnawing at me all night.

I had had very little sleep, and at seven o'clock I began to prowl around the bungalow, waiting for the boy to deliver the newspapers. For reasons best known to him, he didn't arrive until past eight. As I went out to pick up the papers he had tossed on to the porch, Toti, my Filipino servant, arrived.

Afraid to look at the paper, while he was around, I told him to wash up the coffee things and then get off.

'I'm not going to the office this morning, Toti.'

He looked at me in concern.

'You sick, Mr Scott?'

'No. I'm just taking the weekend off,' I said, moving towards the terrace, the newspapers burning my hand.

'You look sick,' he announced, continuing to stare at me.

'Never mind how I look,' I snapped. 'Get rid of the breakfast things, and then get off.'

I was frantic to look at the papers, but I somehow managed to control myself. Toti was a smart boy. I didn't want him to suspect anything was wrong.

'I planned to clean up the kitchen this morning, Mr Scott,' he said. 'It needs it. I won't be in your way.'

Speaking slowly and controlling my voice with an effort, I said: 'Leave it till Monday. It's not often I have a weekend off, and I want to potter around here on my own.'

He shrugged his shoulders.

'Okay, Mr Scott, anything you say.'

Again I started towards the terrace.

'Oh, Mr Scott ...'

'Well? What is it?'

'Could I have the key to the garage?'

My heart skipped a beat. He would naturally want to know what the Pontiac was doing there and where the Cadillac was. The Cadillac was one of his great prides. He kept it clean, and it was due to his continual attention that the car still looked brand new after eighteen months of hard driving.

'What do you want it for?'

'There's some cleaning rag in there I want to take home, Mr Scott. My sister said she'd wash it out for me.'

'For the love of Mike, don't bother me with that!' I snarled at him. 'Forget it! I want to read the papers.'

I went out on to the terrace and sat down. I didn't move until I heard him go into the kitchen, then with an unsteady hand I unfolded the papers.

In banner headlines splashed across the front pages, the newspapers screamed that this was the hit-and-run case to end all hit-and-run cases. This, they yelled, was the most callous, ruthless motor killing of all time.

According to the *Palm City Inquirer*, Patrol Officer

Harry O'Brien, the dead man, had been one of the most popular officers on the City's force. All three newspapers carried a picture of the dead man who looked a typical hard, brutal cop: a man around thirty years of age with small, granite-hard eyes, a lipless mouth and coarse heavy features.

The *Palm City Inquirer* said he was a good Catholic, a good son to his parents and a hard-working, conscientious police officer.

'Only two days before he was so ruthlessly struck down, O'Brien had told friends that he was planning to get married at the end of next month,' the account went on. 'It is believed his *fiancée* is Miss Dolores Lane, the popular entertainer at the Little Tavern nightclub.'

The editors of all three newspapers shrilly demanded that the City's Administration should find the driver of the car and punish him as he deserved.

But it wasn't the hysterical yapping of the press that really scared me. The attitude of the police was far more menacing.

John Sullivan, Captain of Police, in a press interview held late last night, said that not one of his men would rest until they had found the driver who had killed O'Brien.

'Make no mistake about it,' Sullivan had concluded in a ten-minute speech in which he had extolled O'Brien's qualities, 'we will find this man. This is no ordinary accident. There have been police officers in the past who have been unlucky enough to have been killed in motoring accidents, but the drivers involved have faced up to a court hearing. They didn't run away. By running away, this man has branded himself as a killer, and I will not tolerate killers in this city. I will find him! We know his car is badly damaged. Every car in this city is going to be checked. I mean exactly that. Every car owner will be given a clearance certificate. Any driver damaging his car after the time of the accident must report the damage to the police or he will find himself on a hook. He will have to convince my men just how the damage was done, and if he can't, then I'll talk to him and I'll be sorry for him if he can't convince *me*. Road blocks have been set up. No car can leave the city without being checked for damage. I am satisfied we have the killer's car trapped. It's hidden somewhere and we only have to find it. And when we've found it, I'll teach the owner it is damn bad medicine to kill one of my boys and run away.'

So by the time it was ten minutes to ten, by the time I had got rid of Toti, by the time I had thought over what I had read, I was glad to drink two double shots of whisky.

It seemed incredible to me that the police should be planning to check every car in the city. The task would be enormous, but then I remembered once reading of how a police force had searched practically every refuse bin in a city while hunting for a murder weapon, and after four days of incredible labour and patience, had found it. I told myself it would be dangerous to underestimate Sullivan. If he really meant what he said, and if he wasn't just putting on a show for the press, it might perhaps be possible to check every car, even if it did take weeks.

At ten o'clock, I went down the path and stood at the gate to watch for Lucille.

I hadn't had much time to make up my mind what my immediate moves should be, but I had come to two important decisions. I decided there was no question of going to the police and telling them the truth. I also decided that if the Cadillac was found, I would have to take the blame for the accident.

It wasn't entirely my infatuation for Lucille that prompted me to take this decision. It was obvious to me I had little choice. There was no point in both of us getting into trouble, and besides, I felt I was really to blame. If I hadn't lost my head and had behaved as I had done, she wouldn't have driven off on her own.

If I let her take the blame, the truth would come out and I would not only lose my job but I could go to prison as an accessory. If I kept her out of it, and I was lucky to get off with a light sentence, it was possible Aitken would give me back my job after I had served my sentence.

I was still brooding about this when Lucille arrived.

I put her bicycle in the garage and then took her into the lounge.

'You've seen the papers?' I said as I shut the door.

'Yes, and it's on the radio this morning. Did you hear what they said?'

'The radio? No, I didn't think of that. What did they say?'

'They are asking for information.' Her voice was unsteady. 'They want anyone who saw a damaged car on the roads last night to come forward. They're asking all garages to report at once if anyone asks them to repair a damaged car.' She stood, staring at me, her face white and drawn. 'Oh, Ches ...' Then she was suddenly in my arms, her face against my shoulder. 'I'm frightened. I'm sure they will find me. What am I going to do?'

I held her close to me.

'It's going to be all right,' I said. 'I've been thinking about it. You don't have to be frightened. Let's talk it over. You have nothing to worry about.'

She pushed away from me and frowned at me.

'How can you say that? What do you mean?'

She had on an open-neck shirt and pale green snug-fitting slacks. Even in this crisis I found myself thinking what a beautiful little creature she was.

'Sit down,' I said and I led her over to the settee.

She sat down and I took an easy chair opposite her.

'There's no point in both of us being in this mess,' I said. 'If the car is found, I'm taking the entire blame.'

She stiffened, her hands turning into fists as she gazed blankly at me.

'But you can't do that. It was my fault ...'

'It was an accident. If you had stopped and if you had got help, Lucille, you would have most likely got away with it. But to have got away with it, you would have had to tell the court the truth. You would have had to tell them why you went off in the car. It would have kept you out of prison, but landed you in the middle of a scandal. You can imagine how the press would have picked on us both. Your husband would probably have divorced you, and I would most certainly have lost my job. So even if you go now and tell the police what happened we would be both in a very serious jam. You see that, don't you?'

She nodded.

'I don't intend to tell the police what happened,' I went on. 'There's just a chance they won't find the Cadillac, and I'm going to take that chance. But if they do find it, then I'm going to tell them I was driving and I hit the policeman. It's important to both of us that you are kept out of it. I might be lucky and get off with a light sentence. Your husband seems to think a lot of me, and he might have me back when I come out. But once you are involved, he would blacklist me and I'll never get another job in advertising. So you see I'm thinking of myself as much as you when I say I'll take the blame.'

She sat motionless for a long moment, then her hands suddenly relaxed.

'You really mean it, Ches? You really will tell them you did it?'

'Yes, that's what I mean.'

She drew in a deep breath.

'Well, if you're sure ...'

'I'm sure.'

She lifted her hair off her shoulders, frowning. She didn't look as relieved as I expected her to look.

'Doesn't that make you feel better, Lucille?'

'Oh, yes, of course.' She stared down at her hands, then said: 'There is one thing, Ches. I left my swimsuit in your car.'

I felt a little pang of disappointment. I thought she might have thanked me for letting her out of this mess.

'Well, that's all right. I'm going to check the car when you have gone. I'll get the swimsuit, and when next I come to the house, I'll bring it with me.'

She moistened her lips with the tip of her tongue.

'Could we go now and get it?'

'I'll get it when I check the car.'

'I would like it now.'

Then I realized why she was being so persistent. If the police found the car and the swimsuit, they might trace the swimsuit to her.

'All right. You wait here. I'll get it now.'

'I'd like to come with you ...'

'You'd better not. We can't afford to be seen together.'

'I'd rather come.'

I stared at her.

'What is it, Lucille? Don't you trust me to give it to you?'

She looked away.

'It's very important to me.'

'Of course, but it's also important no one sees us together. I'll get it for you.'

She got to her feet.

'I'd rather come with you, Ches.'

I restrained my rising temper with difficulty. Turning, I walked into the hall. She followed me.

'Wait here,' I said. 'I'll get the car.'

Leaving her on the top step, I went to the garage and drove the Pontiac out on to the road. I got out and looked up and down the road. There was no one in sight.

'Come on,' I said, waving to her.

She ran down the steps, down the path and scrambled into the car. I got in beside her and drove fast the quarter of a mile to Seaborne's house.

We both got out.

Leading the way, I started up the drive towards the garage, then I suddenly came to an abrupt stop. Lucille paused at my side.

The garage door stood ajar.

The previous night I had locked the doors after I had put the Cadillac away. There was no question about that. I had not only locked them, but I had taken care to make certain they had been secure.

'What is it, Ches?' Lucille asked sharply.

'Wait here,' I said, and breaking into a run, I covered the last twenty yards to the garage, pushed open the doors and looked inside.

The Cadillac was still there. The hard sunlight made the bent fender and the broken lamp look uglier than they had looked the previous night in the light of my flash-lamp.

I looked at the lock on the double doors. A chill snaked

up my spine as I saw the lock was bent and twisted. There were claw marks of a jemmy dug into the woodwork.

Lucille joined me.

'What is it?'

'Someone has been here.'

She caught her breath sharply.

'Who?'

'How should I know?'

She caught hold of my arm.

'Do you think it was the police?'

'No. If it had been the police they would have come for me. My name's on the licence tag.'

'The swimsuit, Ches!'

'Where did you leave it?'

'On the floor at the back.'

I moved into the garage, opened the rear door of the car and looked inside.

If she had left the swimsuit on the floor of the car, it wasn't there now.

II

Overhead an aircraft droned: there was no other sound. The silence seemed to me to go on for a long time. I stood by the car looking into the emptiness of the back seat and the floor, aware that my heart was thumping.

Then Lucille said in a small voice: 'What is it?'

I turned and looked at her.

'It's not here.'

Her eyes opened very wide.

'It must be there! Let me look!'

I stood aside and she peered into the car.

'It must be here,' she muttered and got into the car, her hands feeling under the seat.

'Are you sure you didn't leave it on the beach?'

'Of course I'm sure!' Her voice was strident. 'I put it on the floor!'

She got out of the car, her eyes were wide with panic.

'Perhaps you put it in the boot,' I said, and going around to the car, I lifted the boot lid and looked inside. There was no swimsuit. I closed the boot and came back to where she was standing.

'What have you done with it?' she demanded.

I stared at her.

'What do you mean? I've done nothing with it. I didn't even know you had left it in the car.'

She moved away from me.

'You're lying! You've taken it and hidden it!'

'How can you say such a thing! I tell you I didn't even know it was in the car!'

Her face was now tense, and her eyes glittered. She no longer looked young and fresh and beautiful. I scarcely recognized her.

'Don't lie to me!' she said furiously. 'You've taken it! Where is it?'

'Have you gone crazy? Someone's been here! You can see that for yourself! Look at the door! Whoever it was found the swimsuit and has taken it!'

'Oh, no! No one's been here. It was you who forced the door! So that's why you are so willing to take the blame,' she said, her voice low and furious. 'You thought I'd be so grateful to you I'd fall down and kiss your feet, didn't you? You thought you could make love to me, didn't you? I'd be so grateful to you, I'd let you! That was the idea, wasn't it? And all the time you were planning to give me away! You planned to put the swimsuit back in the car so the police would know I had been with you in the car!'

I very nearly slapped her face, but controlled myself in time.

'All right, Lucille, if you want to believe that, then believe it,' I said. 'I didn't take your swimsuit. You frightened little fool! Someone has been here and has taken it, but it wasn't me.'

She stood motionless, staring at me, then she put her hands up to her face.

'Yes,' she said. 'Of course.'

Her voice was so soft I could scarcely hear it.

'What does that mean?' I asked, watching her.

She pressed her temples with her fingertips, then suddenly she gave me a ghost of a smile.

'I'm sorry, Ches. I'm really sorry. I didn't mean to speak to you like that. I didn't sleep last night. My nerves are in a dreadful state. Please forgive me.'

'Oh, forget it.'

'Who could have taken it, Ches? It could have been the police, couldn't it?'

'No. It wasn't the police.'

She looked away from me. I had a sudden feeling I no longer existed for her, that her thoughts had carried her far away.

'There's no point in you staying here, Lucille,' I said. 'It's dangerous.'

She started slightly, looked at me for a moment, her eyes appeared to be slightly out of focus, then a more lively expression came into them as if she was suddenly seeing me clearly.

'Yes. Will you give me a cigarette, please?'

Surprised, I took out my pack of Camels and offered her one. She took the cigarette, put it between her lips and accepted the light from my lighter. She pulled hard on the cigarette, then let the smoke come rolling out of her mouth. All the time she stared fixedly at the oily, concrete floor of the garage.

I watched her. It was like seeing a child after several years: a child that had grown suddenly into a woman.

She looked up and saw I was watching her. She smiled: it wasn't any easy smile, but it made her look very desirable and lovely.

'So we're in this mess now together aren't we, Ches?'

'Not necessarily. It could have been a sneak thief.'

'Do you think so? It could have been a blackmailer.'

I stared at her.

'Why do you say that?'

'It's something I feel,' she said, after a moment's hesitation. 'We are in an ideal position to be blackmailed, aren't we? I for killing this policeman, and you for trying to seduce me.'

For several seconds I said nothing. That angle hadn't struck me, but now she had put it into words, I could see she could be right.

'It doesn't necessarily follow ...'

'No. We must wait and see what happens.' She moved past me to the garage door. 'I suppose I had better get back.'

'Yes.'

We moved out into the hot sunshine. She waited while I closed the garage doors.

'I'll have to come back and fix this lock,' I said after I had tried to wedge the two doors together and had failed.

'Yes.'

She walked down the path, the sun making the lights in her glossy hair glitter. From behind, she made a trim little figure in her slacks and yellow shirt: trim and excitingly feminine.

She got into the Pontiac and sat upright, her slim hands resting on her knees.

I got in beside her, started the engine, U-turned and drove back fast to my bungalow.

During the short run back to the bungalow neither of us said anything.

I pulled up outside the gate.

'I'll get your cycle.'

'I'll come in, Ches. I want to talk to you.'

'Well, all right.'

I followed her up the path and into the bungalow. She went on ahead of me into the lounge while I paused to lock the front door.

As I came into the lounge, she sat down in an easy chair and stared out of the big window at the beach and the sea.

I looked at the clock on the overmantel. The time was a quarter to eleven. It seemed a lifetime since she had come out of the shadows last night and had fainted in my arms. I moved over to another chair and sat down. I looked at her. She was no longer the lovely kid I had been infatuated with when I had seen her for the first time, admiring herself in the mirror. Since then, she had grown a skin: a veneer of hardness. She was still lovely, still desirable, but the innocence and the youth were now missing.

She turned her head slowly and looked at me. Our eyes met.

'I seem to have made a complete mess of this,' she said. 'Thanks to you, I could have ducked out, but leaving that swimsuit puts me back into the picture again, doesn't it?'

'I wouldn't say that,' I said, speaking slowly and carefully. 'It depends who took it. A sneak thief might have broken in in the hope of finding something valuable. There was nothing else in the car except the swimsuit. He might have taken that in the hope of raising a few dimes on it.'

She shook her head.

'I don't think so. You see, the suit had my name on it.'

I looked at her, my heart suddenly beginning to thump.

'Nearly everyone in this city knows how rich Roger is,' she went on.

I felt my hands turn damp. I had really believed that a sneak thief had broken into the garage, but this matter-of-fact utterance of hers lit up a red light in my mind.

'After all,' she went on, not looking at me, and speaking very quietly, 'why should a sneak thief take a swimsuit? Who would want it? I think we are going to be blackmailed, Ches.'

'You're jumping to conclusions ...'

She made an impatient little movement with her hands.

'That remains to be seen.' She turned her head slowly and looked directly at me. 'Would you pay blackmail, Ches?'

'That gets you nowhere,' I said trying to match her quiet tone, but aware that my voice was harsh. 'Once you start to pay blackmail, you have a monkey on your back.'

'I just wanted to know.' She stared down at her hands, turned them and looked at her blood-red fingernails. 'I think I must talk to Roger.'

'He can't do anything,' I said sharply.

She continued to study her hands.

'You don't know him as well as I do. He is very particular about his position and what people think of him. If I told him exactly what had happened and that you were willing to take all the blame, then I think he would pay blackmail.'

I sat staring at her in frozen silence.

'He has a lot of money,' she went on after an interminable pause. 'He can drive a very hard bargain. I don't think it would cost him much. I think he would pay.'

'But he would divorce you,' I said.

'I'd rather be divorced than go to prison.'

I took out my pack of Camels, lit one and noted my hand was steadier than I expected it to be.

'But we don't know yet that we are going to be blackmailed.'

She lifted her hair off her shoulders in a nervous gesture I had come to recognize.

'You think this man took my swimsuit as a souvenir?' she asked with exaggerated politeness.

'You don't have to be sarcastic about it,' I said. 'I'm trying to be helpful.'

'At least you might be realistic.'

'At the moment there is no question of blackmail,' I said, my voice sounding unnaturally loud. 'I said I would keep you out of this, and I mean it.'

She regarded me, her eyes thoughtful.

'Does that mean you will pay this man to keep quiet?'

'What man?'

'The man who took my swimsuit.'

'But he is only a figment of your imagination,' I said. 'We don't even know he exists.'

'Do you think my swimsuit disappeared of its own accord?'

'I think it's possible you left it on the beach.'

'I did not!' Her eyes flashed as she shouted the words at me. 'I left it in the car, and someone has taken it!'

'All right, there is no need to get worked up about it. It could have been a sneak thief.'

She stared fixedly at me.

'Ches, will you swear you didn't take it?'

'Oh, for heaven's sake! Don't start that again!'

'Will you swear you didn't take it?'

'Of course I didn't take it!'

I met her searching eyes angrily.

She let her hand fall back against the back of the chair and she shut her eyes.

'I thought it was you who called me on the telephone this morning,' she said. 'I thought you were trying to frighten me. It sounded like your voice.'

I stiffened.

'What do you mean? Who telephoned you?'

'This morning, around nine o'clock, the telephone rang. I answered it. A man asked if it was Mrs Lucille Aitken speaking. I had an idea it was you. I said it was. Then he said, "I hope you enjoyed your swim last night," and then he hung up.'

I stubbed out my cigarette, feeling suddenly cold.

'Why didn't you tell me this before?'

'I thought it was you. That's why I was so anxious to go with you to get my swimsuit.'

'It wasn't me.'

She opened her eyes and stared at the ceiling.

'That's why I say I think we're going to be blackmailed.'

'But there was no one on the beach. We couldn't have been seen,' I said.

'Whoever it was knew I had been in for a swim.'

'And you think this man is the one who has taken the swimsuit?'

'Yes.'

I got slowly to my feet and walked over to the liquor cabinet.

'Will you have a drink?'

'Well, all right.'

'Whisky or gin?'

'Oh, whisky.'

I poured two stiff drinks into glasses and dropped in ice cubes. As I picked them up to carry them across the room the telephone bell started to ring.

I felt my muscles stiffen. Slowly I put the glasses down. Lucille was upright in her chair, her hands on her knees, her knuckles white.

We stared at each other as the bell created a strident clamour in the silent room.

'Aren't you going to answer it?' she said, her voice a husky whisper.

I moved slowly across the room and took up the receiver.

'Hello?' I said and my voice didn't sound like my own.

'Is that Mr Chester Scott?'

A man's voice. I had the impression the tone was frivolous. It was like listening to a man who has a secret joke he is reluctant to share with anyone.

'Yes. Who is it?'

'You should have made love to her, Mr Scott. You should never have let her run away. After all, that is what women are given to us for.'

The words were spoken slowly and distinctly. There was no possibility of mistaking them.

'What do you mean?' I said, feeling cold sweat on my face. 'Who is that?'

The steady humming sound in my ear told me I was talking over a dead line.

6

I

The sound the telephone receiver made as I dropped it back on to its cradle was like a minor explosion in the tight silence of the room.

I turned slowly and looked at Lucille.

She was sitting upright, tense and frightened, her hands gripping her knees.

'Who was it?' she asked breathlessly.

'I don't know,' I said, moving back to my chair. I sat down. 'But I can make a guess, I think it was the same man who telephoned you this morning.'

I told her exactly whet the man had said.

She hid her face in her hands.

I was feeling pretty bad myself. This had been a shock, and I stared out of the window, trying to control my shaking hands.

She said: 'Oh, Ches! What are we going to do?'

'I don't know,' I said. 'This is a complication.'

'You see, I was right. He is going to blackmail us.'

'He said nothing about blackmail and until he does there's no point in assuming he's going to blackmail us.'

'Of course he is going to blackmail us! He has the swimsuit, he knows you and I were on the beach together, he knows it was my fault the policeman was killed! Of course he is going to blackmail us!'

'Now wait a moment. We don't know he has the swimsuit and we don't know he knows you killed O'Brien. All we do know for certain is that he saw us on the beach.'

'Of course he has the swimsuit and he's seen the damaged car!'

'We don't know that for certain, Lucille!' I said sharply. 'If these two telephone calls are a preliminary softening-up process for blackmail, we may find he is going to threaten to tell your husband he saw us on the beach together. He may know nothing about the accident.'

She made an impatient movement.

'What does it matter? Even if he doesn't know about the accident, we'll still have to pay him if you don't want to lose your job and I don't want to lose Roger.'

'Don't be so sure about it,' I said, staring at her. 'We could go to the police. They know how to deal with a blackmailer, and they would keep us out of it.'

'How can you talk like that?' she said angrily. 'He's seen the car!'

'We don't know that. He might not have noticed it in the darkness. He might have searched the inside of the car, found your swimsuit and not noticed the damage.'

'You're talking for the sake of talking. I'm sure he knows about the accident!'

'Then why didn't he mention it? That would be a far more powerful lever for blackmail.'

She lay back as if suddenly exhausted, her hands dropping limply in her lap.

'Have it your own way. I know you are wrong, but have it your own way. What are you going to do?'

'Nothing about him for the moment. I admit he's a complication, but he isn't the main danger. The real danger comes from the police. Even if this fella does know about the accident, and he does try to blackmail us, we'll probably be able to buy him off, but we won't be able to buy off the police. They are the real danger.'

'You said you would take the blame,' she said sullenly. 'The real danger for me is this man – not the police.'

'I promised to keep you out of it, but I can't guarantee to do it,' I said quietly. 'You were careless enough to leave your swimsuit in the car; if someone has taken it to the police, then I can't keep you out of it. All I can do is to swear I was driving, but that still makes you an accessory to manslaughter.'

She stared angrily at me.

'I am sure this man has my swimsuit! I'm certain of it! I am certain he is going to blackmail us! What I want to know is are you going to pay him or must I go to Roger?'

'Are you threatening me, Lucille?' I asked quietly. 'That sounds like blackmail too to me.'

She pounded her fists on her knees and cried: 'I don't care what it sounds like! I want to know what you intend to do when he makes his demand!'

'I'm going to wait until he makes it.'

She sank back, her eyes smouldering.

'I believe you're trying to get out of taking the blame. You're beginning to be sorry you made that promise. Well, you're not going to get out of it!'

'Do you ever think of anyone except yourself? Ever since this business started you haven't given me a thought,' I said, and I made no attempt to keep my disgust out of my voice. 'All you have thought about is how you can wriggle out of this mess yourself.'

Her face hardened and she stared at me.

'But for you, I wouldn't be in this mess,' she said in a cold, flat voice. 'Why should I consider you?' She looked away as she added: 'It was your fault. It's been your fault all along.'

I checked my rising temper.

'Are you so sure about that, Lucille? Have you been all that innocent? You knew you were doing the wrong thing by persuading me to teach you to drive. You led me on. It was your idea for us to go down to that lonely beach. The way you have behaved was enough to make any man think you were easy game, and that's what I thought.'

She turned scarlet.

'How dare you say such a thing to me!' she flared.

'Oh, let's skip it,' I said impatiently. 'Quarrelling won't help. I have promised to keep you out of it, and if I possibly can that's what I'll do.'

She leaned forward, her face white and tense.

'You'd better keep me out of it! I don't intend to lose Roger, and I don't intend to go to prison simply because you behaved like an animal.'

I got to my feet and crossed to the window, turning my back on her. I was too angry to speak.

'I'm going now,' she went on after a long pause. 'I'm not going to think any more about this. I'm going to leave it entirely to you. I have your promise, and I expect you to keep it.'

I turned.

'Then you'd better snap out of that pipe dream,' I said. 'I've had as much as I intend to take from you. You're nothing but a selfish, calculating, spoilt little bitch. You're in this mess with me, and the sooner you realize it the less of a jar it will be for you if there is a showdown.'

She got to her feet.

'I should have told Roger last night. I'm going to tell him right now!'

I had got beyond caring, and I smiled at her.

'What's that supposed to do? Make me cringe and fall on my knees in front of you? All right, if you want your precious and influential Roger to be in on this, then we'll both go and tell him, and I'll tell him the facts. I'll tell him you forced yourself on me, you asked me to teach you to drive, you suggested a midnight swim, you tried to invite yourself to this bungalow disguised in a shady hat and sunglasses because you didn't want him to know you were going around with me. When I told you to ask his permission you said he was jealous and silly: those were your words, weren't they? Come on, let's go. Let's tell him the facts and see how he likes them.'

She started to say something, then stopped. She remained motionless, staring at me, her eyes glittering, her fists clenched.

'If you don't want to come with me, then stay here,' I said. 'I'm going. I've had enough of this. One thing I'm damned sure about is I'm not going to be blackmailed by you! If you're bluffing, then I'm going to call your bluff.'

I walked across the lounge, leaving her staring after me, walked into the hall and opened the front door.

'Ches ... please ...'

She came running from the lounge and caught hold of me.

'No ... please ...'

I looked down at her.

'What a fool I've been,' I said evenly. 'What a mug I was to have fallen in love with you. Get away from me! If you want it the hard way, you can have it the hard way!'

'I didn't mean it,' she said tearfully. 'I'm sorry, Ches. You don't know how frightened I am. I'm not going to tell Roger. I'm willing to leave it to you. I do trust you. I just don't know what I'm saying or doing.'

I stared down at her.

'Don't you? I think you do. You keep shifting your attitude: first, you're going to trust me, then you're threatening me, then you're going to run to your husband, then you're trusting me again. Let's get this straight, once and for all: do you want your husband in on this or don't you?'

She shook her head.

'No, Ches.'

'You're sure? You're not going to change your mind and wave him in my face again?'

'No, Ches.'

'Are you willing to let me handle it?'

'Yes, of course.'

'Of course? You change your mind pretty easily, don't you? It wasn't of course five minutes ago.'

'Ches, please don't be angry with me,' she pleaded. 'I honestly don't know what I'm saying or doing. I'm so frightened.'

'You're saying a lot and you are doing nothing. Come back into the lounge. It's time we really talked this thing out.'

She turned around and went back into the lounge and sat down. She put her elbows on her knees and rested her face in her hands. She made a dramatic picture, but I was beyond being impressed by dramatic pictures.

I sat down and lit a cigarette.

'Have you thought about this business, Lucille?' I asked, abruptly. 'Has it occurred to you that there are one or two odd things about it?'

She stiffened, looked up, her eyes question marks.

'What do you mean?'

'For one thing I can't understand what this speed cop was doing on that road. It's no better than a dirt track and it is scarcely ever used. Why should he be down there?'

'I don't know.'

'He must have been there for some reason. I can't imagine he expected to catch any speeding motorist down there. Haven't you any suggestions to make why he should have been there?'

'No. I don't see that it matters.'

'Don't you? I do. Well, all right, let's leave it for now. It's something I intend to look into. Let's go over the whole thing together. After our swim, you returned to the car, changed and left your swimsuit on the floor of the car. Right?'

'Yes.'

'Did you see anyone while you were doing this?'

'No, of course not. There wasn't anyone there.'

'But there must have been. This man who telephoned just now must have been watching us. How else could he have known we swam together? As far as I can remember there was absolutely no cover anywhere except that clump of palm trees where we sat, and yet he must have been there.'

'I didn't see anyone.'

'Yet he must have been there. I think I'll go down and take a look at the ground in daylight. He must have hidden somewhere there. It beats me where he could have been, though. There's no cover as far as I can remember.' I paused, then went on: 'Has it occurred to you that after you had left the swimsuit in the car, this man might have turned up and taken it.'

She stared at me.

'No, it hadn't.'

'If he took it while we were quarrelling, it could mean, of course, that he doesn't know the car is damaged.'

'But the garage door was forced – that was when he took it.'

'Yes, I was forgetting that. All right, let's go on: what happened when you returned to the car and drove away?'

'I was upset. I drove up the road. After I had gone about a mile I heard a man shout ...'

'Don't let's rush this, Lucille. How fast were you driving?'

'Fast. I don't exactly know how fast.'

'Seventy – eighty? It's important.'

'Perhaps seventy. I don't know.'

'You didn't see O'Brien? You had no idea you had passed him?'

'No.'

'You had driven a mile, then you heard him shouting?'

'Yes.'

'You must have passed him on the road, then. He must have been waiting there with his headlamp off, and as you went past, he came after you.'

'I suppose so.'

'Then what happened?'

She moved restlessly.

'I told you. I heard him shout and I swerved. I heard a bang against the side of the car.'

'You didn't hear the motorcycle engine?'

'I think I did.'

'You slackened speed?'

'I lost control of the car. I was startled. I think I must have increased speed.'

'He came up beside you. Did he come up on your onside or on your offside?'

She hesitated, frowning.

'I don't remember.'

'Did you see him as he came alongside you?'

'I saw the light from his headlamp, that startled me and made me swerve.'

'Now think: was the light on your offside?'

Again she hesitated, then she said: 'Yes. He came up and shouted through the window. Yes, I remember now.'

I stared at her. She sat forward, looking away from me, her hands gripped tightly between her knees.

'Are you sure?'

'Yes, of course I am.'

'But you weren't a moment ago.'

'I am now. It was on my offside. I am sure of it.'

Was she deliberately lying or was she sincerely making a mistake? The damage to the car had been on the onside. O'Brien couldn't have come up on her offside.

'You can't be right, Lucille. The onside lamp was smashed. He must have been on your onside, and besides, he just wouldn't have come up behind you on your offside. It would be inviting an accident.'

Blood flowed into her face, and then as quickly, went away, leaving her white and taut.

'Then why did you ask me if you knew all the time?' she said angrily. 'I don't remember which side it was.'

I studied her, then shrugged.

'Okay, let it go. You hit him anyway. What happened after you heard the bang?'

She looked away, her face sullen.

'I drove on.'

'It was a pretty violent collision?'

'Yes.'

'You had no doubt that you had hit him?'

'Of course I knew I had hit him.'

'You lost your head, accelerated and drove on without stopping to see if he was hurt?'

She lifted her hair off her shoulders with an exasperated movement.

'Do you have to keep on and on like this? I've told you what happened.'

'I must get this straight, Lucille. You kept on and reached the main road. Then what did you do?'

'I realized I must have damaged the man's motorcycle and I had also damaged your car. I was frightened. I thought I'd better tell you. I didn't want to go back in case I met the policeman, so I decided to go to your place and wait for you.'

I lit another cigarette while I stared at her. She kept her eyes lowered and I could see she was very tense.

'How did you know where I lived?' I asked.

She stiffened.

'I – I had looked you up in the telephone book,' she said, speaking slowly and deliberately as if to give herself time to think. 'I – I once passed your place when I was out cycling. I knew where you lived.'

I had an uneasy feeling she wasn't telling me the truth.

'You had to drive a mile and a half before you reached the road that leads here. Did you pass any car while you were coming here?'

'I don't think so.'

'Are you quite sure about that?'

'I don't remember passing any.'

'I think you must have, Lucille. After all it's a highway. The time was around half past ten. There must have been a number of cars on the road.'

'I didn't notice any.'

'I think you must have passed at least one car, Lucille.'

'Suppose I did?' Her voice shot up. 'I tell you I didn't notice any, but suppose I did? What does it matter?'

'You were driving with only one light: the other light was smashed. An approaching motorist, seeing you, would think you were driving a motorcycle until he was close enough to see you were driving a car. He would remember that.'

She moved impatiently.

'So what does it matter?'

'It does. If the car was seen and remembered, the police will know in which direction you were travelling. It will tell them you weren't leaving town. That's the one thing they can't be sure about: whether the car that killed O'Brien left town before the road blocks were set up. If you were seen, the police will know where to look for the car. Instead of having to search the whole town, they will know the first place to look is on the coast roads – right here!'

If possible, her face went a shade paler than it was already.

'Oh! I hadn't thought of that.'

'That's the main reason why I'm asking all these questions. Will you please try to concentrate? It's more than important. Can't you remember if you passed any cars?'

She shook her head helplessly.

'I can't remember. All I was thinking about was getting to your place.'

'At least you must remember if you met any cars on this road.'

'I'm sure I didn't.'

Thinking about it, it seemed to me the situation was pretty bad. She must have passed a number of cars on the highway. Someone must have noticed she was driving with only one headlamp. Sooner or later this someone would remember and report to the police, and then the search would concentrate on the district where I lived.

'Well, all right, I think that's about all,' I said. 'You'd better go home. There's nothing you can do now. You must leave me to handle it.'

She got hesitantly to her feet.

'But what are you going to do, Ches?'

'I honestly don't know for the moment. I've got to think about it. You have my promise to keep you out of it if I possibly can. If things look as if they are going wrong, I'll let you know. That's as far as I can go for the moment.'

She studied me, her face tense.

'What are you going to do about your car?'

'That's something else I'll have to think about. I don't know.'

'And this man who telephoned?'

'I'll wait until he contacts me again. If you hear from him, let me know.'

'But suppose he asks me for money? I'm sure that is what he plans to do.'

'Let's wait until he does,' I said impatiently. 'If he does want money, tell him you must talk to me first.'

'Can I promise him some money?' she asked, staring at me. I looked at her and her eyes shifted from mine.

'No, you can't promise him anything. If he asks for money, tell him to contact me. I'll deal with him. You know, Lucille, you seem most anxious for him to have money either from you or me.'

'I'm not! I just want to know where I am!' Her voice went shrill. 'I know he is going to blackmail me! I haven't any money! How would you like to be in my place? How would you like to know someone is going to blackmail you, and you can't pay and everything that means anything to you will be taken away? How would you like that?'

'For heaven's sake!' I exclaimed impatiently. 'He hasn't even asked you for anything yet. Will you stop working yourself up? If he does ask for money, let me know. I'll deal with him. Now go home. I have a lot to think about, and I can't begin to think until you have gone.'

She got to her feet. She looked suddenly very young and unhappy and desirable.

'Then I just have to wait, Ches?'

'Call me around ten o'clock tonight. I may have something to tell you.'

Then suddenly she was in my arms, her mouth soft and trembling against mine, her arms clinging to me, her body pressing against mine.

'Oh, Ches ...' she whispered, her hands moving up the nape of my neck. 'I'm so frightened. You will look after me? You will make this come right?'

I made the effort and pushed her away from me, then I turned and walked over to the window while I got myself in hand. The feel of her lips against mine had really got me going.

'I'm relying on you, Ches,' she said. 'I'll call you tonight.'

'Do that,' I said, not looking around.

I heard her move across the lounge, away from me, and again I had to make an effort not to turn around and stop her going.

I stood there, staring out of the window, long after I heard the front door click shut, telling me she had gone.

II

The time was now twenty minutes to eleven.

I sat in the easy chair and my thoughts were busy.

There was something phony about this whole business. I had no doubt that Lucille had hit and killed a policeman, but the way it had happened as she told it and the way it must have happened from the evidence just didn't coincide. For some reason she had lied to me. Why had she insisted on saying that O'Brien had overtaken her on her offside? Why had she insisted that she hadn't met any cars on the busy highway? I had a growing feeling that her story wasn't to be trusted. She was frightened out of her wits and, like a trapped animal, she thought only of escape and she would stop at nothing to save herself.

I had an uneasy feeling that time was running out. Someone must have seen her on the highway, and for all I knew the police might be already concentrating on my district.

Then I suddenly remembered the bloodstains on the Cadillac's wheel. That brought me out in a hot sweat. If the police found those bloodstains, I really would be fixed.

Locking up the bungalow, I went to the garage and collected a bucket and sponge. Amongst the junk I kept with my tools, I found a strong padlock and a hasp. I then got in the Pontiac and drove fast to Seaborne's house.

In the hard light of the sun, I examined the damage to the Cadillac. The onside headlamp was completely smashed and the metal work surrounding it was buckled beyond an amateur's attempt to repair. The two deep scores along the side of the car would have to be handled by a coach-builder. There was nothing I could do about them.

I went around to look at the bloodstains, and there I had a shock. There were no bloodstains. For a long moment I stood and stared, scarcely believing my eyes. I knelt down by the rear wheel and examined it closely, but there were no bloodstains. I straightened and, walking stiff-legged, I went to the other side of the car and examined the offside rear wheel. There, I found the bloodstains.

For a full ten seconds I knelt there while I stared at the red sticky mess on the white rim of the tyre. Here was something that set my mind crawling with suspicion.

I stood up and went to the front of the car and again looked at the headlamp. Then I realized something else. Lucille's story that the cop had come up behind her and she had been startled and had hit him with the side of the car couldn't possibly be true. I was surprised I hadn't realized this before. For the lamp to have been damaged in the way it was damaged, she must have hit the cop head on, and that meant he wasn't overtaking her when the accident had happened. He must have been coming down the road towards her. It meant I had caught her out in yet one more lie and a much more serious one. She had said she hadn't seen the cop, but had only heard him shout at her, and she had been so startled she had swerved and that was how the accident happened. It was obvious to me now that it hadn't happened like that at all. She must have seen the light from his headlamp as it came down the road. She had admitted driving fast. The road was narrow. She had lost control, and before he could get out of the way, she had hit him head on. Her story that he had come up beside her and had startled her had been invented to make me believe the crash hadn't been her fault.

Did she imagine any jury would believe such a story once they had examined the car? Then I remembered my promise to take the blame. If I admitted I had been driving the Cadillac at the time of the accident, a jury would immediately jump to the conclusion that I had been drunk to have had such an accident. The road was straight. I could have seen the approaching headlight. I would have had plenty of warning to slow down. My mouth turned dry as I realized what I had let myself in for.

Then there was this puzzle of the bloodstains on the offside rear wheel. How could they have got there? She had hit the motorcycle on her onside. It wouldn't have been possible for her to run the cop over with her rear offside wheel.

I went back to the rear of the car and again examined the dull, sticky red marks on the tyre. They had to be bloodstains: they couldn't be anything else.

This was a baffler, and on the spur of the moment, I decided to leave the bloodstains. They offered the kind of evidence that could confuse a jury if handled by a clever counsellor, and I felt in my bones I would be asking for trouble to remove such evidence.

I turned my attention to the garage doors. With the aid of the tools I had brought with me, I straightened the lock and got the doors to shut properly. Then I screwed on the hasp and fixed the padlock. I felt fairly confident the police wouldn't attempt to break into the garage. They would contact Seaborne first and ask for the key. That at least would gain me a little time.

I decided to go now down to the beach where Lucille and I had bathed and examine the ground in daylight. I returned to the Pontiac.

By now it was a little after twelve o'clock, and I found the highway crowded with weekend motorists. I had to drive slowly, and it took me twenty minutes to reach the dirt track leading down to the beach.

As I drove down the narrow road with its low, undulating sand hills on either side, I examined the terrain carefully.

Again it struck me how odd it was that O'Brien should have been on this road. There was no cover on either side of the road, no trees or shrubs behind which he could have hidden.

I drove slowly on until I came to a disturbance in the sand dunes on my right. A large patch of ground had been trampled flat, and I decided this must have been the scene of the accident. I stopped the car and got out.

From where I stood I could see the sea and the beach some two miles ahead of me. The ground was flat with only slight sandhills, and no cover except the distant clump of palms where Lucille and I had been.

For some moments I continued to look around, but there was nothing to tell me more than I had seen at first glance, so I got back into the Pontiac. I drove down to the beach and pulled up within twenty yards of where we had parked last night.

The first thing I noticed was the tyre marks of the Cadillac, imprinted in the sand, and that gave me a shock. I saw also Lucille's and my footprints leading down to the palm trees. This was something I hadn't reckoned on, and I wondered if the police had been down here and if they had seen the tracks.

If we had left prints in the sand, then the man who had telephoned us, if he had really seen us on the beach, must also have left prints.

I started to hunt around for them, and although I covered the ground for a three-hundred-yard radius there were no other footprints except mine and Lucille's to be seen.

That told me two things: the police hadn't been down here, and therefore they couldn't have seen the tyre marks of the Cadillac and the man who had telephoned us couldn't have been on the scene either. That set me another puzzle. If he hadn't been down here, how had he known Lucille and I had swam together and then had quarrelled? After thinking about this for some moments, I decided the only possible way in which he could have seen us would have been from some distance away, and he must have watched us with the aid of powerful night glasses. That would explain why Lucille hadn't seen him.

I spent several minutes wiping out the tyre marks in the sand. Then, walking down to the palm trees, taking care to walk in the prints I had made the previous night, I started back to the road, wiping out each print and also Lucille's as I went until I once more reached the road.

I was sweating by the time I had completed the task, but it gave me a sense of security to see there were no tell-tale prints to be discovered if the police did decide to extend their search down here for clues.

Feeling at least I had taken every reasonable precaution not to be traced, I walked over to the Pontiac. As I opened the car door, I heard a car coming and looking around, I saw a yellow and red Oldsmobile turning the bend in the road and coming slowly towards me.

My heart gave a little kick against my ribs, and I waited, watching the car come, thinking if it had arrived three minutes sooner, the driver would have seen me wiping out the prints in the sand.

When the car was within a hundred yards of me, I saw the driver was a woman. She pulled up within ten yards of where I stood and she stared at me through the open window of the car. Then she got out.

She had on a scarlet dress, a small, white hat and white net gloves. She was slightly above medium height and dark: her face had the standard beauty of the Latin-American women you can see any day on the Florida beaches displaying themselves either as ornaments or as commercial propositions depending on who is looking at them.

She got out of the car with a display of long, tapering legs in nylon, smoothed her dress over solid, well-padded hips and stared at me, her black eyes intent and curious.

'Is this the place where the policeman was killed?' she asked, moving slowly towards me.

'I imagine it happened farther up the road,' I said, wondering who she was and what she was doing here. 'I'd say you've passed the actual place.'

'Oh?' She paused near me. 'You think farther back up the road?'

'The papers said he was killed on the road.'

She opened her handbag, took out a crumpled pack of Luckies, put one between her full red lips and then stared at me.

I took out my lighter and moved close to her. As she bent to dip the cigarette end into the flame I sheltered in my cupped hands, I smelt the perfume she had sprayed on her hair.

'Thank you.'

She lifted her head and stared directly at me. At such close quarters I could see her heavy pancake make-up had been expertly put on and she had a faint black line of a moustache that gave her that sensual quality that most Latin-American women have.

'Are you a newspaper man?' she asked.

'A newspaper man? Why, no. I just came down here for a swim.'

She turned her head and looked at the stretch of sand and stared at the smudge marks made while wiping out Lucille's and my footprints.

'Did you make those marks?'

'You mean those marks in the sand?' I tried to sound casual. 'They were there when I came.'

'They look as if someone has been trying to get rid of footprints.'

I turned to stare at the marks.

'Do you think so? They could have been made by the wind. The wind can make odd patterns in the sand.'

'Can it?' Again I felt the dark eyes move over my face. 'I passed a piece of ground that was trampled over about two miles up the road. Do you think that is where he was killed?'

'It's likely. I wouldn't know.'

'I'm not asking out of curiosity. I was going to marry him.'

I looked sharply at her, remembering one of the newspapers had said O'Brien was going to marry a nightclub singer.

'Oh, yes. I read this morning in the paper you were going to marry him.'

'Did you?' She smiled. It was a cold, bitter smile. 'I don't suppose you had ever heard of me before you read that in the paper. I've been in show business now for ten years. It's not very encouraging that the first real publicity I get is when a man I planned to marry gets himself killed because he is too stupid to know any better.'

She turned abruptly and walked back to the Oldsmobile, leaving me staring after her.

She got in the car and U-turned. Then without a glance in my direction, she drove away fast in a cloud of sand and dust.

7

I

I had a sandwich lunch and then drove back to my bungalow. While I ate the sandwiches and on my way back, my mind was busy, but I didn't come up with anything helpful. I was more convinced than ever that there was something very phoney about this accident. I was certain Lucille had lied to me about how the accident had happened. The situation had become more perplexing after I had looked over the ground. It was so obvious now she must have seen O'Brien as he was coming towards her. She could not have slowed down and she must have driven straight at him. With such an obvious set-up, she could expect no mercy from any jury, and it was even more obvious to me now why she was so anxious for me to take the blame.

But my immediate problem was what I was to do with the Cadillac. Sooner or later, if the police search was going to be as thorough as they claimed, they would find it in Seaborne's garage.

The Captain of Police had announced that anyone who damaged his car after the time of the accident would have to report the damage immediately, and explain how it had happened.

I wondered if this ruling could offer me a way out. If I drove the Cadillac hard against the garage door upright, and then telephoned the police, would they accept my explanation that I had damaged the car in this way? Had the damage been done only to the front of the car, I felt I might have been on fairly safe ground, but the two deep scars on the bodywork would not be consistent with ramming into the garage upright, and those two scars could easily arouse the police's suspicions.

But at least it was an idea, and I decided to keep thinking along this line. I was still thinking about it as I unlocked my front door when my mind was abruptly switched away from it as I heard the telephone bell ringing.

I entered the lounge and picked up the receiver.

'Mr Scott?'

I recognized Watkins' voice, and I stiffened, wondering why he should be calling.

'Yes, speaking,' I said.

'Mr Aitken asked me to call you, sir. He said it was possible you would still be at home,' Watkins said. 'If you could spare the time, Mr Aitken would be glad if you could come over.'

'But I'm supposed to be relaxing on the golf course,' I said. 'Can't you tell him you couldn't contact me?'

Watkins coughed.

'I suppose I could, sir, but Mr Aitken gave me to understand the matter was urgent. However, if you think ...'

'No, it's okay. I'll be over. He wants me right away, of course?'

'I believe he is waiting for you, sir.'

'Okay, I'm on my way,' I said and hung up.

For a moment or so I stood staring at my reflection in the mirror over the mantelpiece. I looked a little pale and my eyes were scared.

Had Lucille lost her nerve and told him? Had she got her word in first? Aitken had ordered me to take the weekend off and to relax, so why this sudden summons, unless there was trouble?

I left the bungalow, went down to the Pontiac and drove fast to Aitken's place.

During the drive my mind was as panicky as an old lady's who has heard a noise under her bed.

I parked the Pontiac beside a grey Buick convertible that stood on the tarmac before the marble steps leading up to Aitken's terrace. I got out and walked up the steps.

As I reached the top step and looked along the wide terrace I saw Aitken in pyjamas and a dressing-gown, a rug over his legs, lying in a lounging chair. He had with him a big, broad-shouldered man who sat in an upright terrace chair, his back turned to me.

I paused. My heart was thumping and my nerves were crawling as I looked at Aitken, who turned his head, saw me and waved. His leather, whisky-red face softened slightly into a welcoming grin and I felt suddenly a little sick. The relief of seeing that grotesque smile hit me like a physical blow. He wouldn't be smiling if he were after my blood.

'There you are, Scott,' he said. 'Were you going out to golf?'

The other man turned and I felt a sudden cramping sensation in my stomach. I recognized him immediately. He was Tom Hackett; the man who had seen Lucille and me leaving the bungalow on the night of the accident: Tom Hackett, Seaborne's pal.

He looked at me, then got slowly to his feet, his red, good-natured face lighting up with a broad grin.

'Hello, there,' he said and extended his hand. 'So we meet again. RA tells me you're going to be his head man in New York.'

I took his hand, aware again that mine felt cold in his warm, firm grip.

'Sit down, sit down,' Aitken said irritably. 'Were you on your way to golf?'

'I was about to change when Watkins called me,' I said, moving over to where he lay and sitting down in a chair near Hackett's.

'I'm sorry. I told you to get a game in. I meant you to,' Aitken said, running his fingers through his sparse hair, 'but when Hackett turned up, I thought you should meet him.'

I looked politely at Hackett, then back to Aitken again. I had no idea what it was all about, but at least it didn't seem to be trouble.

Aitken looked over at Hackett and grinned his sneering little grin.

'This young fella's been working too hard,' he said. 'I told him to take the weekend off: to play golf and find a pretty woman. You turning up like this has spoilt it for him.'

Hackett laughed.

'Don't you believe it. He may have missed his golf, but he didn't miss out on the other thing.' He turned to me with a wide grin. 'Did you, boy?'

My smile was stiff, but I somehow managed to keep it in place. I didn't say anything.

Aitken looked sharply at me, then at Hackett.

'Oh? What do you know about what he's been up to?'

I found my hands were turning into fists and I put them in my trouser pockets.

'Never mind: the guy's got a private life, hasn't he?' Hackett said and winked at me. 'The fact is, Scott, I'm coming in on this New York venture. I'm putting in some of my money. When RA told me you were going to handle the office, I wanted to meet and talk to you. That's about it, isn't it, RA?'

Aitken scowled. He disliked anyone taking charge of the conversation just as he disliked being side-tracked, but he said in a fairly genial tone: 'Yes, that's it. Well, here he is for you to talk to.' He turned to me. 'Hackett is putting up a hundred thousand dollars, and he naturally wants to make sure you're the man to look after his money.'

'From what RA tells me, you must be okay,' Hackett said, leaning back in his chair, 'but there are one or two points I'd like to cover with you. You don't mind answering a few questions, do you?'

'Why, no,' I said, relaxing a little. 'I'd be glad to.'

'They won't touch on your private life,' he said and smiled. 'How a man lives outside the office is no concern of mine, unless, of course, he gets mixed up in some mess or scandal.' The jovial face was still jovial, but the eyes were now a little too steady and searching for me to meet. I took out my cigarettes and hid behind the business of lighting up. 'I don't suppose you aim to mix yourself up in any scandal, do you?' he went on.

Aitken moved impatiently.

'There's nothing like that about Scott,' he growled. 'You don't imagine I employ men who get mixed up in scandals, do you?'

'I'm sure you don't,' Hackett said and, leaning forward, he slapped me on the knee. 'I'm a great little kidder. Don't pay any attention to it. Now, suppose you tell me about your qualifications?'

Maybe he was a great little kidder, but he wasn't kidding me. He knew something or suspected something. I was sure of that. Had he guessed the girl he had seen me with was Lucille?

I told him about my qualifications, and then answered a series of searching questions to do with my career. He also asked me questions about my plans for the New York office, the staff I would need, where the office would be located and so on. Finally, he seemed satisfied and he sat back, nodding his head.

'You'll do. You're a regular RA man, and that's good enough for me.' He glanced over at Aitken. 'And he's putting up twenty thousand?'

Aitken nodded.

'And he's to get five per cent on the gross as well as his salary?'

'Yes.'

Hackett brooded for a moment, and I was expecting him to say he didn't agree with the percentage, but he didn't.

'Okay. They're damn good terms, Scott, but I bet you'll earn them. When do you put the money up?'

'Next Thursday,' I told him.

'Okay, RA. You'll have my cheque at the same time. Okay?'

'Suits me fine. I'll have the whole thing fixed through Webster. You know him, don't you?'

'Yeah – a good man.' Hackett got to his feet. 'Well, we mustn't keep Scott from his golf.' He offered me his hand, 'I'm sure you're going to make a big success of the job. I wish you luck.'

'Thank you.' I shook his hand, then turned to Aitken. 'If that's all ...'

I broke off as Aitken stared past me down towards the long twisting drive.

'Now what the devil is this?' Aitken growled.

I looked in the same direction.

A dark blue car with a red flasher and a siren horn on its roof was coming fast up the drive.

I felt myself turn rigid.

There were four men in the car – all cops.

II

A big man, wearing a grey, crumpled suit and a lightweight hat pushed to the back of his head got out of the police car. His fleshy face was hard and sunburned. There was a mass of freckles across his short flat nose. He looked what he was: a tough, cynical, suspicious cop.

He looked up at Hackett and me as we leaned over the balustrade, then he started up the steps, moving slowly as if he had plenty of time and was in no hurry to reach us.

Two uniformed cops had spilt out of the car and now stood around in the aimless way cops have. The driver remained at the wheel.

The plain-clothes man finally arrived at the top step and came over to us, moving slowly and deliberately.

I watched him come, my heart beating fast, my mouth dry. I wondered, the way all guilty people must wonder at the sight of a cop, if he had come here to arrest me.

He walked across the terrace, his big feet coming down on the hot stonework with a slight slapping sound, and he stopped in front of Aitken.

'Detective-lieutenant West, City police, sir,' he said. 'The Captain's compliments. We are asking for your co-operation.'

Aitken stared up at him, his expression puzzled. 'What is it? What's the Captain want?'

'It's to do with this hit-and-run case. Maybe you've read about it in this morning's papers.' West's voice was slow and heavy. 'The Captain aims to check every car in the city for damage. If it's okay with you, Mr Aitken, we'd like to look your cars over.'

Aitken started to get a bloom on his face.

'Look at my cars? Why? You don't imagine I had anything to do with it, do you?'

I looked quickly at Hackett. He was leaning against the balustrade, his heavy face showing his interest.

West tilted his hat a little farther to the back of his head. His forehead was glistening with sweat.

'No, sir, we don't think that. But we're checking every car in town. You have a chauffeur. Maybe he used one of your cars last night. I didn't say he did, but a check would clear him. The Captain said if you objected, I wasn't to bother you.'

Aitken's face took on a deeper hue.

'My chauffeur didn't use any of my cars last night,' he grated. West's face became expressionless.

'Okay, sir, the Captain said not to persist, but if your chauffeur didn't use any of your cars, someone else might have.'

'None of my cars have been out since I broke my leg,' Aitken said, his voice tight with rage. 'You're wasting your time.'

West lifted his heavy shoulders.

'It's what I get paid for. If you object to me looking at your cars, that's okay with me. I'll leave it and report back to the Captain.'

'Listen to him!' Aitken exploded and turned to Hackett. 'This is a fine example of how these guys waste our money! Four men to check four cars! I'll write to Sullivan about this! Just because some fool got himself knocked over and killed, there's all this uproar.'

'The driver didn't stop,' Hackett said mildly. 'You can't blame this officer, RA. He's only doing his duty.'

Aitken drew in a long breath.

'Okay, go and look at my cars! I don't give a damn! Go ahead and waste the money I pay out in taxes. Go on: but get off this terrace!'

'Thank you,' West said, his face expressionless. 'Would you tell me where the garage is?'

Aitken turned to me.

'You know where my garage is?'

I said I did.

'Then take this man and show him, will you? And keep with him. See none of his men kick a panel in. Just watch out there's no evidence manufactured to get my chauffeur into trouble.'

I walked to the head of the steps and West plodded after me. We went down the steps to where the uniformed men were waiting. West shook his head at them, and we went past them, leaving them standing motionless in the sun.

When we were out of sight of the terrace, West said quietly: 'Do you work for that guy?'

'That's right.'

'Rather you than me.' He took off his hat and wiped his forehead with the sleeve of his jacket. 'I thought my chief was the world's worst, but I can see he's not even trying compared to this guy Aitken.'

I didn't say anything.

We walked past the Pontiac and the Buick. West paused and stared at the two cars.

'Know who they belong to?'

I had taken the precaution of removing Seaborne's licence tag and substituting my own, but I knew if he wanted to he could easily check the licence number against the tag, and then I'd be sunk, but I didn't dare tell him I had borrowed the car. I hesitated only for a split second.

'The Pontiac's mine. The Buick belongs to Mr Hackett, the guy up on the terrace.'

Moving slowly and deliberately, West walked around the two cars. He stood staring at them for some seconds, then moved back to where I stood, tense, my hands gripped behind my back.

'Well, there's nothing wrong with either of them, is there?' he said in a conversational tone. 'You said yours was the Pontiac?'

'That's right.'

'May as well give you a clearance certificate now: save my boys calling on you. What's your name?'

I told him.

He took a pad of printed forms out of his packet and began to write.

'Address?'

I told him.

He looked over at the car, wrote some more, then ripped the sheet from the pad.

'This is the Captain's idea,' he said. 'Maybe it's not so lousy. This certificate clears your car from this date. If you dent your fender or damage your car in any way, you don't have to bother to report to us. If you get stopped, all you have to do is to show the certificate. This is quite a job; checking every damn car in town.' He pushed the form at me and I took it. 'Don't lose it. It might save you a headache.'

'I won't lose it,' I said and put the paper away in my wallet as if it were a million-dollar bill.

'The Captain's full of bright ideas,' West went on. 'That's why he's a Captain, but then, of course, he doesn't have to do the work. He sticks his fat backside into a chair and keeps it there. Not that I blame him, you understand. I dare say I'd do the same if I were a Captain. Right now he has every man on the force hunting for this hit-and-run joker. Can you imagine? Everyone on the force, calling on houses, turning over garages, setting up road blocks, going around in circles until they don't know their brass from their oboes, if you will pardon my French.' He was staring sightlessly at me, not seeing me, half talking to himself. 'Know what our Captain is? He's a newspaper cop. He loves publicity. He thrives on it. Did you read the crap he handed out to the press this morning? About O'Brien?' He suddenly got me into focus and his eyes looked into mine. 'Between you and me, O'Brien was the worst man on the force, and we have a few choice specimens, believe you me. He was lazy and a no-good and spent most of his time trying to dodge his work. He took bribes and he wasn't above a little blackmail if he thought he could get away with it. He was a punk right through. The Captain knew it. Only last week, he told me he was going to get rid of him. And instead, the punk has to get himself run over, and we have to run ourselves ragged to find the guy who killed him. Know how much sleep I've had since he was killed? Exactly one hour and ten minutes, and that's only because I took a nap in the car, and I'll be lucky if I get any more tonight.'

I stood in the hot sun, listening to this. As I had never heard a police officer talk this way before, I was as bewildered as I was surprised.

West suddenly grinned, showing his big white teeth.

'You don't have to take me too seriously, Mr Scott,' he said. 'Every now and then I sound off. It does me good. Although I know O'Brien was a no-good punk, and although I know when he died it was good riddance, I intend to find the guy who killed him. It's a bad thing for the force when one of its men gets killed. An effort has to be made, and we're making it, and we'll find him. It'll probably take time, and it won't be easy, but we'll find him, and then I'll be able to relax again.' He dropped his cigarette on the ground and put his foot on it. 'Now let's go and look at your boss' cars, not that they had anything to do with it, but I have to give him a clearance certificate. Just where are they?'

'By the swimming-pool, just around here,' I said.

'A swimming-pool, huh? How the rich live!' West shook his head and started to walk along the drive while I trailed after him. 'You like working for a rich man, Mr Scott?'

'I can take it or leave it,' I said.

'Yeah, I guess that's the only way. He could be a bastard. There's that look in his eyes the Commissioner has. Money gives a guy an inflated feeling of power. I don't like guys with power. I don't like guys with a lot of money. When they get that way, they have to throw their weight around. I bet Mr Aitken leans on people pretty heavily every so often.'

I didn't have to think up a suitable remark to this as we turned the corner and came upon the four-car garage and the swimming-pool.

Standing poised on the high-dive board was Lucille. She was sideways on to us and she didn't see us. She wore a white bikini that just concealed those parts of the body not suitable for public viewing. The rest of her body was a golden brown and her thick chestnut hair lay around her shoulders and reached nearly to her waist. She made a picture standing up there that brought West and me to an abrupt stop as if we had walked into a brick wall.

She raised up on her toes, swung her arms wide, then launched herself off the board.

She went down in a graceful, perfect dive and hit the water with scarcely a splash and came up, shaking her hair out of her eyes. She turned on her back with her hair floating out around her and swam slowly towards the steps leading out of the bath.

'Well,' West said and drew in a slow breath.

He removed his hat, took out his handkerchief and wiped the sweat band while he watched Lucille climb out of the bath, and then walk along the side of the bath, the water glistening on her brown skin, the white bikini plastered to her body like a second skin.

We stood there like stone men, watching her until she disappeared into one of the cabins.

Then West turned and looked at me. His small grey eyes were sleepy and his thin, hard mouth was curled into a small incredulous smile.

'That his daughter?'

'That is Mrs Aitken.'

'Mrs Aitken?'

'Yes.'

'You mean she's that old punk's *wife*?'

'She is Mrs Aitken.'

He blew a long silent whistle.

'She doesn't look more than twenty.'

I was losing patience as well as getting jittery with these remarks.

'Well, that's scarcely my fault, is it?'

He stared at me, momentarily surprised, then he nodded.

'That's right, it's not your fault. Well, well, the guy certainly makes use of his money, doesn't he?'

Leaving me, he strolled over to the garage, swung up the tilt-up doors and went in to examine the cars.

I stood in the sun and waited.

Lucille came out of the cabin. She was now wearing a scarlet halter, white shorts and pair of sandals. She carried the two little pieces of wet rag that made up her bikini and she walked quickly around the bath towards me.

I realized the effect West would have on her unless I warned her before she ran into him, and I went towards her.

She looked up and saw me.

Out of the corner of my eye I saw West come out of the garage. I quickened my pace and reached her as West shut the garage doors.

'This man is a police officer,' I said, speaking fast. 'He's not looking for you. He's only checking the cars. There's nothing to worry about.'

Maybe I shouldn't have jumped it on her like this, but I hadn't much time. Anyway, she went as white as a fresh fall of snow, and for one awful moment I thought she was going to faint.

Her eyes grew large and dark and, under her heavy tan, the change of colour gave her an odd mottled look.

Then I heard the gentle slapping of West's feet as he came towards us. He didn't seem in a hurry, but he reached us quicker than I would have thought possible.

He came up beside me, his breath whistling down his thick nose, and I knew he was staring at Lucille, and when I turned, that was what he was doing.

She stared back at him like a rabbit staring at a snake.

My voice sounded husky as I said: 'This is Lieutenant West. Lieutenant, this is Mrs Aitken.'

West said in his slow drawl, 'Good afternoon, madam. I've just been checking the cars, I expect you've read …' but that was as far as he got.

Lucille turned abruptly and walked away. She didn't exactly run, but her slim brown legs took her over the ground at quite a pace.

West turned and watched her go. Neither of us said anything until she had run up the steps and out of sight.

'Sort of snooty, huh?' he said, cocking his head on one side. 'High-hat, would you say?'

'What's a police officer to her?' I said, trying to sound casual. 'After all she's a rich man's wife.'

'That's right.' He took off his hat and wiped the sweat band with his handkerchief. It seemed to be a habit of his. 'Now I wonder what was on her mind. Did you see how she changed colour?'

'Did she?'

I began to move towards the terrace, my heart bumping unevenly against my ribs.

West fell in step beside me.

'Yeah. She changed colour. Quite a doll. With a shape like that it seems a waste to have married an old guy like Aitken.'

'If it worries you all that much, why don't you take it up with him?' I said curtly.

West glanced at me and smiled a tired smile.

'I'm not all that in love with my job, but I don't aim to lose it. Would she have a lover, do you think?'

'Why not ask her, if it's any of your business?' I said, turning to glare at him.

He rubbed his big hand over his sweating face and stifled a yawn.

'I'd like to, but I don't imagine she'd tell me. Does she ever use any of Aitken's cars?'

My heart skipped a beat.

'Did you find any of them damaged?'

'No. The chauffeur keeps them nice. He probably has to.'

'Then it's no business of yours if she uses them or not. But if it will set your mind at rest, she hasn't a driving permit so the answer is she doesn't use them.'

He squinted at me.

'Just because she hasn't a driving permit,' he said slowly, 'doesn't mean she doesn't take a car out sometimes. Some people take chances. How come she doesn't drive?'

I was suddenly scared I had said too much.

'Maybe you'd better ask her,' I said. 'What business is it of yours?'

'Look, friend,' he said quietly, 'you don't have to get touchy. It's my job to ask questions. I wouldn't do it if I didn't have to. I'm a cop. When something happens out of the way, I wonder why. I'm wondering why she turned into a ghost when she saw me. A girl with her looks and her shape usually has plenty of confidence. It should take more than a cop to fazz her, but she was fazzed all right. Why? What's on her mind? You don't turn that colour at the sight of a cop unless your conscience is taking a beating. What's biting her, I wonder?'

'How should I know?' I said through stiff lips.

He patted my arm absently.

'That's right. How should you know?'

He moved past me and headed towards the terrace.

I went after him, but kept far enough behind him so as not to enter into another conversation with him.

He gave Aitken four certificates, clearing his cars.

Aitken took the certificates and tossed them contemptuously on the terrace table. West then gave Hackett a certificate for his car.

'I guess that's about all,' he said, looking around at us. 'Thanks for your help, sir.' This to Aitken. 'And for yours too.' His small eyes moved to me. Then in a silence you could lean on, he plodded across the terrace and went down the steps to the waiting police car.

'Well, I must say that's a wonderful way of wasting taxpayers' money,' Aitken growled. 'Of all the damned nonsense I've run into ...'

'Would you say that?' Hackett asked, lifting his heavy eyebrows. 'They're trying to find the man who killed a policeman. To them it is important. They know the killer's car is damaged. This is the surest way of finding his car,' he waved his certificate. 'Sooner or later, they will come across a car that is damaged and hasn't a certificate, then they will have found the killer. Personally, I think it's a smart idea.' He turned to me. 'Well, we're holding you off from your golf.' He stretched his massive frame. 'And I've got to be running along too.' He looked over at Aitken. 'The wife will be wondering where I've got to. So long, RA, this venture of ours is going to be a lot of fun,' and he shook Aitken's hand.

'I hope so,' Aitken said. 'A lot depends on Scott.' Hackett slapped me on the shoulder. 'He'll handle it. Well, I'll get off. Look after that leg, RA. The sooner you're up and about again the better.'

There was more talk before Hackett and I crossed the terrace together and walked down the steps to where our cars were parked.

'You won't forget to come over to my hotel,' Hackett said. 'I'd like you to meet the wife.'

'That's nice of you,' I returned. 'The trouble is RA expects me to come here every night and that limits my time.'

'Yes, I can see that. But try and find time.' He paused beside his Buick, looking over at the Pontiac. 'I see you're still using Jack's car.'

I kept my face expressionless with an effort.

'Yes, but not for much longer. I should have my car back soon.'

The shrewd eyes moved over my face.

'What did you say was the matter with it?'

'It's leaking oil.'

He nodded.

'Cars can be hell. Coming down here, I blew a gasket. It doesn't seem to matter how much one spends buying a car, something or other goes wrong sooner or later.'

I wasn't kidding myself he was talking because he liked the sound of his voice. I was sure a punch line was coming and I tensed myself, waiting for it.

'Have you met RA's wife?' he asked abruptly and his eyes were sudden searchlights on my face.

I hadn't expected that punch to be quite so direct nor so hard. I flinched. There was nothing I could do about it. It had been hard enough to get under my guard.

'I – I've seen her.'

He nodded.

'I've seen her too.' He looked away from me as he opened his car door. 'Some girl. I've often wondered why RA married her. She's a young man's girl. He's much too old for her. When a girl that young marries a man nearly forty years older than she, she becomes rank poison to any young fella who happens along.' He grinned cheerfully at me. 'Though why I'm sounding off like this to you I can't imagine. A sensible guy like you wouldn't go for rank poison, now would you?' He patted my arm and got into the car. 'Don't forget to come and see us when you have time,' he went on, poking his genial face out of the car window. 'So long for now: hope to see you soon.'

I remained motionless as a shop-window dummy and watched him drive away.

I knew then he had recognized Lucille as she had come out of my bungalow last night, and in his odd, kindly way, he was waving a red light in my face.

I was aware my breathing was coming fast and hard as I walked over to the Pontiac and got in. For several tense seconds I sat staring through the windshield, then leaning forward, I stabbed at the starter button and drove fast down the drive and headed towards my bungalow.

8

I

During the afternoon I had a long, lonely session with my thoughts. Hackett's hint bothered me, but as he didn't seem ready to make trouble for me, I felt I had to get that out of my mind and concentrate on the main problem, which was the Cadillac. I was sure that if I could think of a way to get the car repaired, I could cope with the rest of my problems.

It wasn't until late in the evening that I suddenly saw how I could do this in safety. I happened to take from my wallet the certificate Lieutenant West had given me, and on examining it, I suddenly realized he had unwittingly handed me the solution.

In completing the form, he had put down only the licence number and had omitted the make of the car. I saw then that if I put the Pontiac's number plate on the Cadillac, the certificate would clear me if I were stopped while taking the Cadillac to my local garage to get the damage repaired.

For several seconds I stared at the certificate, scarcely believing the solution could be this simple. There was a risk that if I were stopped by a policeman he might check my licence tag against the number plates. If he did that, I'd be sunk, but I decided I would have to take this risk.

I decided it would be too risky to change the number plates before dark. I had still a couple of hours ahead of me before sunset, and it occurred to me, while I was waiting, to call Lucille and tell her I had found a possible solution. I knew her nerve had been badly shaken by West's unexpected appearance and I wasn't going to take the risk of her losing her nerve at the last moment just when it looked as if I had the problem licked.

I crossed over to the telephone and called Aitken's house.

Lucille herself answered.

'Ches here,' I said. 'Can you talk?'

I heard her catch her breath sharply.

'Yes. What is it?'

'I wanted you to know I've found a way out,' I said. 'I think it's going to be all right. I think I've really got it fixed.'

There was a pause. I could hear her quick breathing.

'Do you really mean that?' she asked finally.

'Yes. It's going to be all right. We're both going to be in the clear.'

'But how?'

'I can't talk over an open line. I wanted you to know right away. It's going to be fixed, and you don't have to worry any more.'

'I see.' Her voice sounded curiously flat. 'Well, all right.'

'You can relax now,' I said. 'You just take it easy.'

'All right,' and the line went dead.

I put down the receiver, frowning. Her reaction puzzled me. I had expected her to have been pleased and relieved. It was almost as if she were disappointed that I had found a solution.

As it was still too light to go out to Seaborne's place, I sat on my terrace and brooded, waiting impatiently for the sun to go down. It wasn't until half past eight that I got the darkness I had been waiting for.

I left the bungalow and went down to the Pontiac. Then I drove over to Seaborne's house.

It took me a little time to get the licence plates off the Pontiac. I had to work by my flashlight and the screws had rusted in, but I got the plates off finally. Then I went up the drive to Seaborne's garage, unlocked the doors and shut myself in before turning on the overhead light.

The rear number plate on the Cadillac came off easily enough and I put on the Pontiac's plate. Then I came around to the front of the car. There I found the screws on the front plate were badly rusted in and I had a struggle to shift them.

I was lying on my back, half under the car, struggling with the screws when suddenly I heard a faint noise outside.

I froze, gripping the spanner, while I stared up into the darkness of the Cadillac's engine. I heard nothing except the faint sound of the sea coming in-shore and the sighing of the wind in the palm trees. I remained motionless, my ears straining, my heart thudding, still sure I had heard a sound outside, but not quite convinced that my imagination was playing me tricks.

As I heard nothing, I finally decided I had imagined the noise and I bent once more to the task of shifting the last of the obstinate screws.

I had just got the screw free when I heard the garage doors creak.

My heart seemed to turn a somersault. From where I lay I could see part of one of the doors: it was opening! I knew it couldn't be the wind. I had pushed the doors shut. It could mean only that someone was forcing the doors open.

I began to wriggle out from under the car. Before I could get clear of the front bumper, the overhead light in the garage went out. Then I heard the garage doors swing wide open.

It was too early for the moon. The sky I could see through the open doors was inky black with only a few stars. I was in a hell of a panic as I forced myself out from under the car.

Then, just as I was getting to my feet, the Pontiac number plate clutched in my hand, there was a blinding flash of light followed instantly by complete darkness.

For a second or so I crouched motionless, completely witless, then I heard the sound of someone running away, and immediately my mind adjusted itself and I realized what had happened.

Someone had crept up on me with a flashlight camera and had taken a photograph of me as I crouched before the damaged Cadillac, the Pontiac number plate in my hand.

A surge of fear and rage ran through me. I dropped the number plate and ran out of the garage.

Whoever it was who had taken the photograph was now running up the road. I could hear the sound of the footfalls distinctly, and from the sound I knew it must be a man running. No woman could run as fast and as evenly as that.

I went after him. Rage gave me added speed, but the darkness of the moonless night hindered me.

At least I knew the road. I knew a couple of hundred yards or so beyond my bungalow was a big clump of flowering shrubs and palm trees. Beyond this clump was the open road, and it remained open until it reached the highway. On either side of the road were sand dunes that offered no cover. If this man got beyond the clump of shrubs, I must catch him, unless he could run a lot faster than I, and I doubted that.

I hared down the road faster than I've ever run before. And then as I drew near the clump of shrubs and palm trees, I pulled up, panting, to listen. I heard nothing, and that told me the man had run off the road and had taken shelter in the shrubs.

I had no doubt that this man was the one who had telephoned Lucille and then me this morning. This man was set to blackmail me. He had a photograph of me now that could get me a ten-year sentence, and I was determined he wasn't going to slip through my hands. I'd fix him if it was the last thing I did.

I wished now I had brought my flashlight with me. The darkness pressed in on me, and I could only see the dim outline of the palms against the dark, night sky. Somewhere just ahead of me, this man was hiding. I moved forward, being careful to make no sound as I reached the clump of shrubs. It was then I realized the difficulty that faced me. The shrubs loomed out of the darkness as a big dark mass. I was sure he was in there somewhere, but, without a light, he was going to be difficult to flush.

The noise I made as I moved into the shrubs must have told him I was in there looking for him.

I got halfway into the undergrowth, then I stopped to listen. There was no sound. I was sure he was close by, probably within touching distance, crouching in the darkness, probably as scared as I was and hoping I would pass him.

Without a light, my only chance of finding him would be to walk directly on to him. The dry leaves of the shrubs brushed my face as I moved forward. My groping hands reached out into the darkness and I listened, hoping to hear him start out of his cover.

Then suddenly my foot touched something that yielded under my weight. I heard a quick gasp that could have been made only by a man startled into sudden sound. I reached out into the darkness and my hands touched a face. I was dimly aware of a shadowy figure that rose up out of the shrubs. I pulled back my arm, clenching my fist, but I was a shade too late.

I heard a swish of something that came down violently towards me. I swayed to one side, throwing up my arms in an attempt to protect my head. Something hard smashed down on my shoulder, driving me to my knees. Before I could recover, there was another swishing sound and I received a violent blow on the top of my head.

I felt myself falling forward into a lonely vacuum of darkness.

II

Somewhere in the far distance, a clock struck nine. The gentle musical beat-beat-beat of its chimes came to me from a long way off, but it was a familiar sound. I was vaguely surprised to realize I was listening to the chimes of my own clock that stood on the overmantel in my lounge.

I opened my eyes. The lighted white ceiling rushed down at me, then as abruptly, receded. There was a throbbing going on inside my head with the violence of a hammer beat.

I hurriedly shut my eyes and kept them shut until the clock had stopped chiming, and then, more cautiously, I opened them again.

I was lying on my settee. I put my hand to the back of my head and felt a hard lump and a dry knot of blood. As I slowly sat up, I heard myself give a grunting groan, and again I had to shut my eyes. The hammer beat inside my head began to lessen, and after a minute or so, I was able to sit upright and stare around the lounge.

All the lights were on. On the occasional table near by was a bottle of my best whisky and a container of ice. This whisky I had been keeping for a special occasion, and I vaguely noticed that a quarter of it had gone.

I looked slightly to my left. It came as no surprise to see a man sitting in one of my lounging chairs. He sat in the shadows. My eyes weren't yet in focus and he was just a shadowy figure, but I knew instinctively that this was the man who had telephoned Lucille and me and who had taken my photograph as I was changing the licence plates and who had hit me over the head as I had stumbled on him in the darkness of the shrubs.

Again I shut my eyes, my hands holding my head. I remained motionless for some minutes, then, getting a grip on myself, I looked up and stared at the man seated opposite me.

Slowly he swam into focus.

He was powerfully built, around twenty-three or four, blond, with a heavy suntan. He had a Grecian nose, green eyes and a pencil-lined moustache. His hair was neatly set about his well-shaped head and needed cutting, although maybe a woman might have thought it cute as it was.

He was wearing a bottle-green sports suit with brown buckskin shoes and around his wrist was a solid gold bracelet that supported a solid gold watch. In his right hand, he held a glass three-quarters full of whisky, clinking with ice, and he regarded me with a tolerant little smile that made me want to jump across the room and plant my fist in his face.

'Hey, buster,' he said cheerfully, 'I was beginning to wonder if I'd hit you too hard.'

My hand cautiously investigated the lump at the back of my head and I winced as the hammer beat started up again.

'I bet it hurts,' he went on and his grin widened. 'Want a drink?'

'Who are you? What are you doing here?' I growled.

'I thought I'd better bring you home,' he said, stretching out his long legs. 'It's time we had a little talk. You and I are going to form a beautiful friendship. My name's Ross. My friends call me Oscar. Do you feel like a cosy little chat, buster?'

'I feel like shoving your nice white teeth through the back of your head,' I said, slowly sitting bolt upright.

He laughed. He seemed genuinely amused.

'I don't blame you, but I wouldn't try it if I were you. Bigger guys than you have thought they could take me, but they found out different. Don't let's get unfriendly. This is a business deal. I've got something to sell that you will want to buy. It's as simple as that.'

So Lucille had been right. We were going to be blackmailed. I stared across at the man who called himself Ross and I tried to make up my mind just how dangerous he could be. My first move was to find out how much he knew and how much he wanted to keep his mouth shut, then I could decide what to do about him.

'And what do you imagine you have to sell?' I asked.

'There's a nice strip of beach not far from here,' he said, 'where boys and girls go for a little fun. I have a hide-out there and when I want a little extra money, I go down there and wait around. I'm not always lucky, of course, but the other night I was. I saw the wife of a well-known advertising magnate and a member of his staff having a work-out on the sands. It struck me this fella might be willing to part with a few bucks rather than have me call up his boss and tell him what had been going on. You'd be surprised at the number of suckers I catch in the course of a year this way. It helps quite a bit to increase my income.'

I reached for a cigarette and lit it.

'Not much of a deal,' I said. 'It's your word against mine.'

He nodded.

'That's right. Usually, they're willing to part with fifty bucks just to keep the whole thing quiet, and I didn't expect to make more out of you, but then there was this accident. The wife of this advertising magnate resented your advances and she ran away. She took your car and she hit a cop. You've probably read about it in the papers. I arrived on the scene two minutes after she had hit him. She didn't stop and she damaged your car. It was a smart idea of yours to change the number plates, but I have been camping outside your place for more hours than I care to remember with a camera and flashlight equipment. I now have a picture in the camera that can send you and the girl away for a ten-year stretch. Maybe if you're unlucky and draw a tough judge, you could go away for fifteen years. It seems to me I could make a nice slice of money out of you if you want to avoid going to jail and if you want to save her from going to jail too.'

I sat there, staring at him, realizing I was really in trouble.

'Don't look so sad, buster,' he said, grinning at me. 'After all, money is only money. There are more important things in life than the dollar. Even if you had a million bucks, you couldn't have any fun if you were in jail. Let's get down to business. I need money. I've got to get out of town. We'll make a one-payment job of it. Cash down and I don't tell your boss you've been fooling around with his wife and I don't send the photo to the cops. How's that?'

'Then you'll come back for more.'

He sipped his whisky, his grin widening.

'Well, of course, that's a risk you'll have to take, but for a nice fat payment, I could forget about you.'

I braced myself.

'How much?'

'Between the two of you,' he said, sinking lower in his chair, 'I should imagine you could scrape up thirty thousand bucks. She must have a few diamonds she could hock, and I bet you've salted away a sackful of the stuff. Yeah, let's settle for thirty thousand. It's cheap at the price.'

I felt a cold sensation snake up my spine.

'You're crazy! I haven't anything like that. I'll buy the photograph for five thousand – not a nickel more.'

He finished his whisky and then set the glass down.

'That's damn fine Scotch. I'll give you to the end of the week to collect the dough. I'll call you and tell you where to deliver it. Thirty thousand in cash.'

'I tell you I haven't got it! Five is my top.'

He leaned forward and took a cigarette from the box on the occasional table and lit it.

'Be your age, buster. You can sell this bungalow. That'll bring in fifteen thousand. She can raise some dough too.

You want to get organized. This is a one-payment job. I'm not coming back for more.' He laughed suddenly. 'I'm not coming back for any more because I'm going to convince myself there won't be any more to come back for. Now listen, buster, when I throw a hook into a sucker I make certain it goes in deep and it stays in. You'll either go to jail for fifteen years and take her with you, or you'll find thirty thousand bucks. You have six days. Think about it. I'll call you on Thursday to see how you are making out. What you have to decide is whether it is better to pay me the dough or to spend fifteen years in jail: it's as simple as that.' He got to his feet. 'I know what I'd do, but maybe you don't think the way I think. But don't let it spoil your dreams, buster. After all what is money?' He began to move across the room, a little swagger to his shoulders. 'Sorry I had to hit you, but you did ask for it. We'll be getting together again so don't pine for me. So long, and thanks for the drink.'

I watched him walk to the door where he paused to look back at me. I stared at him. My head was beginning to ache again and I felt pretty bad.

'And no funny business, buster,' he said. 'You can kick a little. That's only natural, and it won't do any harm, but what you want to get clearly into your head is you are on the hook. You'll find out fast enough the hook is in good and deep and it'll stay in.'

He went away, and after a moment or so, I heard a car start up and drive away fast.

I got unsteadily to my feet. I fetched a clean glass from the liquor cabinet and poured myself a stiff whisky. I drank it, then went into the bathroom and ran a basinful of cold water. I shoved my head into it. I felt slightly better by the time I returned to the lounge. I poured another shot of whisky, carried the glass to an armchair, sat down and lit a cigarette.

I stared up at the ceiling and thought: so this is what it is like to be blackmailed. Ross had said the hook was in and wouldn't come out. That was what he had said, so I took a look at the hook to see just how deep in it was.

After a little thought, I decided it was in pretty deep.

It seemed to me whichever way I moved, I was caught. If I went to Aitken and told him the truth, he would throw me out. If I went to the police and told them the truth, they would grab Lucille and Aitken would fix me for giving his wife away. If I somehow managed to scrape up thirty thousand dollars, I would be finished as far as the new job was concerned.

As Ross had said, the hook was in.

So what was I to do?

I stubbed out my cigarette and then lit another.

There is only one thing to do, I said to myself. You are going to get off this hook. You're not only going to get off it, but you're going to fix Oscar Ross so he can't fix you. You have no alternative. You either fix him or you're sunk.

At least I had six days' grace before I had to cope with him. My first move was to make the Cadillac safe.

The time was now half past nine. I went to the telephone and called Sam Lowther, who ran the garage that handled my repairs.

'Sam,' I said when he came on the line, 'I'm sorry to call you so late but I've had a hell of a pile-up with the Caddy. I rammed it into a tree. I want a quick repair job done. How are you fixed?'

'I can take her in right away, Mr Scott,' he said, 'if that suits you. I have a couple of men here who haven't anything much to do and they can get on with it as soon as you bring it in. If it's not all that bad I can let you have it back Wednesday, but I'd like to see the extent of the damage before making a promise.'

'Thanks a lot, Sam,' I said. Although my head was throbbing now like mad, I was determined to get the Cadillac into his hands this night. 'I'll bring it around in half an hour.'

'Okay, Mr Scott, but there's just one thing. You'll have to report the damage to the police. It's this hit-and-run case. I've had instructions not to take in any damaged car without a clearance certificate. I expect you've read about the business in the papers. Can you get a certificate?'

'I've already got it. As soon as I had the pile-up I reported to the police and they fixed it.'

'That's fine, Mr Scott, then you bring her in and I'll get my boys working on her.'

I thanked him and hung up.

There was a slight chance he would spot the changed number plates, but I decided I would have to take that risk. He had dozens of cars through his hands during a working week, and it wasn't likely he would spot I had changed the plates. By going to him rather than a garage that didn't know me, I was much less likely to run into a barrage of awkward questions.

I locked up the bungalow, then walked the three-quarters of a mile to Seaborne's house. I found the Pontiac parked outside as I had left it. I was feeling pretty bad, my head aching as I walked up the drive to the garage.

Everything was as I had left it when giving chase to Ross. I shut myself in and completed fixing the front number plate. Then I went around to the rear of the car and took a look at the dried blood on the fender and the tyre. I had to get rid of it. I couldn't risk Sam seeing it. I had a feeling that I was destroying evidence that might react in my favour if ever I came up for trial, but I just couldn't leave the bloodstains there. I fetched a bucket of water and washed the bloodstains off. Then I drove the Cadillac out on to the road and put the Pontiac into the garage. When the job was done I locked the garage and drove the Cadillac fast along the beach road to the highway.

I had no alternative but to drive with one light. It so happened the highway was practically deserted. The few cars that passed me appeared to take no notice of the single headlight, and I arrived at Sam's garage without meeting a patrol officer.

As I drove into the big, dimly lit shed, I saw Sam in his office, talking to two of his mechanics.

He came out and shook hands with me: a big, powerfully built man with a fleshy sunburned face and humorous eyes.

'Evening, Mr Scott,' he said and looked at the Cadillac. 'Phew! You've certainly given her a knock.'

'Yeah. I guess that comes of having an arm around a girl and driving too fast,' I said, sure this sort of explanation would be right for him.

He grinned.

'I know. You don't have to tell me. I've done it myself. Women can be hell at times. Well, this isn't anything that can't be fixed, but I don't think I can get it done before the end of the week.'

The mechanics came over and stared gloomily at the car.

'These two scratches have gone deep,' Sam went on, examining the side panel. 'You boys had better get busy.

Get the door off and fix that first.' He turned to me. 'Got the police certificate, Mr Scott?'

As I put my hand in my pocket to get out my wallet, I heard the sound of an approaching motorcycle, and looking around, I saw a patrol cop pull up outside the garage.

My heart stood still for a second and then began to race. Somehow I managed to keep my face expressionless as the cop stalked into the garage.

'Just a second,' Sam said to me and went across to meet the cop whom he appeared to know. 'Hey, Tim. What do you want?' he asked the cop.

'Got a damaged car here?' the cop growled.

'Why, sure. Mr Scott has just brought in his Caddy. He's had a pile-up against a tree.'

The cop shot me a hard stare, then stalked over to the Cadillac. He looked at the smashed headlamp.

By now I had pulled myself together and had got the certificate out of my wallet.

I walked over to him.

'I have a certificate for the damage, officer,' I said. 'Lieutenant West gave it to me.'

The cop turned slowly and deliberately and held out his hand, while his small, hard eyes moved over my face. It needed an effort of will to meet those probing eyes, but I did it.

He studied the certificate.

If he checked the licence tag with the number plates I was sunk. There was nothing I could do but stand there and wait, and the next few minutes were about the worst I have lived through.

He looked at the number plates, then again at the certificate, then he pushed his cap to the back of his head and blew out his cheeks.

'When did you see the Lieutenant?' he demanded.

'He was out at Mr Aitken's place. I work for Mr Aitken,' I said. 'The Lieutenant cleared Mr Aitken's cars and mine.' I was aware my voice didn't sound too steady. 'Sam knows me. He's handled my car often enough.'

'How did you do this?'

'I rammed it into a tree.'

Sam joined us.

'Mr Scott was cuddling a girl,' he said, his face one vast expansive grin. 'Done it myself when I was his age, but I went clean through a shop window.'

The cop didn't seem amused. He shoved the certificate at me.

'I have a mind to take you in,' he growled, glaring at me. 'You might have killed someone.'

'I know. That's what the Lieutenant said.' I tried to sound humble. 'I told him I wouldn't do it again.'

The cop hesitated. I could see he wanted badly to make something of this, but I felt sure that by mentioning West's name I would block him off and I was right.

'You'd better not do it again,' he said, then turning his back on me he went on to Sam: 'I thought I'd caught up with that joker who killed O'Brien. I had a report from a driver who had seen this car. Well, okay. I'll get on,' and he stalked out of the garage.

When he had driven away, Sam winked at me.

'You were smart to mention Lieutenant West, otherwise that big head would have run you in. He's a guy who looks for trouble.'

I gave him the certificate.

'You'll want this.'

'That's right.' Sam put the certificate in his pocket. 'Can I lend you a car, Mr Scott?'

'I'd be glad if you would.'

'Take the Buick over there. I'll get the Caddy fixed by Friday. You bring the Buick in on your way home and the Caddy'll be ready for you.'

I thanked him, got in the Buick and drove out on to the highway.

I didn't feel like returning to my bungalow. The time now was twenty minutes to eleven. I was still feeling pretty shaky from my encounter with the patrol cop and the thought of sitting in my lonely lounge with so much on my mind was something I just couldn't face up to. So I drove into town.

I parked the Buick and went into a little bar Joe and I used sometimes when we felt a drink might help us get a few new ideas.

The barman, an elderly, fat humorist we called Slim, nodded to me as I came up to the bar.

'A double Scotch,' I said, climbing up on the stool.

There were only four men in the bar and they were at the far end, shooting crap.

'Right away, Mr Scott,' Slim said. 'You're late tonight.'

'Yeah,' I said, 'still, tomorrow's Sunday.'

'That's a fact: my favourite day.' He poured the Scotch, dropped ice into the glass and placed it before me. 'Heard the latest on the hit-and-run case?'

The muscles in my stomach suddenly cramped up.

'No. What's new?'

'On the radio: ten minutes ago. A man and woman were seen driving off the highway and going down the beach road where the cop was killed about the time of the accident. The police are asking them to come forward. They seem to think they might have seen the car that killed O'Brien or maybe they did it themselves.'

I took a long pull at my whisky.

'Is that right?' I said, not looking at him.

'I bet they don't come forward. A man and woman don't go down that kind of road to admire the view.' He winked at me. 'I bet those two aren't going to get themselves on the front pages of the papers.'

'That's a fact. Well, they're certainly making an effort to catch the guy who did it,' I said, trying hard to sound casual.

'Yeah. Seems a lot of fuss to me. People get killed every second of the day, but when it's a cop, it's got to be special.'

I sat and listened to views about the police for several minutes, then I asked him suddenly: 'Would you know a guy who calls himself Oscar Ross?'

Slim looked surprised.

'Why, sure. He's a barman at the Little Tavern nightclub out at Mount Cresta. You know him, Mr Scott?'

'No, but someone was saying he was the best barman in town.' I was careful to keep my face expressionless although this unexpected information had me seething with excitement. 'I just wondered what was so special about him.'

'I bet a lady told you that,' Slim said, his face registering contempt. 'The best barman in town! That's rich. Why, he's just an amateur. The martinis he throws together would make a cat puke. I tell you what he's got: he's got looks. I'll say that for him. The dames go for him in a big way. He really gives them the works when they come into the bar: you know the stuff: the steady stare, looks up and down them, strokes their behinds when he helps them up on the stools. They love it, but he hasn't any talent as a barman. I wouldn't have him in this bar, not if he offered to work here for nothing.'

'The Little Tavern? Isn't that where Dolores Lane sings?'

'That's the joint.' Slim picked up a cloth and began to polish the bar. 'You ain't missed a thing by not going there. She's nothing to lose sleep over either.'

'Wasn't she supposed to be engaged to this cop who was killed?'

Slim scratched the back of his neck and stared blankly at me. 'Yeah, I believe you're right, but maybe it's just a newspaper story. What would a nightclub singer want to marry a cop for?'

I finished my whisky.

'You're right. I only believe half of what I read in the newspapers,' I said as I slid off the stool. 'Well, I've got to be getting home. So long, Slim.'

'Always glad to have you in here, Mr Scott. Have a nice weekend.'

I went out to the Buick. Getting in, I lit a cigarette.

By the merest chance I had picked up a piece of information that had to be important. So Ross and Dolores Lane worked at the same nightclub. Dolores had told me she was going to marry O'Brien. As Slim had said, why should a nightclub singer hook up with a cop? It didn't make sense. It certainly deserved to be investigated.

On the spur of the moment, I decided to take a look at the Little Tavern nightclub.

I thumbed the starter, moved the Buick into the evening traffic, and headed out to Mount Cresta.

9

I

The Little Tavern nightclub was a typical roadside joint with a circular drive-in, a lot of coloured neon lights, a gaudy doorman and a big parking lot crammed with the less expensive cars.

I found space in one of the rows, cut my engine and turned off my lights.

Then I walked back between the alley of cars to the entrance of the nightclub.

The doorman turned the revolving door for me, touching his cap as he did so.

I entered a large ornate vestibule. A hat-check girl, clad in a frilly thing that showed her knees, hip-swayed towards me, showing her even white teeth in a smile of welcome. The smile slipped a little when she saw I had no hat and had nothing to leave with her for her to earn a possible dollar tip.

I moved around her, giving her one of my boyish smiles, but for the impression it made on her, I might be offering a beggar the time of day. She turned and hip-swayed back to her station. For build, she and Marilyn Monroe had a lot in common.

I went up the red-carpeted stairs to a passage lit by ceiling lights and headed towards a pale-blue neon light that flashed Bar at me.

I paused in the doorway and surveyed the scene.

The room was big, with a horseshoe-shaped bar at the far end, and a lot of tables and chairs to cope with the hundred odd people who were getting liquored up for the night.

It wasn't what I would call a smart crowd. None of the men were in tuxedos. The women were a mixed lot: some of them looked like businessmen's secretaries out for the night in return for past services rendered; some of them looked like slightly soiled young ladies from the back row of unsuccessful musicals; some of them were obviously professionals, and they sat alone at various tables, discreetly distant from each other, and there were a few elderly women waiting impatiently for their gigolos: the usual crowd you can see any night of the week in the less smart nightclubs of Palm City.

I looked over the bar. There were two barmen coping with the rush: neither of them was Ross: two small men, Mexicans to judge by their sleek, black hair, their dark oily skins and their servile, flashing smiles.

I didn't expect to find Ross serving behind the bar. I guessed it was his night off.

As I looked around I was aware that at least ten of the women on their own were staring pointedly at me. I took care not to meet their inviting eyes.

I wandered over to the bar and waited my turn beside a fat man in a slightly creased, tropical white suit who was being served with a rum and lime juice and who looked three parts drunk.

When my turn came, I ordered a Scotch on the rocks, and while the barman was fixing the drink, I asked him what time the cabaret started.

'Half past eleven, sir,' he said, sliding the drink over to me. 'In the restaurant, second on the left down the passage.'

He went away to serve a tall, bony blonde in a sea-green evening dress whose elderly escort seemed to begrudge her the champagne cocktail she was whining for.

I glanced at my wrist-watch. The time was twenty minutes past eleven.

The fat drunk next to me turned and grinned sheepishly as if to apologize for intruding. He said on a rum ladened breath: 'You don't want to waste good money on the cabaret, friend. It's the worst swindle in town, and that's saying a lot.'

'No girls?'

He made a face.

'Well, yes, there are girls, if you can call them girls.'

I twiddled my glass.

'I heard this Lane dish is worth catching.'

He sucked up some of his rum and lime juice, and then closed a heavy eyelid.

'If you could catch her, I'd say she would be pretty satisfactory, but she's hard to catch. I've tried, and all I've got out of it is a couple of evenings listening to her sing, and that's something she can't do.'

'So what's good about this joint?'

He looked over his shoulder to see if anyone was listening, then leaning close and lowering his voice, he said: 'Between friends, they have a roulette table upstairs. The table stakes are up to the ceiling. All the rest of the muck here is just a front. But keep it under your hat, friend. I'm doing you a favour, telling you.'

'Maybe I might see what I can lose.'

He lifted his fat shoulders.

'They're pretty strict who they let up there. It's strictly illegal. You might have a word with Claude: he manages the joint. You can mention my name if you like: Phil Welliver.'

'Thanks. Where do I find him?'

He nodded across the bar to a door.

'In there.' Then he pushed himself away from the bar. 'I've got to move along. I promised the wife I'd take her out tonight. Went right out of my mind until five minutes ago. I'd better not be too late.'

I watched him lurch across the bar, and when I was sure he had gone, I went the same way, again aware of the twenty staring eyes on me as I walked to the exit.

I found the restaurant on the left of the passage: an oval-shaped room with dim lighting, rose-pink mirrors and blue décor. There were about sixty people finishing dinner, and the room was full of the hum of voices and cigarette smoke.

The head waiter, a jaded young man with red-gold wavy hair, came up to me, his face set in a professional smile.

'I wanted to catch the cabaret,' I said, 'but I don't want the dinner.'

'Certainly, sir: perhaps a drink and a sandwich ...?' He let his voice die away as he waved his hands apologetically.

'Sure,' I said. 'I'll have a whisky sour and a chicken on rye bread.'

He led me around the back of the tables to a small table a little too near the band for comfort, but I didn't argue about it.

He went away and I sat down.

The band was a four-piece job: four well-built Negroes: a trumpet, drums, double bass and a saxophone. They played as if they needed a vacation and were going to strike at any moment if they didn't get it.

After a while the waiter brought my chicken sandwich and my drink. The rye bread was a little dry and the chicken looked as if it had had a sharp attack of jaundice before departing this earth. I let the sandwich lie. I've drunk worse whisky sours in my time, but not much worse.

Around quarter to twelve, the floor was cleared and four girls came prancing in. They wore G-strings, halters and guardsmen's hats. They were pretty terrible, and there was one of them who had dirty knees. They were strictly for the drunks, and after they had shown themselves off and made eyes at the *habitués*, they bounced out more enthusiastically than they had bounced in. As my rum and lime juice friend had said: as a cabaret, it was a swindle.

A little after midnight, Dolores Lane came in and stood holding a microphone the way a drowning man hangs on to a lifebelt.

She was wearing a gold *lamé* dress that fitted her like a second skin, and she looked pretty good as she stood there under a white spotlight. She sang two Latin-American songs. Her voice was small, but at least she could sing in tune. Without a microphone, no one would have heard her. She sang listlessly as if she were bored with the whole thing, and the applause she collected could have been packed into a thimble without overflowing.

She went away, her eyes glittering, and then the crowd began to dance again.

I found a scrap of paper in my wallet and wrote the following message:

Will you have a drink with me? I hope you didn't get sand in your shoes this morning.

A nutty note to send her; but I had an idea it might hook her. I grabbed a passing waiter, gave him the note and a five-dollar bill and told him to get some action. He made sure the bill was for five dollars before he said he would fix it.

I was working on my second whisky sour when the waiter came back.

'She'll see you in her dressing-room,' he said and gave me a curious stare. 'Through that door, turn left, and it's the door ahead with a star on it.'

I thanked him.

He paused just long enough for me to reach for my wallet if I felt inclined, but as I didn't, he moved off.

I finished my drink, settled the check which was three times too much, and then made my way through the door the waiter had indicated into a typical behind-the-scenes passage.

Facing me was a shabby door with a faded, gold star on it. I rapped and a woman's voice said: 'Come on in.'

I turned the handle and stepped into a small room with a lighted mirror, a small dressing-table, a cupboard, a screen in a corner, two upright chairs and well-worn carpet on the floor.

Dolores was sitting in front of the mirror doing things to her face. She had on a red silk wrap which fell open above her thighs to show me her sleek legs in nylon stockings.

On the dressing-table was a bottle of gin, half full, and a glass with either gin and water in it or just gin.

She didn't turn, but looked at my reflection in the mirror as I closed the door and moved over to the upright chair.

'I thought it would be you,' she said. 'Want some gin? There's a glass somewhere around.'

I sat down.

'No, thanks. I've been on whisky. The idea was for me to buy you a drink.'

She leaned forward to peer at herself in the mirror. She picked up a rabbit's foot and dusted the powder off her dark eyebrows.

'Why?'

I had an idea she was a little drunk, but I wasn't sure. 'I liked your act. I thought it was worth a bottle of champagne,' I said, watching her. 'Besides, I wanted to talk to you.'

She put the rabbit's foot down and drank from the glass. By the way she grimaced, and then shuddered, I knew the glass contained neat gin.

'Just who are you?'

Her eyes were slightly glassy and slightly out of focus. That told me she was three parts drunk, but not drunk enough not to know what she was saying or doing.

'The name's Chester Scott. I live and work in this city.'

'Scott?' Her eyebrows came down in a frown. 'Chester Scott? Where have I heard that name before?'

'Have you?'

She screwed up her eyes, grimaced, then shrugged.

'Somewhere ... so you liked my act?' She held out her hand. 'Give me a cigarette.'

I gave her one, gave myself one and lit hers, then mine.

'The act was fine, but the background didn't jell.'

'I know.' She blew smoke to the ceiling, then took a little more gin. 'Did you hear the way they applauded? You would think to hear them, they had blisters on their hands.'

'It's the wrong crowd for you.'

She grimaced.

'An artist who is worth a damn can handle any crowd,' she said and turned back to examine her face in the mirror. She picked up an eyelash brush and began to stroke up her eyelashes with quick, deft movements. 'What were you doing down there this morning? I didn't fall for that swim story.'

'Looking the place over. What were you thinking about, marrying a cop?'

She put down the eyelash brush and turned her head slowly. Her glittering eyes were now more out of focus.

'What's it to you who I marry?'

'Nothing much. It seemed odd to me a girl like you should want to marry a speed cop.'

Her lips curved into a smile.

'But then he was a very special cop.'

'Was he?' I reached forward to drop ash into an empty tobacco tin that stood on the dressing-table. 'How special?'

She put her hand to her mouth to cover a gentle belch.

'He had money.' She got to her feet and crossed over to the screen and went behind it. She moved unsteadily. 'Have you any money, Mr Scott?'

I edged my chair around so I could stare at the screen. I could just see the top of her head as she stripped off her wrap which she tossed on the floor beside the screen.

'I have a little money,' I said. 'Not much.'

'The only thing in this world that means anything, that has any importance, is money. Don't let anyone kid you otherwise. They say health and religion are good things to have: but I'll settle for money,' she said from behind the screen. 'If you haven't got it, you might just as well buy a razor and slit your throat. Without money you're nothing. You can't get a decent job; you can't go anywhere worth going to; you can't live in a place worth living in; you can't mix with the people who are worth mixing with. Without money, you're just one of a crowd, and that's the lowest form of life to my thinking – being one of a crowd.'

She came out from behind the screen. She now had on a red silk dress that showed off her curves to advantage. She moved unsteadily to the dressing-table to fix her dark hair.

'I've been in this racket for ten years,' she went on as she ran a comb through her hair. 'I have a small talent. The words aren't mine. They were dreamed up by my drunken agent who hangs on to me because he can't find anyone else to bleed. But the small talent doesn't bring me in any money worth speaking about. It provides me with a living if you can call it that, and that's all. So when this red-faced cop started to work on me, I let him, because he had money. For the past ten years I have been in practically every nightclub along this lousy coast, and although I have been propositioned countless times, I have never had an offer of marriage. Then this cop comes on the scene. He is tough and crude and utterly horrible, but at least he wanted to marry me.' She paused and finished the gin in her glass. 'He had money. He gave me presents.' She pulled open a drawer in her dressing-table and fished out a gold powder-compact. She held it in her hand so I could see it. It was an expensive, impressive ornament. 'He gave me this and he didn't expect me to throw my clothes off the moment I got it. He gave me a squirrel coat and I still had my clothes on. He said if I would marry him he'd give me a mink coat for a wedding present.' She paused to pour more gin in her glass. She sipped and grimaced with disgust at its taste. I guessed she wouldn't be talking like this if she hadn't been three-quarters tight, but I was listening: listening as hard as I could. 'He had a bungalow out at Palm Bay. It was nice. There was a terrace overlooking the sea and the rooms were tricky: one of them had a glass floor with lights under it. I would have married that man if he had stayed alive long enough, even though he was so crude he used to come in here with his hat on, put his feet up here on the dressing-table and call me "Baby Doll". But he had to be dumb enough to get killed.' She finished the gin and put the glass down, shuddering. 'He had to be dumb enough just when he and Art Galgano ...' She broke off, squinting at me, as if trying to get me in focus. 'I guess I'm drunk,' she said. 'What am I talking like this to you for?'

'I don't know,' I said. 'People talk to get things out of their systems. You're not boring me. He couldn't help getting killed. You should feel sorry for him.'

'Should I?' She stubbed out her cigarette. 'You mean I should feel sorry for myself.' She splashed more gin into her glass. 'Are you looking for a wife, Mr Scott?'

'I can't say I am.'

'What are you looking for?'

'I'd like to find out how O'Brien got himself run over.'

She lifted the glass of gin and sniffed at it.

'This is filthy stuff. It's only when I've done my act and get the applause I got tonight, that I use it.' She peered at me. 'What's O'Brien to you?'

'Nothing. I'm just curious to find out how he got run over.'

'No reason – just curious?'

'Just curious.'

She studied me.

'What did you say your name was again?'

'Scott.'

'And you want to know how Harry got himself run over?'

'That's right.'

'I could tell you.' She sipped the gin, then with a movement of disgust, she crossed the room and poured the gin into the small, grimy toilet basin. 'I could tell you. How much is it worth to you, Mr Scott?'

I dropped my cigarette into the tobacco tin.

'You mean how much in money?'

She leaned her solid hips against the toilet basin and smiled at me: it wasn't a nice smile, and it made her look as hard as if her face had been hacked out of stone.

'Yes, I mean how much in money. Chester Scott – of course. I know who you are now. You're the man Oscar is blackmailing.'

'What makes you think that?' I asked, keeping my face expressionless.

'I hear things,' she said. 'I don't approve of blackmail. I need money, Mr Scott. I can give you information that can take you off Oscar's hook, but it'll cost you. I won't rob you. I'll put you wise for five hundred. It's cheap. I know what Oscar's asking. Five hundred is nothing.'

'What information?'

'Have you five hundred dollars, Mr Scott?'

'Not on me.'

'Can you get it tonight?'

'I might.' I thought of the eight hundred dollars we kept in the safe at the office. I could borrow that and pay it back when the bank opened on Monday. 'What makes you imagine the information you have would be worth all that to me?'

'Give me another cigarette.'

I crossed over to her, gave her a cigarette and lit it. As she dipped the cigarette end into the flame of my lighter, she put her hand on mine. Her flesh felt hot and dry against mine.

I moved away from her, watching her draw in smoke, then let it out slowly down her nostrils.

'I can get you off Oscar's hook,' she said. 'I know the whole set-up. You can have it for five hundred. I've got to get out of this town and I want a get-away stake.'

'How do you get me off the hook?' I asked, wondering if she were taking me for a ride.

'I'll tell you when you produce the money and not before. When you get bitten by a snake, you use an antidote. I can give you the antidote to Oscar's bite. If you don't want to spend five hundred to save thirty thousand, then you're a fool. Can you give me the money tonight?'

If she really knew how I could fix Oscar, five hundred would be a give away price.

'Yes, I can get it.'

'I'll be home just after two,' she said. 'You'll find me at apartment 10; Maddox Arms. So you know where it is?'

I said I knew where it was.

'Bring the money with you, Mr Scott, and I'll give you the antidote. Be there sharp at two. I have a train to catch.' She went over to the door and opened it. 'I've got to sing to those lousy drunks again. See you later.'

I moved past her into the passage, then turned and looked at her. Her face was tense and her eyes were glittering in the hard, ceiling light just above her head. I had an idea she was frightened.

We stared at each other for a long, steady moment, then she gently closed the door in my face.

II

As I drove out of the parking lot, I noticed a black Clipper edge out of the second row of cars and move after me.

I thought nothing of it at the time even though it kept behind me all the way back to town and only passed me when I pulled up outside my office block, but I was to remember it later.

The time was now a quarter to one. I had a key to the

main door, but I knew if I opened the door I'd set the alarm off, so I rang for the janitor, hoping he hadn't gone to bed.

He came eventually and peered through the plate-glass door at me. Then he turned off the alarm and let me in.

'I hope I didn't get you out of bed,' I said. 'I forgot some papers I want to work on over Sunday.'

'That's okay, Mr Scott,' he said cheerfully. 'I was just about to turn in, but I wasn't in. Will you be long?'

'Five minutes,' I said.

'Then I'll wait for you here and shut you out. You certainly work late hours.'

I made a noncommittal remark and crossed over to the elevator.

It took me only a few minutes to unlock my office and open the safe. I exchanged an IOU slip for the five hundred dollars I took from the cash box.

During the run down from Mount Cresta I had been doing some thinking. Dolores had said she would give me an antidote to Ross' bite. That could only mean she was going to give me information that I could threaten him with so he wouldn't dare use the information he had against me.

As I stowed the five hundred dollars away in my hip pocket, I wondered what the information was and just how far I could trust Dolores. Going down the elevator I recalled that Ross had said he had to leave town. Dolores had said she needed money to leave town. Could these two have been hooked up in some racket that had gone sour now that O'Brien was dead?

Obviously O'Brien was a character worth investigating. A speed cop who can promise a mink coat and who owned a bungalow with a glass floor must have a pretty handsome private income, so why had he remained a cop?

The janitor was patiently waiting for me as I crossed the lobby. I said good night to him and he let me out.

As I walked to where I had parked the Buick I saw a man standing in a shop doorway on the opposite side of the road. As I looked at him, wondering what he was doing there, he drew back into the shadows.

By the time I had reached the Buick and was driving towards the residential quarter of Palm City, I had forgotten him, but, like the black Clipper, I was to remember him later.

Maddox Arms was a block of apartments on Maddox Avenue in the less fashionable quarter: a brown stone building that had been put up some fifty years ago, and looked as if nothing had been done to the outside since then.

I climbed fifteen steep steps to the front entrance and walked into a dimly lit lobby with a line of mail boxes on the right, an ancient elevator facing me and a door marked *Janitor* on my left.

I learned from the wall indicator that apartment 10 was on the third floor. As I got into the elevator, I glanced at my wrist-watch. The time was three minutes to two o'clock.

The elevator dragged me up to the third floor in a way that made me feel that any moment the cage might part from its cable and plunge me down into the basement. I was glad when it came to a creaking standstill and I got out.

I stepped into a narrow passage: at either end were doors. The one on the left was the door to apartment 10.

I went down the passage and paused outside the door. There was a card fixed to the door panel with a thumb tack which read: *Miss Dolores Lane.*

I pressed the bell push and heard a bell ring sharply somewhere inside the apartment.

There was a pause while I stood there, pretty tense and wondering if within the next ten minutes I would be in a position to fix Oscar Ross.

Then I heard the sound of movement behind the door, which opened an inch or so and came to rest on a chain lock.

'Who is it?' Dolores asked, not showing herself.

'Scott,' I said. 'Who did you think it was?'

The door closed for a moment while she slid off the chain, then she opened up.

She was wearing a lightweight travelling coat over a grey dress. Her expression was tense, but she managed to give me a small, meaningless smile.

'Come in. When you live alone in a dump like this, you have to be careful who you open the door to at two o'clock in the morning.'

I stepped past her into a fair-sized room, sparsely furnished with the kind of furniture you will see only in furnished apartments: junk that no one in their right minds would buy for themselves. It told me that she was living the hard way, and had probably been living like that for some time.

'Don't take any notice of this,' she said, seeing me look around. 'Thank goodness I'm leaving it. The only thing in its favour is it's cheap.'

I moved away from her.

There was a door standing half open near me. Through the open doorway the room beyond appeared to be a bedroom. At the foot of the bed was a fair-sized suitcase. It looked to me as if she were ready to go.

'Did you bring the money?' she asked and I caught an anxious note in her voice.

'I brought it,' I said, 'but I'm not parting with it until I'm satisfied the information you have is worth buying.'

Her lips twisted into a bitter smile.

'It's worth buying. Let me see the money.'

I took from my hip pocket the wad of bills and held them so she could see them.

She stared hungrily at them.

'Five hundred dollars?'

'Yes.'

'Now I'll show you what I've got,' she said and moved over to a shabby desk that stood in one of the corners of the room. She pulled open a drawer.

All along, at the back of my mind, I had an idea I couldn't trust her, but I was vain enough and stupid enough to believe, because she was a woman, I could handle her.

She dipped her hand into the drawer, then turned to face me. She had a .38 automatic in her hand which she pointed at me, and there was an expression in her eyes that sent a chill crawling up my spine.

'Don't move,' she said softly. 'Put the money on the table.'

For a long moment I stared at her and at the gun. It was pointing rock steady at my chest.

This was the first time in my life that anyone had ever pointed a gun at me and I didn't like it. The gun looked terribly dangerous and horribly lethal.

I had often read in detective thrillers of the hero being held up by a gun, and I have accepted the author's impression that his hero could face such a situation without turning a hair. I now discovered that I wouldn't be much of a hero in fiction. I found my mouth had turned dry and there was a cold, empty feeling in my stomach.

'You'd better put that down,' I said huskily. 'It might go off.'

'It will go off if you don't put the money on the table.'

There was a scraped, bleak look on her face and her dark eyes were glittering. She moved slightly to her left, keeping me covered. Her hand groped behind her, found the control knob on the old-fashioned radio that stood on a table against the wall and turned the set on.

'There's no one on this floor to hear the shot,' she went on, speaking rapidly. 'The old fool below us is deaf. He'll think it's a car back-firing or he probably won't hear anything.'

The room suddenly became full of the sound of strident, violent jazz as the station came through the loudspeaker.

'Put the money on the table or I'll shoot you,' she said, a vicious hiss in her voice.

I continued to stare at her. My heart gave a little bounce when I saw the expression in her face and saw she wasn't bluffing. I saw too the skin of her knuckles tighten as she started to take up the slack on the trigger. I had a bleak feeling that any second the gun would go off.

She drew in a sharp breath and slightly lowered the gun. Even with her pancake make-up, I could see she was sweating.

'Back up against the wall!'

I backed up against the wall and watched her scoop up the bills and stuff them into her overcoat pocket.

'You won't get far,' I said, speaking as evenly as I could, which wasn't anything to be impressed about. 'The police will pick you up.'

She smiled at me.

'Don't kid yourself. You tell the police about me and I'll tell them about you,' she said. 'Oscar isn't the only one who knows about you. I know too. Don't think I like doing this. I'm not a thief and I'm not a blackmailer, but I've got to get out of this town and this is the only way I can do it. Don't turn suddenly brave and try to stop me leaving here or you'll get shot. Now turn around and face the wall and don't move.'

There was a ruthless, frightened expression in her glittering eyes that warned me she would shoot if I didn't do what she said. I turned around and faced the wall.

I heard her go into the bedroom and then come out almost immediately. By the heavy way she walked, I guessed she was carrying the suitcase.

'So long, Mr Scott,' she said. 'You've been useful to me. Sorry for the double cross, but if you're fool enough to fall for it, you can't blame me.'

The door banged shut and I heard the key turn.

I moved away from the wall and taking out my handkerchief I wiped my sweating face. Then I crossed the room and snapped off the radio. The sudden silence in the room was almost as violent as had been the strident jazz.

I was moving towards the door when I heard Dolores, outside in the passage, suddenly scream out: 'No! Keep away from me! No ... don't ...'

I stood there, my heart beginning to thump. The note in her voice was loaded with terrified panic.

Then she gave a piercing scream that went into me like a knife thrust. The sound was followed by a scuffling noise and then the sound of a heavy fall.

She screamed again: a scream I still hear from time to time in a nightmare.

Then there was silence.

I stood there, tense, my heart hammering, listening.

I heard the grille of the elevator slam shut and then the creaking noise of its cable told me the elevator was descending.

After a long, tense minute the creaking stopped, and then faintly, three floors below, I heard the grille slam back.

Somewhere on the street a car started up and drove away fast. I still stood there, feeling sweat on my face, listening to the silence that now cloaked the whole of the apartment block, then faintly, I heard a horrible gasping sigh that came from the other side of the door: a sound that turned my blood cold.

10

I

As I stood there, staring at the locked door, the telephone bell started into life. Its sudden violent ringing made me start convulsively.

I looked quickly across the room to where the telephone stood on the desk, then, while the bell continued to ring, I tried the handle of the door, but the door was firmly locked on the outside.

It was a solid door, I couldn't hope to batter it down without making a lot of noise, and besides, it would take some time.

I ran over to the window, pulled aside the curtain and looked down at the street, three storeys below. There was no way out that way.

I went into the bedroom and looked out of the bedroom window: still no way out.

I came out of the bedroom and back into the living-room. The strident sound of the telephone bell, ringing continuously, jarred on my nerves.

Across the room was another door. I opened it and glanced into a kitchen bathroom. The window, high up, was too small for anything larger than a cat to pass through.

The persistent ringing of the telephone was now more than I could stand, and I went back into the sitting-room and removed the receiver, laying it gently on the desk.

As I turned back to the kitchen, I heard a man's voice come faintly out of the receiver.

'Dolly! Is that you, Dolly? This is Ed. The goddamn train is leaving in five minutes ...'

I ran back into the kitchen and opened a cupboard, hunting for a tool strong enough to break open the door, but I couldn't find one.

I went back to the locked door. Bending, I peered into the keyhole. The key was still in the lock.

I could still hear the faint voice, like a ghost voice, coming from the receiver.

I looked around the room. There was a newspaper on one of the chairs, and I tore off a sheet and slid the sheet under the door. There was a fair-sized gap between the bottom of the door and the floor.

I ran back into the kitchen, my heart thumping with panic and started a frantic search through the drawers in a cabinet. In the fourth drawer I was lucky enough to find a pair of thin pliers. I snatched them up and returned to the living-room. With a little manipulation I managed to force the key out of the lock and I heard it drop on to the sheet of newspaper.

Very gently I began to pull the sheet back under the door and with it the key.

I snatched it up.

As I did so, I heard the telephone click and then the dialling tone start up. I went over to the desk and replaced the receiver, then returned to the door, thrust the key into the lock with a shaking hand and opened the door.

I stepped out into the dimly lit passage.

Dolores was lying face down by the elevator, her grey travelling coat rucked up: her long slim legs sprawled grotesquely in death.

No one could lie like that unless they were dead, and I turned cold at the sight of her.

For a full half-minute I stood in the doorway, looking at her, then I reached into the sitting-room, turned off the light and closed the door.

Moving slowly, hearing my breath rasping in my throat, I went down the passage to where she lay.

I reached her and bent over her. Her face was turned away from me, but I could see now there was blood in her hair.

Although I knew she must be dead, I had to make sure.

I took hold of her shoulder and pulled her over on to her back.

Someone had hit her a crushing blow on her right temple, smashing her skull. It had been a terrible blow and must have killed her instantly.

I shut my eyes while I struggled with my nausea. It took me several seconds to fight off the cold, horrible feeling of sickness and before I could nerve myself to look at her again.

I reached in her coat pocket, but of course the five hundred dollars had gone: gone too was her suitcase.

I straightened. Taking out my handkerchief I wiped my face and wrists, then I moved away from her, thinking, in a grip of panic, that if anyone found me here, they would jump to the conclusion that I had killed her.

With one thought to get out of the building, and get as far away as I could before she was found, I started down the stairs.

I was half way down the second flight of stairs when I

suddenly saw a girl turn the bend in the stairs and come up towards me.

For a split second I stopped, my mind screaming to me to turn around and bolt up the stairs, but somehow I managed to keep control of myself and I went on down.

The stairs were badly lit, but I could see enough of the girl to know her again, and I guess that would go for her too if she ever saw me again.

She was young and blonde with a tired, pale, uninteresting face and heavy smudges under her eyes. Under the black coat that hung open she wore a flowery evening dress you can see in any cheap dress shop on Arcade Street, and there was a limp, red carnation in her hair.

She looked at me as she passed, her eyes indifferent, and she went on up the stairs.

I kept on down.

If she went up to the third floor she would walk right on to Dolores' body, I thought, and her screams would bring the police before I could get out of the district.

When I reached the turn in the stairs, I started down the rest of the flight at a run.

I reached the hall and crossed to the front door, then I paused to listen.

I heard a door slam somewhere upstairs, but there were no screams. Her apartment must have been on the second floor, I told myself, and I cautiously opened the front door and looked up and down the long, deserted street.

Then, shutting the front door behind me, I walked quickly down the steps and to where I had left the Buick some fifty yards farther down the street.

I got in and fumbled for the ignition key. I felt pretty bad. The shock of finding Dolores now hit me, and for several seconds I had to sit still, my eyes closed, while I fought against the sickness that nearly swamped me.

Then I heard a car coming down the street. The sound pulled me together, and feverishly, I got out the ignition key and sank it into the wheel-lock.

As I started the Buick engine, a taxi passed me, swerved to the kerb and pulled up outside the Maddox Arms. A man got out, carrying a suitcase. He paid the driver, then ran up the steps and entered the lobby.

I hesitated, watching the taxi drive away.

Was this man Ed who had spoken on the telephone?

I pulled away from the kerb and drove fast down the road, but at the first turning, I braked and swung the car into the side street where there were a number of cars already parked. If this man was Ed, I would be a fool not to get a look at him, I told myself.

I parked the Buick, got out and ran back to the intersection, then I started down Maddox Avenue, walking slowly.

When I was within fifty yards or so of the entrance to the Maddox Arms, I stopped, and stepping into the shadows, I waited.

Five or six minutes crawled by, then I saw the man with the suitcase come hurriedly from the apartment block.

I moved out of the shadows and started down the street towards him, walking briskly like a man returning from a late party and anxious to get home.

The man with the suitcase paused as he reached the sidewalk and looked towards me. I saw him give a violent start at the sight of me, then turning quickly, he set off fast down the street.

I kept on behind him, slightly increasing my stride so as not to lose sight of him, but not going so fast that he could think I was following him.

He reached the intersection, looked back at me, and then he turned left.

As soon as he was out of sight, I broke into a run, running on my toes, and I was just able to spot him as he crossed the main street and turned down a dark side street.

As soon as he was out of sight, I ran across the street, then paused at the corner to look cautiously around.

I spotted him heading for a taxi rank where three taxis were in line, and I saw him get into the first taxi that moved off.

I raced down the street, jerked open the door of the second taxi and scrambled in.

'Follow that taxi,' I said to the driver. 'There's five bucks in it for you if you can keep it in sight. Don't get too close. I don't want the fare to know we are following him.'

The driver had the taxi moving before I had shut the cab door.

'Not much chance he won't spot us, boss,' he said. 'There's no traffic for us to hide behind. I heard him tell my pal to take him to the Washington Hotel.'

'He may change his mind,' I said. 'I don't want to lose him.'

'Alf will tell me where he goes,' the driver said. 'The best thing is for me to drive straight to the Washington Hotel, otherwise he's certain to spot us.'

I decided he was probably right.

'Okay. Get me to the Washington first then.'

'That's the boy,' the driver said approvingly and swung off down a side street and increased his speed. 'You a private dick?'

'Yes,' I said, knowing that if I said no I would have to explain why I wanted to follow the taxi. 'If I lose this guy,

I'll lose my job.'

'You won't lose him, pal,' the driver said as he flung the cab around a corner so the tyres screamed in protest. 'You sit tight. I'll get you there.'

It took us less than five minutes to reach the hotel. The driver stopped his taxi within fifty yards of the entrance and then turned and grinned at me.

'Well, he hasn't arrived yet, but he will. Want me to wait?'

'Yes.'

I took out my cigarettes and offered him one. We both lit up.

I remained in the cab, peering through the windscreen at the hotel entrance.

The Washington was a fourth-rate hotel, used mainly by travelling salesmen visiting Palm City. Its only asset was that it was close to the railroad station.

We waited in silence for five or six minutes, then just as I was beginning to think I had lost my man I saw the taxi come down the street and pull up outside the hotel.

The man with the suitcase got out, paid the driver and then walked quickly into the hotel.

'There you are,' my driver said, turning to grin at me. 'What did I tell you?'

I gave him five dollars.

'Thanks,' I said. 'I'll go and talk to this joker.'

'Want any help?'

'That's okay.'

I got out of the cab, waved to him and then walked to the entrance of the hotel. I climbed the steps and paused just outside the double glass doors leading into the lobby.

The man with the suitcase was talking to the night clerk, an elderly, bald-headed man who was listening to what he was saying with a look of bored indifference on his face.

They stood either side of the reception desk. There was an overhead light that fell directly on the man with the suitcase.

I took a good look at him.

He wasn't the type of man I would expect Dolores to make a journey with. He was short and thickset and nudging sixty. His fleshy face was covered with tiny, broken veins of a heavy drinker. Now I could get a good view of him in the light, I could see his clothes were shabby and looked as if he had had them for a long time. His blue suit was shiny at the elbows; his grey felt hat was dirty and greasy. The only thing new about his attire was his tie: a gaudy thing of pale blue with horses' heads in yellow.

As he talked to the night clerk, he kept wiping his face with a soiled handkerchief, and even at the distance from where I was standing, I could see he was nervous and upset.

Finally he gave the night clerk some money and the night clerk pushed the register towards him. The man signed the book, took the room key the night clerk dropped on the counter, then, picking up his suitcase, he crossed the lobby and disappeared up a flight of dimly lit stairs.

I stood there hesitating, then I pushed open the double glass doors and walked into the lobby.

II

The night clerk watched me come, his old, jaded face expressionless.

I arrived at the counter and leaned on it. There could be only one way to handle a man like this, I told myself after I had a close-up of him. His threadbare suit and his frayed cuffs told of his poverty.

'I want information about the man who's just gone upstairs,' I said briskly.

Taking out my wallet, I produced a ten-dollar bill, let him get a good look at it before I began to fold it into a neat spill. Then I put it between the first and second knuckles of my left hand so it stuck up like a flag and rested my hand on the counter within three feet of him.

The night clerk's eyes shifted from me to the folded bill. He began to breathe heavily through his pinched nostrils and his face showed slight animation.

'We don't reckon to give information about our clients,' he said, a hesitant note in his voice. 'Who might you be, mister?'

'A man who buys information with a ten-dollar bill,' I said.

He hunched his shoulders and closed his eyes while he appeared to think. Like that, he reminded me of a scraggy, broody hen. Then he opened his eyes and looked once more at the bill.

'You're not a cop,' he said as if speaking to himself. 'And you're not a private dick.'

His jaded eyes shifted from the bill to my face and he searched earnestly for a clue, but it didn't get him anywhere.

'Never mind who I am,' I said. 'What's his name?'

His hand that looked as if he had forgotten to wash it for several days, moved timidly towards the bill. I let him get to within a few inches of it, then I moved it out of his reach.

'What's his name?' I repeated.

He sighed.

'I don't know. I bet it isn't what he has written in the book,' and he pushed the register towards me.

I read: *John Turner, San Francisco*. The name was written in a tiny, badly formed handwriting.

'Turner,' he said thoughtfully. 'If I had a dollar for every John Turner in this book, I'd be rich enough to quit this lousy job.'

'Did he say why he was this late and how long he was staying?'

The night clerk hunched his shoulders again.

'If I held the money, mister, it would help my memory. When you reach my age, you'll be surprised how bad your memory gets.'

I dropped the bill on the counter.

'Let it lie there,' I said. 'You keep an eye on it.'

He leaned over the bill and breathed gently on it, then he looked up and asked, 'What was that you wanted to know, mister?'

I repeated the question.

'He said he had lost the last train out and was catching the first one in the morning. He has a call in for seven o'clock.'

'A train to where?'

He shook his head regretfully.

'He didn't say. It wouldn't be Frisco. There isn't a train to Frisco tomorrow at half past seven. Could be San Diego. The last train to San Diego left at half past two this morning, and the first one out leaves at half past seven.'

I thought for a moment, then asked: 'What's his room number?'

The night clerk put his finger on the bill and very slowly, very gently, began to draw it towards him.

'Room 28,' he said, 'but don't get any wild ideas. No one goes upstairs without they hire a room first.'

'Room 27 or 29 vacant?'

He looked over his shoulder at the line of keys hanging on the keyboard, then without taking his finger off the bill, he reached out his left hand and took the key of room 29 off its hook.

He laid it down before me, and then with a movement as fast as a lizard nailing a fly, he whipped the ten-dollar bill out of sight.

'Two bucks for the night,' he said. 'It's not a bad room: anyway, it's better than his.'

I shelled out the two bucks, then I picked up the key. 'Just in case I oversleep,' I said, 'give me a call at half past six.'

'Okay,' he said. 'Up the stairs, first floor, turn left at the head of the stairs.'

I thanked him, crossed the lobby and climbed the stairs to the first floor.

The passage lights were dim. The carpet I walked on felt paper thin; the doors I passed were shabby and the paint faded. A faint smell of cabbage water, bad plumbing and unwashed bodies hung over the passage. The Washington was obviously not one of the class hotels of Palm City.

As I approached room 27, I stepped lightly and paused outside room 28 to listen. I didn't hear anything, so I moved on to room 29, slid the key into the lock, turned it gently and eased open the door. I groped for the light switch, found it and turned on the light.

I entered a rabbit hutch of a room, careful to tread softly. I shut the door and then looked around.

There was a bed, a toilet basin, a strip of carpet and two upright chairs. On the wall, over the bed, was an engraving of a woman with wings and a wisp of tulle across her fat behind. She was hammering with clenched fists on an iron-studded door. She probably represented love locked out and if love was anything like her, it was a good thing the door looked so impregnable.

I crossed the room and sank on to the bed.

The time by my strap watch was ten minutes to three and I suddenly felt completely bushed. It had been the most eventful and disturbing Saturday of my life and I wondered uneasily where I was going from here.

I was tempted to stretch out on the bed, dressed as I was, and catch up with some sleep. I was actually giving way to the temptation when I heard the ping of a telephone bell: the ping you hear when you lift the receiver. It came from the room next door.

I was immediately wide awake and listening.

The man who had signed himself in the register as Turner, said: 'Send up a bottle of Scotch and some ice, and let's have some service.'

There was a pause, then he growled: 'I don't give a damn. Just let's have it without a lot of argument,' and he hung up.

For several moments I sat staring down at the dusty carpet, then, with an effort, I pushed myself off the bed and tiptoed to the door, eased it open and then turned off the light in the room. I supported myself against the door post and waited.

Maybe ten minutes crawled by: it seemed like an hour. Then I heard slow dragging footsteps on the stairs. I fumbled in my wallet and took out a five-dollar bill. This seemed to be a money spending night, but at least I was getting some return for the outlay.

The night clerk came along the corridor carrying a tray on which stood a bottle of whisky and a container of ice. He walked as if he were having trouble with his feet.

When he got to within touching distance of door 25, I moved out into the corridor and blocked his progress. I held up the five-dollar bill so he could see it, then I pushed it towards him. At the same time I took the tray out of his hand.

He accepted the bill the way a hungry tiger accepts a chunk of meat, then he stared blankly at me, shifted his gaze to door 28, then softly backed away.

I watched him walk down the passage to the head of the stairs. He looked back, stared at me again, then went quietly down the stairs and out of sight.

I lowered the tray to the floor, just outside room 28, and then rapped on the door.

'Who is it?' the man who called himself Turner demanded.

'Room service,' I said and braced myself, leaning against the door panel.

I heard him cross the room, turn the key and then he opened the door.

I heaved my weight against it.

The door slammed open and Turner or Ed or whoever he was staggered back and was in the room.

For a man nudging sixty his reflexes were surprisingly good. He recovered himself, spun around and dived for the bed where a Colt .45 was lying.

I charged him, flattening him across the bed.

His hand closed over the gun. My hand closed over his. For a brief moment we exerted our individual strengths, but age was on my side.

I twisted the gun out of his grip, heaved myself off the bed and on to my feet before he could sit up.

When he did sit up he found himself looking down the barrel of the gun: something I'd rather he experienced than me.

He stared at me, his red-veined, broken complexion turning a dusty purple.

'Relax,' I said, trying to breathe normally but without much success. 'I want to talk to you.'

His tongue that looked like a strip of leather dyed purple moistened his lips.

'Who the hell are you?' he demanded, his voice thick and unsteady.

'Never mind who I am,' I said. 'There's the makings of a drink outside the door: suppose you fetch it in and we can have a conference.'

He must have needed a drink badly, for he shot off the bed and grabbed the tray as if his life depended on it. He carried the tray tenderly into the room and set it on the bed.

While he was pouring Scotch into a glass, I moved around, closed the door and turned the key in the lock.

He shot the Scotch down his throat in one long swallow, then he made a second drink.

'I have mine with ice,' I said gently.

He stared glassily at me.

'Who are you? What do you want?' he growled, clutching on his glass, his eyes going over me. From the puzzled expression on his face, he could make nothing of me.

'I'll ask the questions and you supply the answers,' I said, making my voice sound tough. 'Why didn't you call the police when you found her?'

The colour went out of his face, leaving only the red broken veins against a tallow background.

'You know what happened to her?' he croaked.

'I know. I saw you go in and I saw you come out. Why didn't you call the police?'

'What good would that have done?' he said, shifting his eyes from me.

'What's your name?'

Again the purple tongue came out and moved over his dry lips.

'Turner: John Turner.'

'Okay, if that's the way you want to play it,' I said and picked up the gun. It felt heavy and awkward in my hand. I had read about .45's in detective stories, but this was the first time I had actually handled one. I was surprised to find it this big and this heavy. 'Get up and stand against the wall. I'm going to call the police.'

Some whisky jumped out of his glass and splashed on his knees.

'Now, wait a minute,' he said huskily. 'I don't know a thing about it. I found her. Someone had hit her on the head.'

'What's your name?'

'Ed Nutley. I'm her agent.'

That made sense. I remembered Dolores had mentioned an agent.

'Why didn't you call the police?'

He drank some more whisky. The spirit seemed to stiffen his nerve. He scowled at me.

'What's it to you?' he growled. 'Come to that: who are you? You're not a cop, you're not a newspaper man, and I'll be damned if you are a shamus – just who the hell are you?'

'Look, if you don't want to answer my questions, we'll call the police and maybe you'll answer theirs.'

He wilted.

'I was going to call them,' he muttered. 'As soon as I had got over the shock, I was going to call them.'

'Go ahead and call them now, then,' I said, hoping the whisky hadn't made him reckless enough to do just that thing.

He put the glass down, and for an uncomfortable moment I thought he was going to reach for the telephone, but instead he took out a crumpled pack of cigarettes, stuck one on his lower lip and set fire to it.

'I know you,' he said suddenly. 'I must be losing my grip not to have tumbled to you before. You're the guy who was to have sprung her rail fare.'

I put the .45 back on the dressing-table, then I moved around him, picked up the second glass on the tray and made myself a small drink, I felt I needed it. I carried the drink across the room, then sat down on an upright chair by the window.

'Suppose I am?' I said.

He stared at me.

'Well, for crying out loud! Did you give her the money?'

'You're getting away from the subject,' I said. 'I want to know why you didn't call the police when you found her murdered. You'll either tell me or we'll go down to headquarters and you can tell them.'

He hesitated, then lifted his shoulders.

'I didn't want to get mixed up in anything,' he said, and took out a soiled handkerchief and wiped his sweating face. 'They might think I knocked her off.' He put his handkerchief carefully away. 'It wasn't as if I hadn't warned her ...' He stopped abruptly and frowned. 'I just didn't want to get mixed up in anything,' he conduded lamely.

'What did you warn her about?' I asked.

Again he hesitated, then he picked up his glass and finished his drink. He poured more whisky into his glass before saying: 'I don't know why I'm talking to you. Maybe I'm drunk, but if you're all that interested, I told her she was crazy to think of marrying this cop.'

'Why did you tell her that?'

He sucked down half the whisky, then stared at me with bleary eyes.

'Because he was no good, but she wouldn't listen.' He scowled, turning the glass in his soft dirty hands. 'She never would listen to anything I said. I warned her she was getting involved in some dirty racket, but she laughed at me. A cop couldn't live the way he did unless he was up to his ears in slime. She didn't give a damn. She thought by marrying him she could quit show business, and that's all she thought about.' He took another gulp at his drink. 'Now she's landed up with a broken head.'

'Just what was O'Brien's racket?' I asked, sitting forward on the edge of my chair.

He looked slyly at me.

'I wouldn't know.'

'Why did she want to leave town?'

He blew out his cheeks.

'Well, there wasn't anything more here for her. She wanted to have a look at Mexico.'

'She was anxious to get out. There was more to it than that. What was it?'

He sloshed more whisky into his glass.

'Did you give her the dough?'

'I gave it to her but whoever killed her took it,' I said.

He rubbed his hand over his sweating face, his eyes still trying to focus.

'I guess I'm getting drunk. Let me think about this.' He again rubbed his hand over his face. After a moment he said: 'If you know what's happened to her, you must have seen her before I did. That means you knew she was dead before I did. She had a hook into you for five hundred bucks and you've just told me you gave the dough to her.' He belched softly, putting his hand over his mouth. 'I may be half cut, but I'm not stupid. Maybe it was you who killed her.' He sat back, staring at me. 'Yeah ... could be. Maybe it mightn't be such a lousy idea to talk to the cops. They might be more interested in you than in me. I haven't a motive for killing her, but you damn well have.'

I kept my face expressionless although my heart began to thump.

'I didn't kill her,' I said, looking straight at him, 'and I don't think you killed her either, but if you're so set about it, we'll go down to headquarters and let them decide.'

He gave a weak grin.

'Okay, pal, I believe you,' he said. 'I don't want any trouble. She's dead. Nothing I can do can bring her back to life. Between you and me, I don't care who killed her.' He sat forward, rubbing the heels of his palms into his eyes. 'I've been in trouble with the cops in the past. If they don't hang this on you, they'll try to hang it on me. It's safer to keep clear of it. Suppose you get out of here and let me go to bed? I have an early train to catch and I feel like hell.'

I decided to jump a fast one on him.

'You know this fellow Ross?' I asked.

His reaction was disappointing. He just stared.

'I don't know anyone,' he said, picking his words carefully. 'Take my tip: if you want to stay alive, you won't know anyone either in this lousy town. Now suppose you let me get some sleep?'

'Do you think he killed her?'

His loose mouth curved into a grin.

'Ross? You kidding? He wouldn't have the nerve to kill a fly.'

So I tried another fast one.

'Then you think Art Galgano killed her?'

That scored a bull.

He stiffened, his hands turned into fists and he went white. For a long moment he just sat there, staring at me, then he said in a husky voice: 'I don't know who killed her. Now get out of here!'

I had a feeling I wasn't going to get anything more out of him. I was too tired now to care. I told myself I'd waylay him in the morning and have another crack at him. Right now I just had to get some sleep.

I got to my feet.

'I'll see you before you leave here,' I said as I plodded over to the door. 'I'm not through with you, so don't imagine I am.'

'Aw, forget it,' he mumbled and let the glass of whisky slip out of his hand. It dropped to the floor, making a little dark puddle on the carpet. 'I've had enough of this lousy town. I'll be glad to get out.'

I looked at him as he sat there, sweat glistening on his face, dark rings of fatigue around his eyes, the whisky bottle clutched in his hand. He didn't make a pretty picture.

I went out into the dimly lit corridor and shut the door. Although I didn't want to spend the rest of the night in this sordid, smelly hotel, I just couldn't face the long drive back to my bungalow.

I went into room 29, turned on the light and moved over to the bed. I took off my jacket and shoes, then I flopped on the bed, my bones aching for some comfort.

I tried to think of the events of the day. I tried to analyse what I had learned from Nutley, but I was too tired to care.

In a minute or so I was in a heavy, dreamless sleep.

The crash of gunfire brought me awake with a start that nearly threw me off the bed.

I sat upright, my heart slamming against my ribs, staring into the darkness, knowing that someone had fired a gun.

Then I heard quick, soft footfalls going along the passage. I slid off the bed, crossed the room without turning on the light, gently unlocked the door and opened it.

I peered out into the empty passage.

There was a strong smell of cordite fumes drifting out of Nutley's room. His door stood half open and the light was on.

I moved to the door and looked into the room.

Nutley sat on the floor, huddled in a corner. He was wearing a pair of soiled pyjamas and his feet were bare. Just below the pocket of his pyjama jacket was a splash of blood.

As I stood staring at him, the red stain slowly began to expand.

There was nothing I could do for him: there was nothing anyone could do for him.

He was on his own now.

Somewhere down the passage a woman began to scream.

I felt like screaming myself.

11

I

I seemed to have moved into a nightmare world where I was spending my time running away from dead bodies.

As I stood there in the open doorway, staring at Nutley, I realized I must not be found in this hotel, and I must get away before the police arrived.

The woman was still screaming somewhere along the passage, and another woman on the next floor now added to the din.

The grey, vacant, lost look on Nutley's face told me he was dead. I was so tired it was an effort to force myself to turn and plod down the passage and to start down the stairs.

The screaming woman began to yell: 'Police! Murder! Police!' out of a window. Panic forced me into a run, and I arrived in the reception hall, my nerves crawling, my breath coming in laboured gasps, and there, another shock awaited me.

Lying by the desk, face down, his head resting in a pool of blood, was the night clerk. Someone had hit him viciously on his right temple, killing him as Dolores Lane had been killed.

By now I was getting used to the sight of violent death, and I paused to look at the body, my senses too numbed to care. As I looked at it I heard the sound of a distant police siren and I stiffened, listening. The sound grew louder and menacing.

With my heart thumping, I started towards the double glass doors that led on to the street, then stopped as I realized that if I went that way I would walk right into the approaching police car.

Behind the reception desk was a door marked *Service*.

I ran around the counter, opened the door and stepped into a dimly lit passage. Ahead of me were stairs leading down into a basement. I didn't hesitate. I went down them quickly, arriving in another passage that led to the kitchens. I paused to look into the vast underground cellar with its clutter of pots and pans and plates and dishes. There was no sign of life in there and, moving quickly, I went over to a door marked *Fire Exit*.

I had some trouble in pulling back the bolts at the head and foot of the door, but finally got them back. I eased open the door and looked out into a dark alley.

I pulled the door shut behind and then walked quickly down the alley to the main street. At the end of the alley, I paused to look cautiously up and down the street.

A police car stood outside the hotel entrance, but there was no sign of any policeman.

Keeping to the shadows, I started off in the opposite direction, running with dragging feet, but at least running.

I had gone the length of two streets and had been forced into a walk when I saw a taxi crawling towards me. I realized I would be asking for trouble to stop the taxi, that once the alarm went out, the driver was certain to remember me and give the police a description of me, but I was too tired to care.

I waved and the taxi pulled up beside me. I told the driver to take me to Maddox Avenue fast.

He gave me a hard stare, then opened the cab door and I got in. We reached Maddox Avenue within ten minutes, and as we drove past Maddox Arms, I peered cautiously out of the cab window.

Three police cars stood at the entrance. There were five patrolmen standing by the cars and a plain-clothes man. I had an idea the plain-clothes man was Lieutenant West, but as he was in the shadows, I could have been mistaken. At the corner of the next intersection, I told the driver to stop and I paid him off. When the cab had driven away, I walked down the street to where I had left the Buick.

As I edged away from the kerb, I heard a clock strike half past three. It had been a hell of a night, I thought, as I headed back to my bungalow. I was now mixed up not only in the accidental death of a cop, but I was also mixed up in three murders. It was the kind of situation one only encounters in a nightmare, but I was too tired to accept its full impact.

All I could think of now was to get home and get to bed.

I eventually arrived outside the bungalow as the hands of the Buick's clock shifted to five minutes to four.

Leaving the car parked outside, I walked stiffly up the path, unlocked the front door and walked into the dark hall. I didn't bother to turn on the lights. Crossing the hall, I made my way down the passage to my bedroom. I opened the bedroom door and stepped into darkness.

I paused there, a creepy sensation suddenly crawling up my spine. There was a faint smell of perfume in the still air, and that was something I had never smelt in my bedroom before.

I reached out and turned on the light. I felt my heart give a sudden sharp kick against my ribs.

Lying in bed, her chestnut hair half hiding her face, her bare arms outside the sheet, either dead or asleep, was Lucille.

I slumped against the wall while I stared at her. I couldn't see any movement nor could I see if she were breathing. The shock of finding her in my bed was bad enough, but inside me began to grow a sick feeling of fear that she was dead.

Three people had died this night, and she could be the fourth. I had been able to walk out and lose myself after finding three bodies, but I knew if she were dead, I couldn't walk away and forget her. She was in my bed and in my bungalow.

I made the effort. Pushing myself away from the wall, I crossed the room until I reached the bed. With a shaking hand, I very gently touched her arm.

She moved, giving a little sigh, and she turned slightly, pushing her face into the pillow as if to screen her eyes from the light.

I stepped back, drawing in a deep breath of relief. Then I saw her clothes scattered on the floor: a pair of lemon-coloured slacks, a white shirt, a pair of white panties and a brassiere on a chair.

I was beyond caring why she should be in my bed, and of the consequences if she were found here. So long as she was alive I didn't care what happened.

All I wanted was sleep.

I went into the spare bedroom, stripped off my clothes, jerked the cover off the bed and slid under the sheet.

As my head dropped back on to the pillow, I began to drift off. The dead bodies, Lucille in my bed, the damaged Cadillac, the fear of the police and the menace of Oscar Ross dissolved into a heavy, dreamless sleep, and while I slept my problems and my fears sat at the foot of the bed, waiting to greet me when I awoke.

II

The hands of the bedside clock stood at five minutes past eleven when I opened my eyes. Hot sunshine was coming through the slats in the wooden shutters, making sharp patterns on the carpet.

For some moments I lay still, staring up at the ceiling, not quite convinced that I had been experiencing a horrible dream or if the events that now suddenly jumped into my mind had actually happened. Then as I became more awake, I realized this was no nightmare, and I threw off the sheet and slid out of bed. I took the spare bathrobe from the cupboard and put it on, then I went down the passage to the bathroom.

After I had shaved, I felt a little more capable of coping with the situation. As I came out of the bathroom, I heard movements in my bedroom, then the door jerked open and Lucille paused in the doorway.

We stared at each other.

'Hello,' I said. 'Couldn't you have used the spare bed or had you designs on me?'

She flushed scarlet.

'I'm sorry. I waited and waited, but you didn't come.' Her voice was breathless. 'I got so tired I lay on your bed and I must have fallen asleep.'

'Then in your sleep you threw your clothes all over the room and managed to get under the covers,' I said, smiling at her. 'Well, I hope you slept as well as I did. I got in a little late and thought it would be uncharitable to wake you. Was there any particular reason why you are here or did you decide a change of beds would break up the monotony of your life at the Gables?'

She stared blankly at me.

'You said you had found a solution. You didn't say what it was. I wanted to know. I came down here and waited for you in the hope you would come back.'

'I see, and how did you get in here?'

Her eyes shifted away from me.

'I – I found a window open.'

'That was careless of me.' I ran my fingers through my hair and winced as I touched the lump at the back of my head. 'Look, I'm not feeling quite myself this morning. Would you be a nice girl and get on your bicycle and go away? I want a little peace and quiet around here this morning.'

'Ches, please ...' She began to beat her clenched fists together, a sign I had come to recognize as evidence she was agitated. 'I must talk to you. This man who phoned ... he's been to see me. He intends to blackmail us.'

'Yes, I know about him. Well, all right, then we'll have a talk, but not before I have had some coffee. Will you oblige me by going into the bathroom and making yourself look glamorous? Right now you look as if you've been sleeping in a hedge. I'll get the coffee, then we can have a conference.'

Leaving her staring after me, I went into the kitchen and put on the kettle. I heard her go into the bathroom and, after a moment or so, I heard the shower going.

By the time I had the coffee, orange juice and toast on the table, she had come out of the bathroom. There was a fresh glow to her skin now and her hair looked silky and neat. She had rolled up the sleeves of my dressing-gown, and with that extraordinary knack most women have, she somehow had made herself look lovely and desirable even when wearing a man's dressing-gown that was several sizes too large for her.

'Sit down and drink your coffee,' I said. 'Don't let's talk yet. There's plenty of time.'

'But, Ches ...'

'I said we wouldn't talk yet. I want a little peace while I drink my coffee. Just relax, will you, and try to keep quiet?'

She sat down opposite me, her face suddenly sulky, and poured the coffee.

I savoured the situation. If I had no troubles, if Aitken dropped dead and if she were to marry me, this could be the set-up for the next twenty years or more: she sitting opposite me, looking lovely and a little sulky every morning while we drank coffee. I found the picture a lot less exciting than I had imagined it would be.

We finished our coffee in silence. From time to time we looked at each other across the table. It was a pretty odd breakfast, but I was determined not to listen to her troubles before the first cigarette of the morning.

When we had finished the coffee, I pushed a box of cigarettes towards her, got up, walked over to the settee and lay down on it. I lit a cigarette and stared up at the ceiling. I now felt more or less ready to cope with whatever she had to tell me.

'Okay,' I said, not looking at her. 'Let's have it. You're now being blackmailed – is that it?'

She sat rigid, her clenched fists on the table, her eyes wide open.

'Yes. He came yesterday evening. I was swimming. He suddenly appeared as I was getting out of the bath.'

I let smoke drift out of my open mouth.

'If you were wearing the bikini I saw you in, I'm surprised he had the heart to blackmail you.' I lifted my head to look at her. 'How did you like him? He struck me as the type most girls would rave about.'

'I thought he was hateful,' she said in a cold, flat voice.

'Really? Perhaps that was because he wanted money from you. I'm sure if he asked you to go out to dinner with him, you would have found him enchanting.'

'Ches! Will you please stop talking like this! He is demanding thirty thousand dollars! He said you and I could find that amount!'

'I know. He seems to have a certain child-like faith in our ability to raise such a sum. He has put the same proposition to me. He has given me until the end of the week to find the money. Do you think you could find thirty thousand dollars?'

'Of course not!'

I reached out and tapped ash off my cigarette.

'How much can you find – '

'I don't know. I have a diamond ring. It's the only thing I really own. Roger gave it to me before we were married. It must be worth something.' She began to twist a ring on the third finger of her right hand. 'I don't know how much. Perhaps you could sell it for me.'

I stretched out my hand.

'Let's have a look at it.'

She stared at me as if she couldn't believe she had heard aright, then she pulled the ring off her finger, got up and came over to me. She handed the ring to me.

I took it, looking up at her.

'Sit down here,' I said, patting the settee.

She sat down, folding her hands in her lap. Her expression was puzzled and worried.

I examined the ring.

It wasn't bad, but there was nothing about it that would excite any jeweller to fall over himself to buy it.

'I'd say you might hock it for five hundred,' I said, 'providing you told the guy your mother was starving, and you were dying of consumption, and if, of course, he believed you.' I dropped the ring into her lap. 'Well, we're making progress. We now have only to find twenty-nine thousand and five hundred dollars.'

'Ches! Why are you talking like this to me?' she demanded angrily. 'What have I done? I warned you we would be blackmailed and you didn't believe me and now you turn against me. It's not my fault.'

'I've had a very trying night,' I said patiently. 'Your problems, Lucille, don't interest me immediately. I have other things to think about.'

'But they are your problems as well!' she flared. 'How are we going to raise the money?'

'That, as Hamlet once said, is the question. Have you any suggestions to make?'

'Well, you – you can find most of it, can't you? You told me you had twenty thousand dollars.'

I looked at her.

She was sitting forward, her eyes frightened and anxious, and she looked very young and lovely.

'I have to give that to your husband. He might be annoyed if I gave it to Oscar instead.'

'Ches! You're not taking this seriously! What is the matter with you? This man says he will tell Roger we were making love on the beach together and he will tell the police

I killed the policeman! He says he has a photograph of you changing the number plates of your car!' She began to beat her fist on my knee. 'You're in this as much as I am! What are we going to do?'

I pushed her hand away.

'We're not going to let this situation stampede us,' I said. 'That's the first thing. The second thing is we're not going to pay Mr Oscar Ross, and the third thing is you're going to get dressed and go home before someone comes here and finds us together in an obviously compromising situation.'

She became rigid, her clenched fists between her knees.

'You're not going to pay him?' she said, her eyes growing round. 'But you must! He'll go to the police! He'll tell Roger ... you must pay him!'

'There's no must about it. We have until the end of the week: that's six days. I'll be surprised if I don't find something in that time about Ross that will discourage him from pressing his claim. A man like that must have a past. He's anxious to leave town. I'm going to dig into his past, and I'm going to find out why he wants to leave town. I may turn up something. I'm certainly not going to pay him a dime until I'm convinced I must pay him and I'm far from convinced at this moment.'

She stared at me, aghast.

'But if he finds out you are investigating him, he may not like it. He may go to the police ...'

'He won't. Now will you be a nice girl and get dressed and go home? I have lots of things to do and you're in the way.'

'But you're not really serious? You'll only antagonize him. He – he may raise the price.'

'He won't,' I said. 'He's no fool. He knows thirty thousand is as much as he can hope for. Now will you please go home?'

Slowly and reluctantly she got to her feet.

'Don't you think we'd better give him the money, Ches? We – we may go to jail if you try to be clever.'

I smiled at her.

'Will you relax and leave this to me? We have time and we may be lucky.'

'I don't like it,' she said, staring down at me. 'I think it would be better to pay him and get rid of him.'

'Naturally you would think that because it's not your money. If you're so anxious for him to be paid why don't you ask your husband if he will lend you thirty thousand dollars? There's a slight chance that he might.'

She made an angry movement with her hands, then turned and went quickly out of the room.

I reached for the telephone book, turned the pages until I came to the Rs. I found Oscar Ross had a place called Belle Vue on Beach Boulevard: not perhaps the best district in town, but at least as good as mine.

Out of curiosity, I checked to see if Art Galgano was in the book. I wasn't disappointed nor surprised to find he wasn't.

I put the book down, got to my feet and poured another cup of coffee. My head was beginning to ache again, and I went into the bathroom, found some aspirin and washed down the three tablets with the lukewarm coffee.

I went back to the settee and sat on it while I did a little thinking. After ten minutes or so, Lucille came out of my bedroom. She made an attractive picture in her lemon-yellow slacks and white shirt. In her right hand she carried a white wrap-over handbag.

She stood in the doorway, obviously showing herself off, with the lost little girl look on her face that made her look cute enough to eat.

I regarded her and wished she wasn't Aitken's wife, that she wasn't such a barefaced liar and that she wasn't so completely untrustworthy.

'Ches,' she said in her small, little girl's voice, 'we really must be sensible about this. I've been thinking ...'

'Save your breath,' I said. 'I know exactly what you have been thinking. You have decided, for both our sakes, I should hand over every nickel I own, but there is one point you have overlooked. Once you pay blackmail, the blackmailer always comes back for more. Ross will gladly accept the money and perhaps we won't hear from him for a year or so, then one day when we think all is well, he'll turn up with a hard-luck story and put on the bite. This is my money, Lucille. I may eventually be forced to part with it, but I'm going to be quite sure there is no other way out of this mess before I do part with it.'

She began to move restlessly around the room.

Finally she paused and said without looking at me: 'Then perhaps I should tell Roger. I am sure he would pay this man rather than let me go to prison.'

'We've played this scene before and it's still corny,' I said, smiling at her. 'Go home before I get annoyed with you.'

She gripped her handbag until her knuckles turned white and she marched over to me, her eyes stormy.

'We've got to pay this money! If you won't, then I'll tell Roger! I mean it!'

'The last time you acted out this little scene you said finally you didn't want to tell him and you wouldn't throw him in my face again. It seems you have a short memory.

Well, all right, if you are so anxious to tell him, we'll both go and tell him, and I'll make sure he gets the facts right.'

She went white with anger.

'I hate you!' she screamed at me and took a swipe at my face with her handbag.

I got my hand up in time and took the blow on my wrist. The contact was so violent that the handbag shot out of her hand, flew across the room, hit the wall and burst open, its contents scattering on the floor.

An object from the bag caught my eyes.

'Well, what do you know!' I exclaimed.

She darted across the room and snatched up the object and thrust it inside her shirt, then she backed away, her eyes wide with fear and dismay.

For perhaps a second or so I stood rooted, staring at her, then as she turned and bolted for the door, I shot after her.

I grabbed her as she reached the hall. She broke free, dodged around me and tried to open the front door. I grabbed her arm and swung her around. She closed with me, kicking, punching and trying to bite. She was surprisingly strong, and before I could smother her arms, I had collected three or four punches in the face that hurt and made me pretty mad.

She squealed as I forced her around so her back was to me and I brought her down on her knees.

She squirmed away from me, got to her feet and dived towards the front door. I grabbed her again. Panting, she twisted around and aimed a kick at me, but this time I was ready for her and I got out of the way.

She tried to butt my face with the top of her head, then wrenching one wrist free, she managed to rake her nails down the side of my neck.

This was turning into quite a scrap and I was fast losing my temper.

It was like trying to hold on to a wild cat. Somehow she managed to get her knee up and slam it into my chest, breaking my grip on her wrists. She squirmed away from me, but as she did an object fell to the ground.

I picked it up.

It was a driving permit.

I examined it.

It was made out in her name and dated two years back.

I turned to look at her.

She didn't move. She crouched there in the corner, her face hidden in her hands.

Then she began to weep.

12

I

Putting the driving permit in my pocket, I turned my back on the weeping girl and made my way into the bathroom. I ran the water into the toilet basin and bathed the scratches on my neck. They were pretty deep and painful. I stopped the bleeding. Staring at myself in the mirror, I saw it was pretty obvious that I had been in a fight.

I went into my bedroom and changed my pyjamas for an open-neck shirt and slacks, then I went into the lounge and sat down and looked across the sands at the sea and the distant palm trees.

I was thinking and smoking when I heard a movement behind me and I looked around.

Lucille stood in the doorway.

We stared at each other.

'Ches ...' Her voice was a thin quaver. 'I can explain ... Really I can ...'

'Well, come on in and explain,' I said. 'This should be worth hearing. You've proved to me you are a pretty fluent liar, but now this is where you can win an Oscar if you take the trouble.'

She moved towards me and sat down in a chair near mine.

'Please, Ches ... I know how angry you must be, but I haven't ever lied to you. I really haven't.' There was now a saintly expression on her face that made me itch to haul her over my knee and belabour her with the nearest weapon I could lay my hands on. 'If you had asked me for the permit, I would have given it to you. There was no need for you to have behaved like that.'

'Look, don't try me too far.'

She touched her lips with her tongue and the saintly expression gave way to alarmed weariness.

'I'm sorry, Ches. I didn't mean to annoy you,' she said meekly. 'If you don't believe me when I say I have never lied to you ...'

'Oh, skip it,' I said impatiently. 'Let's have your explanation. This business about wanting to learn to drive was just a gag?'

She began to walk the first and second finger of her left hand along her thigh to her knee. This was to convey a little girl's embarrassment, but it cut no ice with me.

'You see, Ches, I fell in love with you the moment I saw you,' she said in a low voice and she looked up, her eyes large and starry.

That cut no ice with me either.

'And when was this moment?'

'When I saw you watching me that night – the night you first came to the house.'

I thought back on that moment: it seemed a long, long way back into the past.

'When you were admiring yourself in the mirror? Was that the time?'

'Yes.' She walked her fingers back from her knee along her thigh, then examined them carefully to see if they had suffered damage during the walk. 'I was lonely, Ches. You can't imagine what it is like to be married to an old man. Roger is so dull. I wanted to get to know you. I was sure you would be fun. So I thought it would be a good idea if I pretended I couldn't drive and asked you to teach me. I only did it so I had the excuse to get to know you.'

I flicked my cigarette butt out into the garden.

'Well, that's really something,' I said admiringly. 'So you just wanted an excuse to get to know me?'

She looked at me, then modestly looked away.

'I would never have told you this, Ches, only I feel you should have an explanation. It's something a girl doesn't like to admit.'

'I can understand that. So you fell in love with me the moment you saw me?'

She bit her lip, looking away from me.

'Yes.'

'But I remember when we were on the beach together and I asked you if you loved me, you not only seemed surprised at the idea, but you even seemed angry.'

She moved uneasily.

'I – I thought it might be dangerous to admit I loved you. I – I didn't want to ...' Her voice died away.

'Well, I won't embarrass you, Lucille. But I must get this straight. You pretended you couldn't drive only because you wanted to have some fun with me. Is that right?'

Again she moved uneasily.

'Well, not exactly. I wanted to get to know you. I thought you would be interesting to know.'

'Well, now you know me, do you find me interesting?'

She flushed a little.

'Of course. It's nice to know a man is in love with you. Love is an important thing in a girl's life. Roger doesn't love me.'

'Did you discover that before or after he married you?'

She looked up, and for a brief moment, her eyes glittered, then she remembered the role she was playing and her expression changed to hurt bewilderment.

'It was after I married him. He just isn't interested in me any more.'

'I wonder why?'

She shifted in her chair, frowning.

'He's old. We don't have the same interests,' she said, looking away from me.

'That I can understand. So naturally you looked around to find someone who would be interested in you and you picked on me.'

She flushed angrily.

'I know how you must be feeling, Ches,' she said, trying to speak gently. 'I would probably feel the same if I were in your place. I don't blame you for feeling bitter. I'm sorry. A lot of this is my fault. I was so lonely. You made my life come alive.'

'Well, you certainly managed to shake up my life, too,' I said. 'Now I've had your explanation for what it is worth, let's examine it a little more closely. So you have been driving for two years?'

Her hands suddenly turned into fists.

'Oh, no. I haven't. I have had a permit for two years, but I haven't driven much. Roger wouldn't let me use his cars. I only drove for a week or so, then he said I drove too fast, and he wouldn't let me drive again.'

I smiled at her. She had been quick enough to have seen the trap and avoided it.

'So you were really starting again when you asked me to teach you?'

Her hands relaxed.

'Yes.'

I tossed the driving permit into her lap.

'I hope you can prove it. I hope your husband's chauffeur will be ready to perjure himself if he is asked if you ever use your husband's cars. I suspect you do, Lucille. It is one thing for a beginner to kill a cop, and another thing for an experienced driver to kill one. When the judge takes a look at your permit, he will need a lot of convincing.'

She stiffened.

'Don't talk like that! You know you're only trying to frighten me!'

I stared at her.

'I wish I could frighten you, Lucille. You're so sure you are getting away with this, aren't you?'

For the first time her eyes showed she was losing confidence and she began to look irritated.

'I don't know what you mean,' she said sharply.

'Don't you? Do me a favour, will you? Will you take your frustrations, your interests and your difficulties out of here? Will you remove your sex appeal, your little-girl attitude and your attractive body out of my sight and temptation? I'll admit I fell for you when you were displaying yourself in your nice little nightie. I also fell for you when I found you waiting for me in my car. I fell again when you lay on the sand and seemed to be offering yourself to me, free, gratis and for nothing, but since those moments I have got wise to myself. I'm no longer interested. I think you are a cheat. I know you are a liar. I am equally sure you are in need of money for some reason best known to yourself, and I am certain you're not going to get it from me. So go away. Find some other sucker. There must be thousands of men who will fall for you as I did. Try again, but pick a guy who hasn't much intelligence. Take my advice and give me up as a dead loss. If you work fast, you'll find someone else and I wish you luck. Now, take your nice little body out of here and leave me in peace.'

She sat motionless, staring at me, her hands gripped between her knees, her face suddenly white, her eyes hard and glittering.

'I don't know what you mean,' she said finally, and her voice was now breathless and hard. 'How can you talk to me like that? We are being blackmailed! You are in this as much as I am! I have explained why I have a driving permit. But that doesn't alter anything. This man wants thirty thousand dollars or he'll tell Roger about us, and he will go to the police and tell them about the accident! How can you speak to me like this?'

I got to my feet.

'Tell me something, Lucille,' I said, moving over to her and squatting down by her side. I looked directly at her. 'How long have you and Oscar been working together? How many suckers have you taken for a ride? Tell me that before I take you by your lying little neck and throw you out of here!'

Her face twisted into an expression of savage rage. Her hand in the shape of a claw swung at my face, but I was ready for her this time. I caught her wrist, jerked her out of the chair, and twisted her arm behind her.

She gave a little squeal of pain as I pulled her up on her feet. I spun her around, let go of her wrist, then caught hold of her arms while I stared down into her furious, glittering eyes.

'Well? What's the answer?' I said, giving her a little shake. 'How long have you two been working together?'

She tried to break free, but I tightened my grip.

'You're making a mistake,' she gasped. 'I'm not working with that man! How could you think such a thing?'

I let go of her.

'You're not kidding anyone,' I said. 'It sticks out a mile. You trapped me into going down to that lonely beach. There was no one there. I went and looked the place over yesterday. There are no footprints except yours and mine, and that told me Ross couldn't have been there. He knew what happened because you told him. You two are after the twenty thousand I'm putting in your husband's business. He told you about it, didn't he? That's why you were so interested in asking questions about it when we first met. You told Ross, and you two planned to get it from me by blackmail. When I called you on the telephone and told you I had found a way out, you weren't pleased. I spotted that in the tone of your voice. As soon as I hung up, you called Ross and told him. He came down here fast to see what I was up to and he brought a flashlight camera with him. Now lie yourself out of that little lot if you can!'

She slumped down in her chair and hid her face in her hands and began to cry.

I crossed the room and mixed myself a highball with lots of ice in it. By the time I had carried the drink to my chair and had sat down, she had stopped crying and was wiping her eyes on the shirt sleeve like any little gutter child who has had a hiding and now feels sorry for herself.

'Ches ...'

'Here we go again,' I said, leaning back in my chair and looking at her. 'Now what yarn have you cooked up?'

'Ches, please be kind to me,' she said and wrung her hands. This was something new, and if I weren't sick to death of the sight of her, her despair might have moved me a little – not much, but maybe a little. 'I couldn't help it. He – he's been blackmailing me for months.'

I drank a little of the Scotch. It tasted fine: strong enough and cold enough and with just the right bite in it.

'You mean Oscar has been blackmailing you for months?'

'Yes.'

'So you thought it would be a bright idea if he blackmailed me as well?'

'I couldn't help it.' Again she wrung her hands. As a repeat performance it wasn't quite so convincing. 'He found out you had all this money …'

'You mean you told him?'

'No, I didn't. I swear I didn't!' She stared at me, tears still on her pale face, her eyes wide and miserable. 'He found out.'

'Look, don't give me that stuff,' I said angrily. 'For heaven's sake, try to make your story convincing. He couldn't have found out. Only you and Aitken knew how much I was going to put into the business. Aitken wouldn't have told him, so you must have.'

She squirmed in her chair as she tried desperately to keep ahead with her lies.

'I – I didn't mean to tell him, Ches. You've got to believe me. We were talking together, and I said I knew someone who had a lot of money and I wish I had it. I never thought he would … It just happened … it slipped out. I didn't intend to tell him.'

'But you told him?'

She went back to the trick of squeezing her hands between her knees.

'Yes, but I didn't meant to.'

'Why has he been blackmailing you for months?'

She hesitated, looking away, moving uneasily.

'I can't tell you that, Ches. It – it's private. It was something I did ...'

'Like taking some interesting man down on a lonely beach?'

'Of course not. I – I've never done that before.'

'Well, all right, let it ride. So he was blackmailing you, and in spite of that you used to have little chats with him like telling him about your husband's employees and how much money they have.'

'It wasn't like that at all ...'

'I bet it wasn't. Okay, don't look so indignant. Anyway, I bet it was his idea for you to persuade me to teach you to drive and to take you down on the beach.'

'Yes.'

She lifted her hair off her shoulders. That was a trick she hadn't tried for some time.

'And you have no idea why you were persuading me to go down to the beach?'

'No. He – he didn't tell me.'

'And because he blackmails you, you do what he tells you?'

She fidgeted with her hands, blood rising into her face.

'I have to do what he tells me.'

'Do you pay him money?'

She flinched.

'No – I haven't any.'

'He extracts his blackmail by making you do what he tells you?'

'Yes.'

'After you had acted out your little scene with me,' I went on, watching her, 'you drove off and somehow managed to kill a policeman. You promptly drove to the nearest telephone and called Oscar and told him what you had done. He saw this was a much more powerful weapon to use against me and instructed you to go to my place and stage another little scene, persuading me to take the responsibility, then he assured you he would move in and collect the money. You, because you have to do what he tells you, followed his instructions to the letter, even trying to persuade me by threats of telling your husband if I didn't pay up.'

She began to beat her fists together again.

'It didn't happen like that at all, Ches! I didn't telephone him. I came straight here.'

'I don't believe you, Lucille. I don't believe Ross is blackmailing you. I think you and he are working on this thing together.'

'You're wrong, Ches! I swear we're not,' she said. 'It is exactly as I told you.'

I studied her, convinced she was lying.

'Okay. I'll tell you what we'll do. We'll go together and talk to Ross. I'd like to hear what he has to say if we come on him unprepared. You wait here. I'm going to change, and then you and I will go and talk to him.'

I went out of the lounge, shutting the door before she could protest, walked down to my bedroom, opened the door but didn't go into the room. I slammed the door shut, then stepped quickly into the spare bedroom, pushing the door ajar and listened.

I heard the lounge door open gently. Looking out, I saw Lucille step into the hall and stare down the passage at my closed bedroom door, then she stepped back into the lounge again and shut the door. A moment later I heard the faint tinkle of the telephone bell as she began to dial.

I had set the trap for her and she had walked into it.

I crept down the passage and listened against the door panel.

I heard her say: 'What shall I do? I don't think he's going to pay. No ... I can't handle him any more. You'll have to do something ...'

I turned the door handle and walked into the room.

Lucille hurriedly replaced the receiver and moved quickly away from the telephone.

'All right, all right,' I said, 'don't look so guilty and embarrassed. I heard you. Now will you admit you're working with him?'

She turned slowly and stared at me. Her face was white and her eyes showed her hatred of me. She was no longer young nor fresh nor beautiful. She looked older, defeated and trapped.

'You think you're smart, don't you?' she said, her voice stifled with hatred. 'Well, all right, I admit it. But you're going to give us the money! You can't prove I was with you! You can't prove I was driving! We've got a picture of you and the car. That's something you can't do anything about! If you don't pay up, we'll send the picture to the police. If you try to bring me into it, it'll be your word against mine and you have no proof. I've got an alibi. I've got people who will say I was with them when he was killed. There's nothing you can do but pay up and that's what you're going to do!'

I stood looking at her hard, vicious little face, and my mind jumped to the bloodstains on the offside rear wheel of the car and I felt a cold chill snake up my spine.

Those stains had baffled me, but I realized now what they meant. This hadn't been an accident. O'Brien had been murdered as Dolores and Nutley had been murdered.

'You and Ross murdered him, didn't you?' I said. 'The crash was faked. You knocked him on the head and you ran him over with the rear wheel of the Cadillac. You were jittery enough to make a mistake. You killed him with the wrong wheel. You should have run him over with your onside wheel and not your offside wheel, Lucille. It's a mistake like that that lands a killer in the gas chamber.'

She backed away from me, her face suddenly grey.

'I didn't kill him!'

'You and Ross did,' I said. 'You planned to kill two birds with one stone, didn't you? You planned to get rid of O'Brien and get thirty thousand dollars out of me.'

'It's not true!' she said hoarsely. 'You can't prove anything! I didn't kill him! If you don't give me that money ...'

'You're not going to get it,' I said and I moved over to the french windows, undid the two curtain cords and pulled them free. 'I have a busy afternoon ahead of me,' I went on, looking at her. 'I want to find out why you had to kill O'Brien. I don't want you in the way. I'm going to tie you up, Lucille, and keep you here, until I find out what I want to find out.'

Her eyes opened very wide and she began to back away.

'Don't you dare touch me!' she exclaimed. 'You're not keeping me here!'

'You will either submit gracefully or you will get hurt,' I said, moving towards her. 'Don't kid yourself our little scrap just now meant anything because it didn't. This time if you get rough, I'll get rough too.'

She whirled around and bolted towards the open french windows, but she had started a shade too late. I reached out, grabbed her arm and spun her around. I was now past the stage of chivalry. As she tried to rake my face with her nails, I knocked her hands aside, and hit her on the side of her jaw. Her eyes rolled back and she slumped into my arms.

Then, moving quickly, I fastened her wrists behind her and then tied her ankles together. I picked her up and carried her into my bedroom and laid her on the bed.

Then going to my wardrobe, I put on a tie and jacket and changed my shoes. By the time I had finished dressing, she began to move.

I went into the kitchen and got a length of clothes line, returned to the bedroom and fastened her securely to the bed.

I went over to her and looked down at her.

After a moment or so, she opened her eyes and stared up at me, her eyes dazed.

'I'm sorry, but you asked for it,' I said. 'I'm also sorry to leave you like this, but there is no other way. You may have a long wait. I'll get back as soon as I can. Just lie quiet and you won't come to any harm!'

'Let me go!' she said furiously, struggling to get her hands free. 'I'll make you pay for this! Let me free!'

I watched her for a moment or so to make sure she couldn't break loose, then, satisfied, I moved to the door.

'Don't leave me!' she screamed out, struggling frantically. 'Come back!'

'Take it easy,' I said. 'I'll try not to be too long.'

I went out and shut the bedroom door.

As I hurried down the passage and into the hall, I heard her scream out after me: 'Ches! Don't leave me! Please, don't leave me!'

Ignoring her cries, I locked the bungalow and then ran down the path where I had left the Buick.

13

I

When I reached town, I bought a couple of Sunday newspapers and took a quick look at the headlines as I walked back to the Buick. I expected to find the murders of Dolores and Ed Nutley plastered over the front page, but there was, as far as I could see, no mention of them.

I got into the car, and as I was in a no-parking zone, I drove fast to Slim's bar where I could examine the papers and have a sandwich and a beer before deciding on a plan of campaign.

The bar was nearly empty, but sitting in one of the booths with a man I didn't know was Joe Fellowes. Both were drinking beer and eating hamburgers. Joe spotted me before I could duck out of sight.

'Hey, Ches! Come on over.'

There was nothing I could do but to wave to him and say I'd be with him. I ordered a sandwich and a beer from Slim, then carried the drink and food over to Joe's booth.

'I thought you were playing golf,' Joe said. 'Sit down. Meet Jim Buckley. He's the star man on the *Inquirer*.'

'Only the *Inquirer* doesn't know it,' Buckley said and grinned. He was short, fat and middle-aged with a pair of probing ice-blue eyes.

He stared pointedly at the scratches on my neck.

'Boy!' he said in wonder. 'She certainly sold her honour at a high price.'

Joe too was staring.

'Don't get ideas,' I said. 'One of those things. There was a guy bothering a girl, and like a dope, I interfered. It turned out she liked him bothering her and didn't like me interfering. It's a wonder I got away with my life.'

They both laughed, but Joe looked wonderingly at me, his eyes puzzled.

'What are you doing here on a Sunday?' I asked him, to change the subject.

'I had arranged to spend the day on the beach with this louse,' Joe said, jerking his thumb at Buckley, 'and now he tells me he has to work. So we eat together and I go on the beach alone unless you have nothing to do and will keep me company.'

'I'd like to, Joe,' I said, 'but I'm tied up.'

'So long as she's tied up too, that'll make a pair of you,' Buckley said and bellowed with laughter.

I thought of Lucille lying on my bed. He was unconsciously getting a little too close to the truth.

'Is that the *Inquirer* you've got there?' he went on, looking at the paper I'd laid on the seat.

'Yes. You want it?'

'I haven't had a chance to see what they did with the stuff I filed last night.' He reached out, took the paper, shook it open and glanced at the front page. He snorted, opened the paper, turned several pages, then paused. Finally, he refolded the paper and handed it back to me. 'Three thousand words, written in blood and Scotch, and the black-hearted punk cuts it down to two hundred. Why I work for this rag beats me.'

Joe said: 'Jim's covering this hit-and-run case.'

I bit into my sandwich and chewed.

'Is that right?' I said. 'I haven't had time to read the paper this morning. Anything new?'

Buckley took a long swig from his glass, sat back and lit a cigarette.

'New? Listen, bud, this is going to be one of the major sensations of the year. This is going to be something that could get the whole of our beautiful Administration tossed out on its fat neck.'

'Suppose you skip the build-up and let's have the dope,' Joe said. 'If it's all that hot, why isn't it hitting the headlines?'

'Because we're not ready yet,' Buckley said. 'Wait until tomorrow. We reckon to bust this thing wide open tomorrow if we have any luck.'

'What thing? What are you talking about?' Joe asked impatiently.

'I'll tell you,' Buckley said. 'If O'Brien hadn't been killed no one would have got on to him for maybe years. All that crap Sullivan gave out about what a fine guy O'Brien was sounded all right until we started to investigate him. Then the cloven hoof came to the surface. Know what? O'Brien had a bank balance of a hundred and twenty-five thousand bucks, and he owned a bungalow out on Palm Crescent that is about as fancy as any movie star could wish to own. When a cop lives like that, there's only one explanation – graft. There were two people who might have known what his racket was. The woman he planned to marry: a nightclub singer, and her agent, a guy named Nutley. Know what happened to them last night?'

Joe was staring at him with round eyes.

'What happened to them?'

'They were both knocked off. Nutley was found in the Washington Hotel, shot through the heart and the night clerk bashed over the head. The killer walked in, persuaded the night clerk to tell him in which room Nutley was, then killed him. He then walked upstairs and shot Nutley to death. He killed the girl as she was leaving her apartment.'

'It's not even in the paper,' Joe said indignantly.

'Yes, it is. It rates ten lines; but boy! it's going to hit the front page tomorrow. We're working on it now. We're trying to get a line on O'Brien's racket. The police commissioner thinks he was hooked up with some gang. Sullivan thinks he was a blackmailer.'

'How about the guy who ran over him?' I asked. 'Haven't they found him yet?'

Buckley shrugged his shoulders.

'They have twenty-three damaged cars at police headquarters and they're checking every driver's alibi. They reckon they'll find the killer among these twenty-three drivers, and I guess if they do find him, they should give him a medal. If O'Brien hadn't been killed, this would never have come out.'

'This girl who was killed last night: didn't she sing at the Little Tavern?' I asked as casually as I could.

'That's the one: a nice-looking wren who couldn't sing for dimes.'

I asked an inspired question.

'Who's behind the Little Tavern?'

Buckley lifted his shoulders.

'That's something I've tried to find out when I have had nothing better to do. It's registered in the name of Art Galgano, but no one seems to know who he is. I don't reckon he lives in town. The joint is run by Jack Claude, who is no better than he could be. What makes you ask?'

'I heard last night there's a roulette table upstairs and the stakes are high.'

Buckley stared at me, then shook his head.

'That's just talk. Gambling is out in this town. A number of smart operators have tried it, but the commissioner has slammed them shut before they have had a chance to wear the shine off the ball. The Little Tavern has been going now for three years. We'd have heard about it if they had a table there.'

'Would you? Sure? I was in there last night, and a guy told me there was a table upstairs.'

Buckley stroked his thick nose. His eyes showed his interest. 'Now wait a minute,' he said, staring fixedly at me. 'O'Brien covered that sector. He could have kept them in the clear. Say, this could be something! Maybe that's where he got his money from! You go there often?'

'I don't go there often,' I said. 'I go there sometimes.'

'You couldn't find out for sure if there is a table upstairs, could you?' Buckley asked, squirming forward on his seat.

'Hey!' Joe broke in. 'You have a nerve, haven't you? Why should Ches do your dirty work for you?'

Buckley waved his hands impatiently.

'I have as much chance of finding out if there's a wheel up there as a cop has,' he said. 'This guy goes to the place. If he feels like it, why shouldn't he help me?'

While they were arguing, I did some quick thinking.

'I'll find out for you if I can,' I said. 'I'll go out there this afternoon, and if I have any luck I'll telephone you.'

Joe stared at me as if he thought I had gone crazy, but Buckley reached forward and patted my arm.

'That's the boy, and let me tell you, the *Inquirer* won't forget. The next time your salesmen come to us for space, I'll see you get what you want.' He took a card from his wallet and gave it to me. 'If I'm not around, ask for Jack

Hemmings. He'll handle anything you give him. If there's a table up there, then we'll really start trouble. Listen, suppose you come down to my office and I'll give you a camera. If you can get a photograph of the table, we'll really have them on ice.'

'I don't imagine they'd stand for that,' I said.

He closed one heavy eyelid.

'Wait until you see the camera. It fits in your buttonhole. All you have to do is to press a shutter release, hidden in your pocket. The lens and the film will take care of the rest. Get us a picture of the table, Scott, and you'll practically own the paper.'

'I'll expect to.'

He patted my arm.

'I'll guarantee it. Come on, let's get the hell out of here. Let's go talk to my boss.'

As I got to my feet, Joe grabbed my arm.

'Wait a minute, Ches,' he said. 'You could be sticking your neck into trouble. Suppose you and me go? What's the matter with that?'

'No, Joe,' I said. 'Two would be a crowd. Take it easy. I'm not walking into anything. I'll handle it.'

'Sure he will,' Buckley said. 'There's nothing to it. It's my bet there isn't a table in the joint, but if there is – boy! won't we shake the commissioner right out of his pants.'

'All the same,' Joe said obstinately, 'I want to go with you. Two may be a crowd but, in trouble, a crowd is pretty cosy.'

'No, Joe,' I said. 'The chances are I won't even get upstairs. Two of us would be a little too obvious.' I slid out of the booth. 'And another thing, the table may not be operating in the afternoon.'

Joe joined me, his expression still obstinate.

'I'm coming with you, Ches. Even if I have to wait outside.'

If I were to get anywhere, I knew I'd only succeed on my own.

'I don't want you around, Joe. I'm combining business with pleasure, and you'll be in the way.'

'Yeah, go and drown yourself, Joe,' Buckley said. 'My pal and me have got business. You go swim in the sea.' He slapped Joe on the shoulder, then, taking my arm, he hustled me out of the bar to where I had parked the Buick.

As we drove to the *Inquirer*'s office I said: 'Have the police any idea who killed the Lane girl?'

'They don't know his name, but he's practically in the bag,' Buckley said. 'They have a description of him and they have his fingerprints. I guess he must have been either a nut or a complete amateur. He left prints all over the place. He was seen leaving the girl's apartment and he was seen leaving the Washington. His prints were found in the girl's room and also in Nutley's room. They say he was a big fellow, dark, around your age; good looking. Lieutenant West reckons it's only a matter of hours before they get him.'

I felt a sinking sensation inside me.

'Is that right?' I said, staring through the windscreen, aware my heart was beginning to thump.

'Yeah. They're driving the girl who saw him around town in the hope she spots him on the sidewalk. Maybe she will. Then all they have to do is to take his prints, and he'll be sniffing cyanide before he knows where he is.'

II

I arrived at the Little Tavern nightclub at a minute or so after two o'clock. The parking lot was crammed with cars and I had trouble in finding a place.

It was one of those hot, airless afternoons you get sometimes in Palm City when you long for a breeze, when the dust gets under your shirt and makes your skin irritable, and tempers get frayed and quick on the trigger.

On the big terrace, packed with tables, men and women in gay weekend clothes were working their way through the elaborate menu.

I walked up the steps. No one paid me any attention, except the doorman, who looked jaded and less impressive in the sunshine than he had done in the moonlight. He touched his cap, recognizing me, and spun the revolving door for me as gently as if it were made of eggshells.

The hat-check girl recognized me. She didn't bother to move out of her station. She gave me a thin smile, then looked away. A guy without a hat was as interesting to her as a man with no arms and legs.

I moved to the bar, but I didn't go in. It was packed tight with weekenders, soaking up liquor, talking in voices just too loud, spending their hard-earned money while they tried to make an impression on the blondes, the brunettes and the redheads they had dragged along with them.

Oscar Ross was behind the bar. The two Mexicans were there too. They were all pretty busy. Ross was concentrating on the female custom. I could see he was making quite a hit with three women who were drinking champagne cocktails.

I moved back a little. I didn't want him to see me, and I looked around the bar, hoping to find my rum and lime juice pal of last night.

I finally spotted him as he moved away from the crush at one end of the bar and headed my way.

'Hello,' I said as he neared me. 'Remember me?'

He was a little drunk, but after screwing up his eyes to get me in focus, his friendly smile told me he had recognized me.

'Hello, pal,' he said. 'Come to drown your sorrows?'

'I've come to see if I can win some money,' I said and moved with him into the lobby. 'Could I get into a game upstairs, do you think?'

'Why not? I'm going up now. Come with me.'

'I thought maybe there would be a little trouble.'

'That's okay. I'm known here. What did you say your name was?'

'Scott.'

He swayed a little, then steadied himself by taking hold of my arm.

'The same as in Great Scott?'

'The same man.'

He bellowed with laughter: a guy who was easily and quickly amused.

'Pretty good. Well, come on, Scott, let's see you lose your money.'

He led me across the hall to a door which he opened. He moved down a passage and I followed him. We reached an automatic elevator, big enough to hold four people. We stood side by side as the elevator took us up two floors with a movement that was gentle enough to be a caress.

While we travelled, Welliver breathed rum fumes over me with the benign air of a bishop blessing his flock.

This seemed a little too easy to me.

I had the tiny camera Buckley had given me, pinned to the back of my coat lapel. The lens just showed through the buttonhole of the lapel. You would have to have the eye of a Davy Crockett to spot it. I fingered the shutter release that lay in my jacket pocket. Just one photograph, Buckley had stressed. There would be no chance to change the minute film. He had begged me not to rush the job.

'A chance in a lifetime,' he had said. 'If we can get a picture of that table – if there is a table – we will tear this city wide open.'

He seemed to have overlooked the fact that if I were caught taking the photograph I would be the one to get torn wide open and not the city.

The elevator came to a silky stop and the doors opened with a whisper of sound.

Welliver moved out into a hall where two bouncers filled up most of the space, flexing their muscles. They looked as if they could have handled Joe Louis and Rocky Marciano in their prime without having to exert themselves into more than a light sweat.

They gave Welliver a hard stare, then their eyes moved to me.

They stared at me the way a Masonic gathering would stare if a bubble dancer had dropped into the middle of one of their most mystic rituals.

Welliver was walking briskly towards double doors that faced us across the hall, and I kept pace with him. I managed to look as unconcerned as anyone out for a Sunday airing.

The bouncers were so taken out of their strides we very nearly made the double doors: very nearly, but not quite.

One of them said in a voice that could have loosened a rusty nut off the propeller of a liner: 'Hey! You! Where do you think you're going?'

The voice hit us at the back of our necks and brought us to an abrupt stop.

Welliver turned and scowled. The voice had shaken him, but, after all, he was a member of the club and he didn't expect to get that kind of treatment.

'You talking to me?' he asked, but beside the bouncer's effort, he sounded as harmless as a kitten.

'No – him!' The bigger of the two moved up to me, making me feel as if I were being crowded by a bulldozer. 'Where do you think you're going?'

'He's a friend of mine,' Welliver said with as much dignity as he could muster, which wasn't much. 'I'm taking him in. Any objections?'

'Mr Claude okayed him?' the bouncer asked.

'Of course he has,' Welliver said, and taking me by the arm, he shoved me towards the double doors, leaving the two bouncers staring suspiciously after us.

We moved into a big room full of men and women, soft lights, cigarette smoke and a buzz of excited conversation.

In the middle of the room was a roulette table. Clustered around it was a bunch of the upper strata of Palm City's social register. Welliver had said the stakes were high. I had only to look at the piles of chips out on the table to see he hadn't been letting his imagination run riot. There could have been around forty to fifty thousand dollars out on the table for this one throw.

'Let this one ride,' Welliver muttered to me after casting an expert eye over the stakes. 'We don't want to tangle with crazy men.'

Everyone's attention was rooted on a fat, elderly man with a vast pile of chips in front of him. As I moved closer, he leaned forward and pushed a stack of chips on number five black.

A number of people, betting small, followed his example, then the wheel began to spin, the ball was tossed in, and after a while it made up its mind and settled in five black.

There was a soft sigh around the table as the croupier, a dark, poker-faced Mexican, scooped in the losers' chips and then shovelled more chips towards the fat man.

I found myself behind a blonde woman who smelt a little too strongly of Chanel No. 5. I edged my way forward until I was against the back of her chair. From there I had an uninterrupted view of the whole table. The lights were strong, and lit up the mass of chips before the big gamblers. It was the perfect angle for a picture.

Buckley had told me all I had to do was to stand square to the table and press the shutter release I had in my pocket. The lens was so fast and the film compensated to such a degree, I couldn't go wrong.

I saw Welliver had moved away from me, hunting for a seat. I got myself in the right position and my fingers closed over the push button of the shutter release. I held my breath and myself steady, as Buckley had told me to do, then I gently squeezed. I was vaguely aware of hearing a very faint click that told me the shutter had operated.

Then things happened.

I'll never know if the guys who were watching the players, keeping check on the bets, spotted me or if I gave myself away by my tense expression or if the croupier had spotted the tiny lens in my buttonhole. Anyway, that is neither here nor there: what mattered was I suddenly felt two hard bodies move against mine. Hands that felt like steel braces caught and held my wrists: a man on each side of me.

With my heart doing a rock 'n' roll, I looked first to the right and then to the left.

These two guys weren't bouncers: they were professionals. Two thin-faced men, almost twins in their cold, remote professionalism. One was a little taller than the other: one was fair and the other dark; both had hatchet-shaped faces; bleak eyes; flat and expressionless; both had lipless mouths and square jaws.

They both looked hard, tough and ruthless, and they both looked very, very lethal.

'Okay, buster,' the fair one said softly. 'Don't let's have any trouble. The boss wants a word with you.'

There was a professional method in which they gently eased me out of the crowd. Both my arms were paralysed in their grips. I suppose I could have kicked and screamed, but the idea didn't occur to me.

Welliver, who had just found a seat at the table, glanced over at me, his face showing surprise, but he had found a seat and he wasn't going to lose it, so he smiled drunkenly at me and said something about seeing me later.

As the two men moved me out of the crowd, I had an unpleasant feeling deep down inside me that I would be lucky if I saw anyone later.

The fair one said: 'Take it easy, buster, let the legs walk. We can handle it if you want to get rough.'

They released my wrists but, like two expert sheep dogs, they managed to keep me moving by jostling me gently forward with their shoulders.

No one in the crowded room paid any attention to us.

I suppose I could have started to sling punches and yell for help, but I was sure it wouldn't get me anything except a blackjack behind the ear while the fair one or the dark one explained to the crowd I was just another tiresome drunk.

So I walked with them across the room to a door which the dark one opened. They eased me through as if I were a millionaire invalid with four days to live and who hadn't as yet paid his doctor's bill.

We went down a short passage to another door.

The fair one knocked while the dark one breathed gently down the back of my neck.

A voice said: 'Come in,' and the fair one turned the handle and pushed open the door.

The dark one nudged me into a room that didn't seem to know quite whether it was an office or a sitting-room. It had a desk by a big window hidden by flame-coloured drapes. There was an executive chair behind the desk and to the right was a steel filing cabinet. The rest of the room was full of lounging chairs, a radio set with a separate corner horn, a small bar and a divan covered with a Spanish shawl.

Behind the desk, in the executive chair, sat a fat, big man in a tuxedo. His hair was a mixture of grey and red; his fleshy face was set in one of those bland expressions that mean nothing; his small, ice-grey eyes were motionless and slightly out of focus as if he were thinking of something pretty important when we interrupted him by coming in.

At a guess, he was around fifty-five to sixty, still in good physical shape in spite of his fat. His hands, slightly freckled and covered with fine red hair, lay relaxed on the snowy white blotter on his desk.

The dark one edged up to the desk while his companion shut the door. I could have been mistaken, but I was pretty sure I heard the key turn in the lock.

I was feeling uneasy by now. If they found the camera on me, I would be in trouble.

The man at the desk stared at me, then looked inquiringly at the dark one and lifted his eyebrows.

'Non-member,' the dark one said in a soft drawl.

The fat man who I guessed would be Jack Claude shifted his ice-grey eyes on me again.

'Sorry about this, friend,' he said in a deceptively mild voice, 'but you can imagine we don't welcome gatecrashers. Could I have your name?'

'I'm Chester Scott,' I said. 'What's all the excitement about? Phil Welliver brought me up here. He's a friend of mine.'

Claude didn't seem particularly impressed.

'Where do you live, Mr Scott?' he asked.

I told him.

He reached forward, picked up the telephone book that was lying on his desk and checked my address.

'Mr Welliver should know by now he can't bring friends up here without my say-so and unless his friends pay the subscription fee.'

I began to get less flustered.

'I didn't know that,' I said. 'Welliver didn't mention a fee. I'm willing to pay it. How much?'

'Twenty-five bucks,' Claude said. His eyes shifted away from me to the dark one who still remained at my side.

'Do we know anything about Mr Scott?'

'He was in last night,' the dark one said. 'He went backstage and talked to Miss Lane.'

I began to sweat again.

A remote look came into Claude's eyes. He shifted in his chair, then, as polite as a dentist asking me to open wide, he said: 'You know Miss Lane, Mr Scott?'

'No. I heard her sing,' I said. 'I thought she was pretty good. I asked her to have a drink with me.'

'And did she?'

'No.'

'But you talked to her in her dressing-room?'

'Yes: we talked. Why all these questions?'

'What did you talk about?'

'This and that,' I said. 'What makes it your business?'

Claude looked at the dark one.

'Anything else?'

'Not that I know of.'

There was a pause, then Claude said: 'Sorry to be bothering you, Mr Scott. That'll be twenty-five bucks.'

I took out my wallet, found two tens and a five and laid them on the desk.

He wrote a receipt and handed it to me.

'We have to be careful, Mr Scott,' he said. 'I don't have to tell you that. I hope we see you here often.'

'You probably will,' I said, not believing it had smoothed out this easy.

The dark one and the fair one had moved away from me. Their faces were now bored and disinterested.

I put the receipt in my wallet and my wallet in my pocket.

'Well, thanks,' I said and began to back away.

Then I heard the door open behind me and I looked around.

Oscar Ross came in.

He had on his barman's coat and he carried a tray on which stood a bottle of Scotch, a glass and a container of ice.

He didn't see me until he was halfway into the room, and then he didn't recognize me until he had put the tray down on Claude's desk. Then he stared at me as if he wasn't sure if he could believe his eyes.

I started across the room to the door, trying not to run, but covering the ground to the exit at a pretty fast clip.

Ross stood rooted, staring at me.

I turned the door handle, but the door was locked.

The fair one moved towards me to unlock the door when Ross said in a strangled voice: 'Hey! Don't let him out of here!'

The fair one paused.

The key was in the lock. I turned it and as I was opening the door, the fair one moved like a swift shadow and his foot jammed against the door.

'What's he doing in here?' Ross demanded.

The fair one, obviously puzzled, looked over at Claude for guidance.

I set myself and slammed a right at his jaw. My knuckles connected and I felt a jar run up my arm. He went over backwards and his head crashed against the wall.

I turned the key and opened the door.

'Hold it!'

This was from the dark one.

I looked quickly at him. He had a .38 automatic in his right fist and it was pointing at me.

I decided recklessly that it was more than he dared do to let off the gun in the confined spaces of the club and ignoring his threat, I jerked open the door.

Ross came at me fast. His hands were seeking me, his eyes were vicious and alarmed.

I got into the corridor as he arrived to close with me. His right fist sailed towards my face as I spun around to grapple with him. I got my face out of the way just in time and I planted my fist in his mouth. He reeled backwards and I turned and hared down the passage to the door into the roulette room.

Something that felt like a tank thudded into the back of my knees and brought me to the floor. I twisted over as the dark one slammed a punch at my jaw. I managed to get my head moving, but the punch connected, just a shade too high up to cause much damage, but hard enough to make me grunt.

I kicked the dark one away and got unsteadily to my feet as Ross came charging out of the room and towards me.

If there was one thing I wanted more than another, it was to get one more bang at him. I slipped the punch he tossed at me, moved in close and hooked him with a right-hand punch that had all my weight and most of my strength behind it.

But that was as far as I got.

I had a vague idea that the dark one had picked himself off the floor and was moving towards me with the speed and the grace of a ballet dancer.

He came at me too fast for me to do anything about it. I started to turn so I could face him, but I was much, much too late.

I heard the swish of a descending cosh and I tried to get my head out of the way.

As the softly lit passage exploded before my eyes, I knew I had shifted that second too late.

After all he was a professional. When he sapped you, you stayed sapped.

14

I

I came out of darkness to feel hot sunshine on my face and a blinding light against my closed eyelids.

There was also a feeling of movement. It took me several seconds to realize I was in a car, being driven somewhere at high speed.

I wanted to groan because the back of my head was expanding and contracting and pain crawled up my neck over the top of my head and into my eyes like a beetle with red-hot feet.

But I didn't groan. I let myself stay limp and slack and I rolled with the motion of the car until I felt good enough to open my eyes and take a quick look around.

I was on the back seat of my hired Buick. There was a man sitting beside me. I recognized the iron-grey suiting of his trouser leg. It was the dark thug: the one who had sapped me.

Sitting in front, driving, was the fair one. He had put on a light grey slouch hat which he wore at a jaunty angle over his nose.

Keeping my eyes half closed, I checked out of the window to see where we were.

We were passing through one of the back streets of Palm City: empty as a hole in the wall on this hot Sunday afternoon.

I kept quiet and wondered where we were going. I didn't have to wonder for long.

The next five minutes saw us leaving Palm City behind us, and we got on to the highway leading to the beach road where I lived. I decided they were going to dump me back in my bungalow.

There was a light travelling rug across my knees to hide my wrists and hands. My wrists were crossed and strapped with what felt like adhesive tape. They were strapped so tightly I could feel the blood pounding in my veins, and although I very gently tried to ease them a little, they were tight against each other as if screwed down in a vice.

'Turn right at the intersection, Lew,' the dark one said suddenly. 'His joint is three hundred yards down on the right: a nice lonely spot for a guy to live in: I wouldn't mind living in it myself.'

Lew, the fair one, laughed without humour.

'Why not ask him to leave it to you in his will?' he said. 'He won't be needing it now.'

'Aw, hell! I don't want it that bad,' the other said.

The car drove on.

I found myself suddenly short of breath, but I didn't have the time to wonder what they meant, for the car suddenly slowed down and finally stopped.

'This is it,' the dark one said.

'Okay, let's get him out,' Lew said.

I remained limp, my eyes closed, my heart slamming against my ribs.

I felt the dark one leave the car, then I heard the offside door open. Hands laid hold of me and pulled me out of the car.

As I slid on to the ground, Lew said: 'You didn't hit him too hard, did you, Nick? He should have come to the surface by now.'

'I hit him right,' Nick, the dark one, said. 'He'll snap out of it in a few minutes.'

Between the two of them they half carried me, half dragged me up the path and dumped me on the front step.

'Got his keys?' Nick asked.

'Yeah. This is the one.'

I heard the lock on the front door snap back, then I was dragged across the hall and into my lounge and dumped on the settee.

'You sure he's all right?' Lew asked.

A hand moved on to my neck: expert fingers touched my pulse.

'He's fine. He should be up and coming in another five minutes.'

'He'd better be.' There was an uneasy note in Lew's voice. 'Galgano will be mad if this punk croaks before he can talk to him.'

'Relax, big head. He's all right. When I tap 'em, I tap 'em right. In five minutes, he'll be dancing the can-can.'

I gave a low groan and moved a little.

'You see? He's coming out of it already. Gimme the rope.'

I felt a cord tighten around my chest, pinning me to the settee. I opened my eyes as Lew was fastening the cord to the legs of the settee. He stared at me, his face expressionless, then he stepped away.

'That fixes it,' he said and leaning over me, he patted my face. 'Relax, buster. The boss wants to talk to you. He'll be along in a little while.'

'Come on,' Nick said impatiently. 'Let's get out of here. Have you forgotten we've got to walk?'

Lew cursed.

'Why couldn't that punk Claude have sent a car?'

'You ask him,' Nick said.

He came over to me and examined the rope across my chest critically, then checked the tapes around my wrists. He grunted, stepped back, and stared at me and a tight, meaningless smile hovered on his thin lips.

'So long, sucker,' he said.

They went across the lounge and out into the hall, pulling the lounge door half shut. I heard them open the front door, then close it behind them.

After a second or so a silence settled over the bungalow that made the ticking of the clock on the overmantel sound unnaturally loud.

I exerted a useless effort for a minute or so against the tape around my wrists and found there was no way of breaking free so I lay still, panting a little from my exertions.

It was then that I remembered Lucille who I had left tied on my bed. Maybe she had managed to get free. Maybe she would set me free.

'Lucille!' I called. 'Lucille! Can you hear me?'

I listened, but there was no sound except the ticking of the clock and the gentle flapping of a curtain against a window as the breeze disturbed it.

'Lucille!' I raised my voice to a shout. 'Are you all right?'

Again silence, and I suddenly felt cold sweat on my face. Had something happened to her? Or had she got free and left the bungalow?

'Lucille!'

Then I did hear something. A soft movement of a door opening: a door somewhere down the passage, possibly my bedroom door.

I lifted my head to listen.

The door squeaked a little and that told me it was my bedroom door. I had been meaning to oil the hinges for weeks and had been too lazy to do it.

'Is that you, Lucille?' I said sharply.

I heard someone move out into the passage: a slow, heavy step, and I was suddenly more frightened than I had ever been before in my life.

Lucille couldn't have moved like that. The slow, stealthy footfalls I was listening to were too heavy for a woman's. It was a man coming down the passage: a man who had come out of my bedroom where I had left Lucille trussed and helpless on the bed.

'Who's that?' I said, my voice off-key, my heart hammering.

The slow, heavy footsteps came down the passage and stopped outside the lounge door. Then there was silence.

I lay there, listening, sweat on my face, hearing gentle, unhurried breathing from the other side of the door.

'Come on in, damn you!' I exclaimed, my nerves crawling. 'What are you skulking out there for? Come on in and show yourself!'

The door began to open slowly.

The man out there intended to frighten me, and he succeeded.

I was practically ready to hit the ceiling as the door swung fully open.

The man who stood in the doorway was massive and tall. He had on a dark blue sports jacket, grey flannel trousers and reserve calf brown shoes. He stood there, his hands in his pockets, his thumbs outside and pointing at me.

I lay staring at him, scarcely believing my eyes, a sudden chill gripping my heart.

The man in the doorway was Roger Aitken.

II

Heavy footed, slow and deliberate, an expression on his face that really put the fear of God into me, Aitken came in to the room.

I was immediately aware that he didn't limp and he was walking as he always walked, and yet a few days back he had fallen down the Plaza Grill steps and had broken his leg.

The whole situation took on a nightmare aspect. It was Aitken, and yet it wasn't Aitken. This tight-set face with glittering eyes made me feel here was another man inside Aitken's skin: a man I didn't know and a man who scared me. Then the familiar voice said: 'I seem to have given you a fright, Scott.'

It was Aitken all right. That voice and that smile could belong to no one else.

'Yes.' My voice was husky and unsteady. 'You certainly did. Your leg seems to have made a pretty good recovery.'

'There was never anything the matter with it,' he said and paused near me, looking down at me, his glittering eyes moving over my face. 'It was something I arranged so you and my wife could get acquainted.'

My mouth was now so dry I couldn't say anything. I just lay and stared up at him.

He looked around, then moved over to a lounging chair and sat down.

'Quite a nice place you have here, Scott,' he said. 'A little lonely but convenient. Do you make a habit of fooling around with other men's wives?'

'I didn't last long and I didn't touch her,' I said. 'I'm sorry. I could explain better if I had my hands free. There's a lot to explain.'

I was wondering about Lucille.

Had she managed to get free? Was she still in the bungalow? If she was still tied up on the bed, then Aitken must know it as he had come out of my bedroom.

Aitken took out his gold cigarette case. He lit a cigarette.

'I think I'll leave you as you are,' he said. 'Anyway, for the time being.'

Then a thought came into my mind: a crazy thought: a thought that made me stiffen and lift my head and stare at him. This was the man Lew had said was coming to talk to me. This man I knew as Roger Aitken was known by Lew and his pal as Art Galgano: a crazy thought, but the facts pointed to it.

'The nickel's dropped?' Aitken said, watching me. 'Yes, you're right. I am Galgano.'

I lay there, staring at him, shocked into silence.

He crossed one leg over the other.

'You don't imagine I can live in the style in which I live from what I get out of the International, do you, Scott? Three years ago I had a chance of buying the Little Tavern, and I bought it. This is a rich town. It is full of rich degenerates with nothing to do but to chase one another's wives and drink whisky. I knew it was a crowd that would gamble if given the opportunity. I gave it the opportunity.

For three years that wheel at the Little Tavern has been spinning and has been making me a fortune. The law against gambling is strict. A lot of people have tried to run a wheel and they have been shut down. I was more fortunate. This man Harry O'Brien was in charge of the roads leading to the Little Tavern. It was his job to report any suspicious gathering of people who might be gamblers. He was the eyes and ears of the Police Commissioner. I made it worth his while to be deaf and dumb, but I knew sooner or later he would get greedy, and he did. The profits from the wheel, instead of coming to me, began to go to him. He bled me white. As a blackmailer he was in a class of his own. After six or seven months, I found I was making less money than I had made before I bought the Little Tavern. His demands became so pressing, I was forced to use some of the International's profits to satisfy him. That was a situation that had to stop.'

The clock on the overmantel suddenly began to strike four o'clock. The afternoon's sun beat against the sun-blinds. The whisper of the sea somehow had a sinister sound.

I lay there, listening, looking at this man who was my boss and who I had thought the tops in the advertising game. He still looked impressive, with his big frame, his well-fitting clothes and his massive, whisky-red face, but he wasn't impressive to me any more.

He reached out and stubbed out his cigarette, lit another and smiled at me.

'There is only one way to stop a blackmailer when he is in O'Brien's class and that's to kill him.' The glittering eyes met mine and the thin lips tightened. 'Murdering a policeman is dangerous, Scott. It is a challenge to the police force and they take extra trouble in tracking down the killer. I laid my plans. As in everything I do, I took the broad view of the situation. If I were to kill a man, I would make a complete job of it, I decided. I badly needed money. I had taken fifteen thousand dollars from the International and I knew I couldn't hide that up for long. I owed money everywhere. It would take me several weeks to recoup from the wheel once I had got rid of O'Brien, and the chances were that his successor would find out what was going on at the nightclub and I would be closed down. So I had to have money quickly. It was then I thought of you. I had heard you had some money. Everything fell into place once I decided to make use of you, Scott. So I prepared the bait of the New York office and you fell for it.'

I lay listening to his quiet, dangerous voice, and I kept wondering about Lucille. I was scared to ask him if she were still in my bedroom in case she had got free and had left the bungalow before he arrived. There was just a chance that she had got free.

'In case things went wrong,' he went on, 'I took the precaution to provide myself with an alibi. Only Mrs Hepple and Lucille know I didn't break my leg. Mrs Hepple has been with me for years and I can trust her. Lucille ...' He broke off and shrugged his shoulders. 'Let me tell you about Lucille. She was one of the dancers at the Little Tavern. When I bought the place, I was careful no one at the club except Claude should know who I was. I used to go there as a customer. The girl appealed to me. A mistake, of course. She was pretty and gay and young, but a man soons gets tired of a girl when she has a head as empty as Lucille's. However, the one thing in her favour is she does what I tell her to do, and so does her oaf of a brother, Ross, who also worked at the Little Tavern when I took it over. I explained to these two what I wanted. I told them if O'Brien continued to blackmail me, the Little Tavern would shut down; Ross would lose his job and Lucille would find herself married to a poor man. It was my suggestion that Lucille should ask you to teach her to drive – a good suggestion, I think.' Again, the thin lips lifted in a sneering smile. 'When I was ready, I told her to take you down that beach road. I had arranged to meet O'Brien down there. His monthly pay-off was due. We met down there. While I was talking to him, Ross came up behind him and knocked him senseless. In the meantime you and Lucille were acting out your little drama. I had instructed her exactly how she was to behave. It was essential that you should attempt to seduce her, thus providing you with a guilt complex. It was also essential that she should run away with your car. I know enough about male psychology to be sure you would act the way I wanted you to act, and you did.' He leaned forward to tap ash off his cigarette. 'Lucille brought the car to me. The accident wasn't difficult to stage. I had O'Brien lying in the road. I ran the car over him. Then I drove the car fast and hard into his motorcycle I had placed on its parker in the middle of the road. It was quite a smash. Then I turned the car over to Lucille and Ross and told them to take it to your bungalow.'

'You made a mistake,' I said. 'All killers make mistakes. You ran O'Brien over with the offside wheel and you hit the motorcycle with the onside front wing. That told me there was something phoney about the accident. It wouldn't have been possible to have killed O'Brien accidentally the way you staged it.'

He lifted his eyebrows.

'It doesn't matter. You obligingly got rid of the mistake by having the car repaired. That was a smart move of yours, Scott, the way you switched the number plates. But it did give Ross a chance to get a photograph of you and when he showed me the photo I knew then I had you where I wanted you.' He stretched out his long legs and stared up at the ceiling. 'It's a pity you got too smart. It's a pity too that you ran into that Lane woman. It complicated things for me. I knew I would have to get rid of her sooner or later as I was sure O'Brien had told her he was blackmailing me, and she would probably guess his death hadn't been an accident. I had my men watching her all the time, and she knew it. She and Nutley were scared. They wanted to get out of town where I couldn't reach them, but they lacked funds. So when you appeared on the scene, she saw her chance of getting some money to leave town. I was told you were going to her apartment. I arrived a little late, but not late enough to hear she had double-crossed you. I was waiting outside her apartment as she came out and I killed her. I very nearly lost track of Nutley, but fortunately one of my men had been watching him and he reported to me that you and Nutley had got together at the Washington. I went along there and shot him. The night clerk had to go too. He cost me a hundred dollars to go up to Nutley's room. On my way out, I had to kill him. He would have known me again.' He rubbed his red, fleshy face and his glittering eyes stared at me.

'Killing comes easily, Scott, after you have killed your first man, but it also becomes complicated. You kill someone, then you kill someone else to cover up the first killing, and then you have to kill again to cover up the second killing.'

'I guess you must be out of your mind,' I said huskily. 'You can't hope to get away with this.'

'Of course I can. At the moment I am lying in bed with a broken leg. It's a perfect alibi. It will never occur to anyone

I have had anything to do with any of this. Besides, I am going to shift the whole thing on to you. I see you have a typewriter over there. I intend to type out the beginning of a confession that will convince the police that you accidentally killed O'Brien, and Ross and Lucille attempted to blackmail you.' He put his head on one side, smiling. 'I forgot to tell you that while my men were bringing you here, I took Ross back to his bungalow and shot him through the head with the gun that killed Nutley. I'm making a clean sweep, Scott. I'm tired of Ross and I am very, very tired of Lucille.' Again he smiled. 'Getting back to your confession, Scott, they will read that the Lane woman and her agent Nutley also tried to blackmail you and you killed them. You have left enough evidence behind you to convince the police that you did kill them. They will read that you went out to Ross' bungalow and killed him and then you returned here, enticed Lucille down here and strangled her with one of your neckties.'

I suddenly felt cold and sick.

'You mean you killed her?' I said, lifting my head and staring at him.

'Of course,' Aitken said. 'The opportunity was much too good to miss. When I found her on the bed, trussed and helpless, it seemed to me the easiest thing in the world to fasten one of your gaudy neckties around her stupid little throat and get rid of her. It's a clean sweep, Scott. I have got rid of Ross and her: both nuisances. I have got rid of a blackmailer who was ruining me. Fortunately Hackett came out of the blue with his hundred thousand, so I now don't need your money. I can start again. Even if I can't keep the wheel spinning at the Little Tavern, with a hundred thousand and my talents I should be able to make a fresh start.'

'You won't get away with it,' I said, staring at him. 'Too many people know about it. Claude knows: his two thugs know ...'

The sneering little smile was in evidence again. 'Claude and his two thugs as you call them are tied in with me. If I go down, so do they, and they know it. Now it only remains for you to become a victim of your conscience, Scott, and shoot yourself. The police won't be surprised that life has become intolerable to you after all these murders and you have ended it.'

He took from his pocket a leather glove which he slipped on his right hand, then from his hip pocket he pulled out a .45 Colt.

'This is Nutley's gun,' he went on. 'It is the gun that killed him and Ross, and now it is going to kill you.' He got to his feet. 'In a way, I'm sorry about this, Scott. I shall miss you. You are good at your job, but there is no other way out of this mess. I assure you it won't hurt. I am told that a shot in the ear kills instantly.'

I was now pretty well ready to hit the ceiling. I was watching him move slowly across the room towards me, the gun hanging by his side when the front door bell rang.

That was a moment in my life I'll never forget.

Aitken stiffened and looked towards the door. I saw his thumb push the safety catch on the gun forward.

He stood there like a stone man, listening.

'They'll know I'm in here,' I said hoarsely. 'The car's outside.'

He looked at me, his mouth curling into a snarl.

'Make a sound and you'll be the first to go,' he said.

Again the front door bell rang, persistently and impatiently.

Aitken moved silently to the sitting-room door and cautiously peered into the hall. His back was now turned to me and to the french doors. I saw a shadow appear, and then the big, massive figure of Lieutenant West suddenly moved silently through the french doors and into the room. In his right hand he held a .38 police special.

He didn't look at me. His eyes were on Aitken's broad back.

As he lifted his gun, he suddenly barked: 'Up with them, Aitken, and drop that gun!'

I saw a shudder run through Aitken's big frame. He spun around, jerking up his gun, his face contorted with rage and fear.

West shot him.

Aitken's gun boomed, but he was already falling and the slug ploughed a groove in my parquet floor. A red stain appeared between Aitken's eyes and he pitched forward, coming down with a crash that rocked the ornaments in the room. He jerked a little as he died, but it was purely reflex. The gun slid out of his limp fingers, and West moved over heavily and ponderously and picked it up.

There was the sound of running feet and three policemen, guns in hand, crowded in.

'Okay, okay, okay,' West said. 'I've fixed him.'

He moved over to me, shoving his gun in his hip pocket and he grinned down at me.

'I bet you were scared,' he said.

I stared up at him, and I was still so scared I couldn't say anything.

As he bent over me and began to unwind the tape around my wrists, Joe Fellowes came in hurriedly. His eyes were bulging and his face was shiny with sweat.

'Hi, Ches,' he said as I sat up, trying to rub life into my wrists. 'Are you all right?'

'Yes,' I said. 'What are you doing here, for the love of Mike?'

'It was me who called the cops,' he said, then stopped short as he caught sight of Aitken's body. His face turned a greenish grey and he stepped hurriedly back. 'Sweet grief! Is he dead?'

'Okay, you two,' West said. 'You get out of here.' He tapped me on my shoulder as I got unsteadily to my feet. 'Go and sit on the porch until I have time to talk to you. You can take it easy. I heard what he said and that puts you in the clear. Go outside and wait for me.'

'Did he kill her?' I asked.

'Yeah,' West said. 'He must have been crazy. Is that right, he operates a wheel at the Little Tavern?'

I put my hand to my coat lapel. The camera was still in place. I freed it and dropped it into his hand. 'There's a picture of the wheel in there. The *Inquirer* gave the camera to me.'

'Looks like I've got a busy afternoon ahead of me. Go out on the porch and wait for me,' and he crossed over to the telephone.

A policeman shoved Joe and me out on to the verandah. We sat down while the policeman leaned against the door post and watched us with bored eyes.

'I saw those two thugs bring you out of the backway of the club,' Joe said. 'I'd followed you, sure you would walk into trouble. I trailed them down here, but they looked too tough for me to tackle on my own so I called the cops.'

'Thanks, Joe,' I said and lay back in the basket chair. I felt pretty bad.

Minutes crawled by, then Joe said suddenly: 'Looks as if we'll be out of a job.'

'We may not be. Someone's got to run the International. This could be our big chance, Joe,' I said, staring out at the sand and the sea.

'Yeah, I hadn't thought of that.' He moved uneasily. 'He must have been crazy. I always thought there was something wrong about him.'

'You heard what he said?'

'I was right outside the verandah door all the time. I was scared to hell he might see me. If that big dick hadn't been with me, I don't know what I should have done.'

'I felt that way myself,' I said.

After that we didn't say anything. We sat there, waiting for maybe an hour, then Lieutenant West came out on to the verandah.

'They got Claude and your two pals,' he said, his face split with a wide grin, 'and they have four wagon loads of the blue blood of this city all going down to the lock-up. This will certainly make headlines tomorrow.' He sat down and stared at me. 'Okay, let's have it from the beginning. There are some points I didn't get. Then you'll have to come down to headquarters and we'll put it in writing. Go ahead and talk.'

So I went ahead and talked.

THE END

James Hadley Chase

An Ace Up My Sleeve

When three very different people come together, all out for the same thing and prepared to go to any lengths to get it, the stakes are likely to be high. But, for a wealthy middle-aged woman, an international lawyer and a young American, games of bluff and counter-bluff quickly develop into a dangerous and deadly battle. As the action hots up, Chase weaves a fast-moving story of blackmail, intrigue and extortion with a hair-raising climax.

The Fast Buck

International jewel thief, Paul Hater, knows a secret that everyone wants to know – and will go to any lengths to uncover. How long can he remain silent?

When Hater is arrested in possession of a stolen necklace, the police use every possible means to persuade him to reveal the location of the rest of the collection. He remains silent and so begins his twenty-year prison sentence. Having exhausted all their leads, the International Detective Agency, acting on behalf of the insurers, must patiently await Hater's release before they can hope to find out more. But just as his day of release approaches, Hater is kidnapped by a ruthless international gang determined to force the secret from him and prepared to go to any lengths to do so...

JAMES HADLEY CHASE

HAVE A CHANGE OF SCENE

Larry Carr is a diamond expert in need of a break. So when his psychiatrist suggests he has a change of scene, he jumps at the opportunity to move to Luceville, a struggling industrial town, and become a social worker. This, he thinks, will give him all the rest he needs...until he runs into Rhea Morgan, a ruthless, vicious thief who also happens to be extremely attractive. He falls headlong into the criminal world and embarks upon a thrilling, rapid and dastardly adventure in true Hadley Chase style.

JUST A MATTER OF TIME

An old lady's will seems to be causing quite a stir. Suddenly everyone wants to get in on the action, everyone that is, including a master forger, a hospital nurse, a young delinquent, a bank executive and, to make matters worse, a professional killer. With such ingredients, a showdown seems inevitable and James Hadley Chase adds enough suspense to keep you guessing right up to the very last page.

James Hadley Chase

My Laugh Comes Last

Farrell Brannigan, President of the National Californian Bank, is an extremely successful man. So when he builds another bank in an up-and-coming town on the Pacific coast, he is given worldwide publicity, and this new bank is hailed as 'the safest bank in the world'. But Brannigan's success came at a price and he made many enemies on his way up the ladder. It seems that one of them is now set on revenge and determined to destroy both the bank and Brannigan himself.

You're Dead Without Money

Joey Luck and his daughter Cindy were small-time criminals going nowhere fast...until they joined forces with Vin Pinna, a hardened criminal on the run from Miami. They began to set their sights higher and turned their hands to kidnapping. But their hostage, ex-movie star Don Elliot, seemed to have different ideas. He wanted in so they formed a 'quartet in crime' and this time the stakes were higher still – eight Russian stamps worth a million dollars.

'realistic and suspenseful' – *Observer*

Printed in Great Britain
by Amazon